# SOULEATER

OTHER BOOKS BY ANTHONY GIANGREGORIO

**THE DEAD WATER SERIES**

DEADWATER
DEADWATER: Expanded Edition
DEADRAIN
DEADCITY
DEADWAVE
DEAD HARVEST
DEAD UNION
DEAD VALLEY

**ALSO BY THE AUTHOR**

DEAD RECKONING: DAWNING OF THE DEAD
THE MONSTER UNDER THE BED
DEAD END: A ZOMBIE NOVEL
DEAD TALES: SHORT STORIES TO DIE FOR
DEAD MOURNING: A ZOMBIE HORROR STORY
ROAD KILL: A ZOMBIE TALE
DEADFREEZE
DEADFALL
DEADRAGE
THE DARK
RISE OF THE DEAD
DARK PLACES
REVOLUTION OF THE DEAD

ACKNOWLEDGEMENTS

I owe my wife and older son a great big thanks for their help with this book. Without their continuing support and input, this book would have never come to pass.

AUTHOR'S NOTE

This book was self-edited, and though I tried my absolute best to correct all grammar mistakes; there may be a few here and here. Please accept my sincerest apology for any errors you may find.
This is the third edition of this book.


Visit my website at www.undeadpress.com


# SOULEATER

# SOULEATER

ANTHONY GIANGREGORIO

# CHAPTER ONE

## October 1987

JASON SHIFTED SLIGHTLY, trying to get more comfortable on his living room couch; the cushions were old and worn, but still somehow gratifying. It was the only couch he remembered since he could walk, and the smell of its old material filled him with a sense of love and contentment.

Across the room, on the television, was a rerun of the Dukes of Hazzard.

Despite the fact it was his favorite show, he still wasn't feeling the love tonight. When the new season started a few months ago, Bo and Luke left after the first episode. They said they were going on the racing circuit and Coy and Vance Duke were going to help around the farm.

Being that Jason was only eleven, but going on twelve real soon, he didn't give much thought to how familiar the two new cousins were to the departing Bo and Luke.

He just sat back and enjoyed the ride.

At least the car chases and stunts were still cool. And Daisy was still there, too. He didn't quite know why, but he liked Daisy…a lot.

His father came into the living room and plopped down next to him, Jason pulling his feet in a little so his dad wouldn't sit on them.

Roger Lawson rubbed his son's hair as he turned to watch the screen.

"Hey, son, any good stunts yet?" He asked while he leaned back on the couch.

"Nah, they've just been running from the sheriff for the last five minutes. 'Sides, it's a repeat and you know the big jump over the river is near the end."

Roger nodded and grinned. "Yeah, I do, just wanted to see if you were paying attention, that's all."

Jason glanced from the television and looked to his father. Roger's attention was on the screen and didn't notice his son watching him. Jason admired the way his father's chin looked, strong and confident. He still had almost all of his hair, despite the fact he was almost out of his thirties.

To an eleven year old, thirty was pretty old.

Roger's eyes gleamed with happiness as he watched the Duke boys drive around a tree and leave poor Sheriff Roscoe in a mud pit.

Jason's heart filled with love in that brief moment.

As corny as it might sound, Jason's father was his best friend. Roger always treated him fairly and seemed to understand whatever hardships Jason might be going through in school or on the playground with his friends.

They would spend hours talking in the backyard while they threw the football back and forth and it was his dad who'd first told him about girls when he had asked him why he felt tingly when he was standing too close to Kathy Milton in school.

He loved his father more than he could ever put into words, and with the exception of his mom, was one of his most favorite people on earth.

"Jason, at the next commercial, I want you to brush your teeth; and when the show's over, its right to bed." His mother's voice floated in from the kitchen.

"Aww, Mom, do I have to? It's Friday night, and I don't have school tomorrow."

"I don't care. I'm sorry, honey, but if you're going to get up early with your father, then you need your sleep."

Jason looked to his dad for some support. Roger just shrugged and smiled.

"Sorry, champ, but your mom's right. If you want to go fishing with me in the morning, you need to get at least a little sleep." Then he leaned closer so only Jason could hear him. "Plus, we both know you're going to stay up reading comic books for at least another hour or so."

Jason's eyes went wide with surprise. "How do you know that?"

Roger just leaned back and grinned. "I was your age, too, son. All the things you do, I've already done before." He turned to look at Jason and winked. "Don't worry, it's our secret. But if you get caught, don't you try using me to get out of your mom's wrath."

Jason sat up and leaned over and gave his father a hug. "Deal," he said, feeling his dad's five-o-clock shadow. He smelled of Old Spice and soap, but to Jason it smelled like security and safety; and of course, love.

The commercial came on and Roger pushed his son off the couch. "Go on, boy; go brush your teeth."

Jason did as he was told, and once he was finished, ran back into the living room and sat back down to watch the last ten minutes of the Dukes. After the usual car jump, the credits began to roll. Jason turned off the television, satisfied the Duke boys had prevailed and Hazzard County was safe for another week.

Leaning over the couch one more time, he gave his father one more hug good night.

"Night, Dad, I love you, and I'll see you in the morning, bright and early."

Roger chuckled at that. "Well, maybe not too early, son. After all, it is one of my only days off."

Jason nodded and went into the kitchen to give his mom a kiss good night. She reciprocated and he left her frowning, wiping her wet kiss from his cheek as he went up the side stairs that led to his bedroom on the second floor.

He paused at his window, preparing to close the shade, and noticed how red the sky seemed tonight. The moon was full and the stars could be seen clearly despite the low cloud cover.

Closing the shade, already forgetting about the night sky, he climbed into bed and reached for his flashlight. Once he was comfortable, he reached under his pillow and pulled out the latest issue of The Amazing Spiderman. Spidey was fighting with the Vulture on the cover and Jason knew it was going to be a good issue.

With the blankets covering his head and body, he relaxed and started to read his comic, the rest of the world forgotten as he became lost in a world of fantasy and superheroes.

*　　*　　*

Jason's closet stood partially ajar on the opposite side of his room. At first the small closet was just darkness and shadows, but as time crept on, a dull, red-orange glow started to seep from under the door.

Something was coming.

When Jason had noticed the odd looking night sky, he had no way of knowing the origin of the strange disturbance.

Jason would have no way of comprehending, how far above his head, way out in deep space; the planets were aligning in a specific pattern. This occurrence only happened about every twenty years, the planets orbiting the sun finally in the perfect position for something miraculous to happen, nay, perhaps even magical.

Tonight, at this precise time, was the next occurrence.

The gravity of the earth was greatly affected on this one night, and while most people would barely notice any difference, in Jason's house this night, strange forces were growing.

Something from another dimension had waited for this one moment in time, gathering the dark energy from its own world, waiting for the perfect opportunity to punch a hole into our world by tearing the very fabric of space-time itself.

Some had names for this creature.

They called him the Boogeyman or the monster under the bed. It had been called many things in its hundreds of years of existence. Even the prey it brought back with it to its own dimension made up names for it.

But one name had always made it smile, despite the fact it did not truly have a mouth in the conventional sense.

Soul Eater.

It liked that name. It most identified to what it was. And yet, he was so much more at the same time.

The energies continued to grow and the creature forced its way into our dimension, the portal flaring brightly for a moment before dying down to a dull glow. The pain was unbearable, but he knew the rewards would be worth it.

With an intake of air in what would be called lungs to a human being, but was as far different anatomically as an ant is to a man, the creature stood up from the floor of the closet.

While he didn't know exactly where it was, he did know that prey would be near. He had always made sure his locater spells brought him close to fresh meat.

In the creature's own dimension, the hunting was slim, others of his kind all but killing every other living animal with the exception of its own kind. And even that taboo had been broken when some of his kin, tired of going hungry, turned on each other, becoming nothing more than cannibals.

But not him. He would never degenerate to that extreme. This was why he had experimented with ways to break the dimensional divide and seek his prey elsewhere.

And it had worked!

After centuries of trial and error, he had finally used the proper incantations and used the dark forces of the universe to push through the rift that divided worlds.

He slowly opened the door that barred the way, the smell of young meat only a few feet away. In just moments he would have his prey and would then return to his dimension to feed at his leisure. The food he would acquire this night, and at many other locations across the planet, would have to keep him fed until the next planetary alignment; his metabolism storing the meat and the essence of the prey's soul. He would have only a few earth days to hunt as much prey as he could find, then the planetary forces would become disrupted and he would have to wait the long years until he could once again go on the hunt.

With the closet door now open, he prepared to strike and kill the small child sitting in front of him on the bed.

Roger walked up the stairs from the living room, planning on using the bathroom, brushing his teeth and then with a quick check on Jason, go to bed.

His right foot landed on the top stair and he turned in the direction of the bathroom, when for no logical reason, his son let out a blood-curdling scream that had Roger's heart in his throat and his pulse doubling.

"Dad, there's something in my room!" Jason shrieked.

He ran for his son's door, for the life of him not imagining what could make him scream like that. He hit the door with his shoulder, forcing it open as he charged into the room and saw something from his worst nightmares.

What stood in front of Jason's bed may have had two arms, two legs and something on its torso that resembled a head, but the resemblance to the human anatomy stopped there.

The shape seemed to shift, catching any available light in the room and absorb it. The head had two slits where eyes would be on a human head and a black tangled mass of hair draped from its shoulders almost like a billowing cape.

"Dad, what is that thing, how did it get in my room?" Jason called, only his head peeking out from the blankets, as if that was all he needed to ward off the evil in front of him. His eyes were petrified with shock as he stared at the creature looming over him like death itself.

Roger was about to answer him, wanting to tell his son to stay where he was and stay calm; that his father would save him. All these ideas went through Roger's mind, but he never had the chance to say any of them.

The creature turned at Roger's intrusion, the orifice on its head hissing at the unplanned disturbance. An arm shot out, curved talons for fingers at the end, throwing Roger across the room where he struck the far wall with a sickening thump. His body became tangled in a coat rack, the jackets cushioning the impact, and in fact the only thing saving him from a broken back.

Roger reached out with his hands, his vision blurry and his mind rattled. His hand wrapped around a wooden baseball bat, the one he'd just given to Jason last week. It was an early birthday present. Despite Jason's birthday being more than a month away, he just couldn't wait and had given it to him early; wanting to see the smile he knew he'd receive for his present.

Picking up the bat, he stood on wobbly legs and moved toward the thing that seemed to want his son.

Despite the fact his body was filled with terror at this unnamable creature in front of him, Roger charged in swinging. The bat hit the creature in the side of its shoulder; the bat passing through the body like it had just struck fog.

Despite this, the creature screamed with rage and jumped away, then lunged at Roger. Off balance when the bat hit nothing but air, he wasn't able to defend himself, and the creature swarmed over him, wrapping its arms around his body, the bat tumbling away. Roger managed to squirm loose and he fell heavily to the floor, rolling away with a scream of fear as he reached out for the baseball bat again.

"Dad! No!" Jason screamed, watching his father battling something that seemed to have jumped out of the pages of one of his comic books.

Jason was frozen in fear, too frightened to move. He could only watch while his father swung blow after blow at the creature's midsection. The one person he loved most in the world was losing a battle for his life and there was nothing he could do about it.

Despite the blows he swung at the creature, Roger was accomplishing nothing but wearing himself out. The creature knew this and was actually just playing with him. It liked to play with its food, like a cat with a mouse.

Less than three minutes had past since Roger had charged into the room and the creature knew it had only moments before this individual portal closed and it would be trapped on this side of the dimensional rift.

Deciding fun and games were over and despite the fact it would have preferred the tender, young meat of the child, it knew it had no more time to waste.

The monster raised itself up to its full height, its head inches from brushing the ceiling. It looked down at the small man still trying to hurt him and decided this game of life and death was definitely over.

Its mouth opened wide, almost a foot in diameter, its mass able to shift and morph as needed. Its head dove down like a striking Cobra and wrapped its black orifice around Roger's head and neck.

With a sound like a tree snapping, Roger's head was separated from his shoulders in one smooth bite.

But the creature wasn't finished. It stood in the same exact position and sucked the blood from Roger's corpse like he was a child's straw in a milkshake. Roger's heart continued pumping the last of his life's fluid until the body was dry, his body dancing under the creature like a rag doll.

Then the creature removed its mouth from the lifeless body and threw the headless corpse over its shoulder, and with the briefest of glances at the child; dove back into the closet and into the portal.

Its body passed through in a flash of light, closing the opening with its passage. The closet grew dark once again.

With the exception of Jason's screams, an overturned coat rack, and an out of place baseball bat, the room was untouched, nothing to show what had just transpired inside the bedroom.

Jason's mother ran into the room, not understanding what was happening. Jason jumped from the bed and ran to her, crying into her arms while trying to tell her what had happened, but the story was so fantastic all she could do was nod and say it was all right. After all, there was no evidence to back up Jason's story other than the tall tale of an eleven-year-old boy. She idly wondered what all of the ruckus was from, but figured her son was just jumping around the room playing superheroes or wrestling.

Jason was brought to the hospital that night. It was believed he'd suffered some form of breakdown.

As for Jason's father, no one ever saw him again. It was believed the man must have run off in the middle of the night, probably with some hussy.

No one would believe Jason's story, and for years he stuck to his tale, but soon realized if he ever wanted to lead a normal life, he would have to push those memories away and try to somehow forget about them.

For years after the incident, Jason saw psychiatrists; the idiots trying to find out why Jason couldn't accept the fact his father had left him and his mom and had never looked back.

By the time Jason was eighteen, he had accepted the fact he must have been crazy to imagine what he thought had happened that October night. With everyone telling him it was impossible, he slowly accepted it as truth and was able to carry on with a regular life. Still, deep down inside, he always wondered if what he'd seen had been real.

So he went to college and met a wonderful girl named Emma.

The two courted for two years and decided to get married when she became pregnant with their first, and so far, only child. The baby was a boy.

Jason had named him Roger, in loving honor of his lost father. Emma was fine with it. And despite having a new wife and child, he managed to finish college and then moved on to a lucrative job in finances.

The three of them settled down only two blocks away from the house he had grown up in. Despite what he told himself, he would always find away to avoid the house, the memories always flooding back and threatening to take away his sanity.

His mother still lived there, but she would always come to his home for visits and holidays. Deep down, she understood what had happened to her son, even if she didn't believe it; the loss of his father a traumatic event no matter what the occurrence.

The years went by and Jason was happy with his family. He made sure to have the same kind of relationship with his son that he'd enjoyed with his father, and the two were good friends.

Jason was so busy living his life; he had no way of knowing that in less than two weeks it would be exactly twenty years to the day his father had disappeared.

While planets realigned, and dark forces gathered, Jason continued hanging Halloween decorations around the house, unaware of what was to come.

# Chapter Two

## October 2007

ROGER JOHN LAWSON, or RJ to his friends, pedaled his bike as fast as he could down the small suburban side street. His eyes tried to look in every direction at once, while he wildly sped down the street, risking a fall at every turn.

He was on the lookout for his arch enemy and the local bully, Ronnie Pasco.

Ronnie lived two streets over from RJ, and every chance he got, the bully would beat RJ up.

RJ's dad had told him to stand up to the big jerk, but when Ronnie was standing in front of him, RJ's legs always felt like water and his stomach felt like he had a hundred butterflies fighting to break loose from their prison.

Ronnie would always punch him in the stomach a few times, and then if RJ was really unlucky, he might get a few slaps or punches to the face. Nothing that would really hurt that bad, but would help to humiliate him further, unless Ronnie was in a bad mood, then things got downright dangerous. After Ronnie was done beating him up, he would always finish by taking whatever money he had in his pockets.

RJ would never tell his dad about the money and he told his father almost everything that had ever happened to him. He just felt too embarrassed.

RJ turned at the next street corner and breathed a sigh of relief. His house was just around the bend in the road. He slowed his frantic pedaling and was about to finally go into a calmer state, when Ronnie and his two goons for friends shot out of a nearby driveway and cut him off. RJ had no choice but to stop or crash into Ronnie's bike.

Ronnie stood on the street, both of his feet firmly planted on the ground with his bicycle between his legs. The bike was a size to small for him and Ronnie could easily stay in that position without ever worrying about the bike falling over.

Behind him were his two goons. They followed him everywhere and were almost as evil as Ronnie was.

Both Kyle and Chris grinned malevolently as RJ screeched his bike to a stop. Thanks to these two, RJ could never stand up to Ronnie even if he wanted too. One time on his dad's advice, RJ had tried to fight the big bully.

The second Ronnie had thought he might not come out on top, he had gestured to his two goons. Immediately, both Kyle and Chris had jumped onto RJ and had held his arms behind his back. Ronnie had then proceeded to punch him in the stomach until RJ felt he wouldn't want to eat for a month. They only let him go when he'd promised to give each of them five bucks, all the money he had in the world at the time; and he was going to spend it on new comics.

So he'd given them the money, because he knew what would have happened to him if he had reneged on the promise.

Now Ronnie stood in front of him again and RJ knew what was coming.

Ronnie lifted his leg off his bike, letting the blue 10-speed fall to the asphalt without a care. RJ happened to know it wasn't even his bike. Ronnie had stolen it from another kid just a week ago. The kid was too scared to tell his mom and so was now walking to school everyday instead of using his bike.

"Hey squirt, where ya goin' in such a hurry?" Ronnie grinned malevolently.

RJ stood perfectly still, speechless. The butterflies were back and he wished he could just lie down.

"Uhm, nowhere, Ronnie, you know, just goin' home. What's up with you?"

Ronnie's teeth showed through his smile. The two front teeth were missing thanks to a stray puck at hockey practice. Ronnie didn't mind. He considered it a badge of honor, like a scar a warrior carries proudly.

"Nothin' much. Hey, Lawson, you got any money?"

RJ's thoughts flashed to the ten dollar bill in his back pocket. He had just earned that money raking Mrs. Miller's leaves and he sure as hell didn't want to give it to this jerk.

"Ah, no, Ronnie, I'm broke, sorry," RJ said apologetically.

Ronnie made a puss on his face, not believing RJ for a moment. He turned to his two goons and then gestured to RJ.

"You, guys, get his arms; I want to check his pockets." Then he looked RJ straight in the eyes. "If you're lying to me, squirt, you're gonna pay."

RJ swallowed at that statement, not looking forward to what was going to happen next.

Kyle and Chris moved over to him, their bikes falling over as they climbed off them. Each boy grabbed one of his arms, holding him fast. Ronnie leaned over and slid his hand into RJ's front pocket, a frown creasing his face when he found them empty.

He was about to check his back pockets when a horn sounded and RJ's heart jumped with relief when his dad pulled up next to them.

"Hey, guys, what seems to be the problem?" Jason Lawson asked.

Both Kyle and Chris immediately let go of RJ, their faces looking like the cat getting caught after eating the canary.

"Uh, nothin', Mr. Lawson. We were just hanging with RJ, here. Weren't we, RJ?" Ronnie asked.

RJ hesitated for a second, then nodded. "Yeah, Dad, that's right, just hangin' around." His eyes pleaded with his father to see he was in trouble and help him.

Mr. Lawson nodded. "Oh, okay then, guys, you take care," he said. Then he started to pull away from the four of them. RJ's heart sank. His father was leaving him alone to be killed! Ronnie's teeth flashed in the sunlight.

Ronnie knew what was going to happen next. And so did RJ, unfortunately.

But just before Mr. Lawson's car had moved four feet, he stopped the car and leaned out the window.

"On second thought, RJ, why don't you throw your bike into the trunk and I'll take you home with me. Your mom's almost got supper on and I could use your help in the yard. That is, unless you'd rather stay with your friends."

RJ didn't hesitate. The moment the last word had left his dad's mouth, he was grabbing his bike and pushing it to the car.

"No, that's cool, Dad, I can see these guys anytime," he said, looking over his shoulder.

Ronnie gritted his teeth, cursing under his breath. "Next time, Lawson," he growled.

RJ pushed his bike a little faster. "Maybe, but not today," he mumbled in return.

His father popped the trunk and RJ picked his bike up and jammed it in. It stuck out a little, but that was fine. They only lived a block away.

RJ ran around to the passenger door and climbed into the car.

His father looked at Ronnie and the other two boys and flashed them a polite smile.

"Now you guys be good, don't do anything I wouldn't do," he joked.

Ronnie waved as Jason turned the car around and headed back to their home.

"We won't, Mr. Lawson. See ya later, RJ," Ronnie spit while the car pulled away.

RJ looked in the rearview mirror as the kids disappeared behind them. He leaned back in the seat and let out a deep breath.

"Wow, thanks, Dad, for a minute I thought you were going to leave me there," RJ said.

Jason's face was grim when he glanced at his son.

"I probably should have, son. You know, sooner or later you're going to have to stand up to that kid. He'll never leave you alone until you do."

RJ sat up in his seat, frustrated. "Don't you think I know that, but how can I get the upper hand when he always has his two sidekicks with him?"

Jason bit his lip while he mulled that one over. "I guess you'll just have to get him alone one day. I know I tell you not to be violent, but one of these days you just might have to take the initiative. You're almost twelve now, son. I know you know what's right and wrong, but sometimes you have to do the wrong thing for the right reasons. Do you understand what I'm saying?"

RJ nodded. "Yeah, I know. It's just that it's hard to get that riled up, even when he's beating me up."

Jason nodded. "Don't worry, son, even if you never do anything, sooner or later the Ronnie's of this world get what's coming to them."

"And what if he doesn't?" RJ asked.

Jason chuckled at that, the car pulling into the driveway of their one-family home.

"Well, that's easy, son, there's always lawsuits and lawyers."

# CHAPTER THREE

E MMA WAS WAITING for them as they walked in the front door. With a big smile on her face, she bent over and gave RJ a big hug and then did the same to Jason.

"So, how are my two favorite men. Where have you guys been? Dinner's on the table and its getting cold."

RJ looked up at his father. He really didn't want to tell his mom that he'd been with Ronnie. Emma hated that boy and would have immediately started chastising RJ about being with him.

She called Ronnie a juvenile delinquent and had no idea that RJ was continually being bullied by him. Jason nodded to his son and winked.

"The boy was with me, honey. I picked him up with the car and we went for a ride."

Emma turned to look at both of them, a curious look on her face.

"Oh, really. And what exactly were you two talking about?"

RJ shrugged. "Ah, you know, Mom, guy stuff.  There's some things I can only talk to dad about."

Emma smiled a little shyly at that. "Oh, I'm so sorry. Sure, honey, I understand. Now go get washed up for supper." Then she turned away and headed for the kitchen to check on dinner.

RJ looked up at his father and sighed. "Thanks, Dad, if Mom knew, well, you know."

Jason chuckled. "More than you know, son, more than you know. Go get washed up like your mother asked and I'll meet you at the dinner table. After supper if you want, I'll kick your butt at Playstation."

RJ laughed then while he turned to go to the bathroom to wash up. "Ha, we'll see about that, old man. The day you beat me will be the day I hang up my controller."

Jason let his son go, their banter making him smile. At moments like these with his son, he couldn't help but remember the same kind of conversations with his own father, except they had played Atari instead of Playstation.

Jason went into the kitchen and kissed his wife on the cheek. He started to wash his hands in the sink and she stopped working to look at him.

"What was that for?" She asked, referring to the unexpected show of emotion.

Turning off the sink and reaching for a dishtowel, he shrugged.

"No reason, just that I love you," he said.

She smiled. "Well, I love you too, honey. Now sit down before the food gets any colder."

Jason did as he was told and a minute later, RJ arrived from the bathroom. Emma sat down and the three of them ate their dinner. Talking about their day and just enjoying being together.

Outside on the street in front of RJ's house, Ronnie was riding around on his bike. He knew what was going on inside RJ's house, the family all eating together, laughing and joking.

Thinking of these things just made Ronnie hate RJ more.

Ronnie was from a broken home. His father was a drunk and liked to beat on him every time he was in a bad mood, which was usually all the time. Ronnie's mother was a small woman who was too scared to protect either Ronnie or herself from his father's tirades.

Then, about a year ago, his father had gotten a little more carried away than usual. He was chasing his mom around the house and she'd slipped in the kitchen, cracking her head against the counter, which caused her to crash head first into the glass kitchen table.

She was cut to pieces.

Ronnie still remembered the day like it was yesterday.

He'd heard her screams of pain when she slipped on the floor and then heard the crash as her body hit the glass table on its way down. Ronnie had been hiding in his room. His headphones were covering his ears while he listened to some AC/DC as loud as it would go. It was still never loud enough, though.

With dread in his heart, Ronnie had ripped the headphones from his ears, dashed out of his bedroom, and ran to the kitchen to see how bad it was this time, figuring his mom just had a black eye or maybe a broken wrist.

Instead he was greeted to the sight of his mother's fractured skull. The glass had cut her face up so bad he could barely recognize her under all the blood. One of her eyes had been punctured by a large shard of the glass table; the eye socket just a mass of oozing ocular fluid.

Ronnie's father was standing over her, the bottle of Jack Daniels still in his hand, swaying back and forth. He looked up at Ronnie and his mouth opened, but nothing came out.

Ronnie screamed to his mother and fell to the floor to try and help her. She had a large gash in her throat, and with each beat of her failing heart, more of her blood shot from the wound. Ronnie had placed his hand over jagged flesh, trying to staunch the flow of blood, but it just shot out between his fingers.

In moments he was covered in his mother's blood, looking like, he too, was suffering from mortal wounds. Ronnie's father had finally snapped out of his stupor and dialed 911. But by the time the paramedics had arrived it was far too late.

His mother was gone.

They had taken her away later that night and the police had asked him a lot of questions. His father had sat across from him on the couch, and Ronnie had known if he told the police what had really happened to his mother, then he would be next.

He had quietly told the detective he had been in his room and had heard his mother fall; when he'd gone to the kitchen to check on her, she was already dead. When the detective asked about his father, he'd just shaken his head no and had said his dad had been sleeping in the living room.

The detective had known something wasn't right, but without evidence, he had to rule his mother's death an accident.

His father had been pretty decent to him after the funeral, as if he genuinely felt guilty for what he'd done. But as the days turned into weeks and then months, he'd quickly turned back into the abusive drunk who Ronnie knew and hated. That was one of the reasons Ronnie was a bully. He had no idea why he liked to beat up on other kids; he just knew it took his mind off his own problems.

He was about to do just that when RJ's dad had arrived. He saw the way the two of them got along and it made him so angry he thought he would explode. Why did RJ get a dad like Jason and he was stuck with an abusive drunk for a father?

Ronnie slowed his bike when he was directly in front of RJ's house. He could see them in the kitchen now, laughing and smiling through the Venetian blinds.

It made him sick.

Right there and then, he decided if he couldn't have life like that, then neither could RJ. Turning his bike around, he pedaled off into the falling night. A plan was forming in his mind, one that would be set into motion soon. He just needed to get a few supplies together.

Then RJ would see how it feels to live in the kind of world Ronnie had to live in every miserable day of his life.

# CHAPTER FOUR

T HE SILENCE OF the Lawson house was shattered, the ringing phone pulling Jason from a restless sleep. Next to him in bed, Emma stirred fitfully.

"It's all right, honey, I'll get it. You go back to sleep," he told her while patting her shoulder. She merely snorted, let out a small gasp, then resumed sleeping.

Jason picked up the phone on the fifth ring. "Hello?" He asked, groggily.

"Ah, yes, my name is Detective Finnegan. I'm with the Malden Police Dept. Is this Jason Lawson I'm speaking with?"

"Yeah, this is him. Who are you again and why are you calling so late?" He looked at the digital clock on the small table near his bed. "Jesus, it's nearly four in the morning."

"Yeah, uhm, I'm sorry about that, but I'm afraid I have some bad news to give you. It seems sometime late last night your mother passed away in her sleep. Now we don't know much else right now with the exception that it seemed to be of natural causes and she didn't appear to suffer. I'll need you to come down to the morgue as soon as possible to identify the...I mean her, and there's a pile of paperwork for you to fill out."

Jason was speechless. He lay there in bed with the phone by his ear. The detective was saying something, but it sounded as if it was coming from far away. After a few seconds he heard his name through the phone and he snapped out of it.

"What, huh, oh I'm sorry, Detective, uhm, Finnegan, you said?

"Yes, sir, it is."

"Right, okay. It's just that it's kind of a shock. Jesus, I just spoke to her the other day. She was fine then."

"Yes, I'm sure it is, the shock that is. I recently lost my father myself and I know how tough it can be. I'm so very sorry for your loss. Look, you don't have to come in until the morning, so if it's possible, try to get some rest. If you decide to come in tonight, though, I'll be at the morgue down at the Meadowview Hospital for a few hours, that's where your mother is. After that you can get me at the station. Do you know where that is?"

"Ah, yeah, sure I do, all right, thanks for your call Detective and I guess I'll see you in a little while."

"Okay, goodnight, Mr. Lawson, and once again, I'm so sorry for your loss." The phone gave a soft click and the line went dead. Jason gently set the phone back on its receiver and lay flat on his back, staring at the ceiling. The streetlamp outside on the sidewalk shone a yellow light into the bedroom where it seeped around the window shade and odd shapes drifted by on the ceiling whenever a car would drive by on the street.

"Who was that Jason; is everything alright?" Emma asked from his side; her voice groggy with sleep.

Jason took in a few breaths, then let them out.

"That was the police. My mother died last night. They think it was natural causes," he stated flatly.

Emma's intake of breath was loud enough for Jason to hear it easily.

"Oh my God, are you all right? Oh, honey, what should we do?" She asked all this even though she had no idea what to do or say.

Jason just lay there. "There's really not that much to do. I have to go down to the morgue and…you know. Then I guess there's the funeral to deal with. Jesus, she was doing fine the last time I talked to her. She'd said she was taking the blood pressure medication and she was feeling pretty good." He sighed again. "Now I'm alone," he said quietly.

"No you're not, Jason. How can you even say such a thing? What about me and RJ?"

He shook his head, dismissing her. "That's not the same thing. Look, you know I love you both with all my heart, but my mother and father were my first family, so to speak. You know about what happened to my dad and, well, my mother was all I had left."

He sat up in bed and slid his feet into his slippers.

"Where're you going?" Emma asked, concerned.

"I'm going to the morgue to see my mom. I sure as hell can't just lay here." He bent over and kissed her on the cheek. "Look, I'll call work in the morning and tell them I'm gonna need a few days off. Don't say anything to RJ, I'll tell him when he gets home from school today, okay?"

She seemed to hesitate for a moment, but then nodded her consent.

"Fine, whatever you say. Just don't forget that I'm here for you, but if you need some space, I can give that to you, too."

He smiled wanly at her for saying that. "Thanks, honey, I guess that's why I love you so much." He kissed her one more time and then went to the bathroom to comb his hair and get dressed.

Once he had his coat on, he stepped through the front door and out into the brisk October air.

One fleeting thought crossed his mind while he walked to his car parked in the driveway. "Well, at least there won't be a lot of traffic on the roads," he mumbled to himself. Then he climbed into his car and drove off into the night.

Somewhere in some cold, dark room, his mother's cold corpse was waiting for him to arrive.

It was still dark when he pulled into the parking lot of the Meadowview Hospital in Medford. The car ride had been blissfully short. Jason had been glad for that. His mood was morose as he thought about his mother, images of what had happened to her constantly forcing themselves through his mind no matter how hard he tried to keep them out.

He parked near the front entrance and walked up the cement walkway. Once inside the main lobby, he noticed there was a fat security guard on duty. The hospital was still on the night shift, only a skeleton crew there to take care of the patients and attend to any emergency's that may arise in the course of the night.

But the Medford, Malden area was usually quiet, with only the usual problems to deal with at night; not like a big city, with their drug deaths and muggings ruling the emergency room nightly.

The security guard looked up when he walked in. He immediately sat up and tried to look a little more efficient, Jason noticed, but the telltale sign of the donut he'd been eating and the cup of coffee gave the phony appearance away.

"Ah, hello, there; I'm looking for the morgue," Jason said quietly.

The lobby was dead silent and it felt weird talking loud.

The guard pointed to a bank of elevators across the lobby.

"Take those to the basement, and then walk straight until you see the desk. There should be a guy there to help you out," he said, politely.

Jason nodded thanks and then did as instructed.

The elevator ride was quick and in less than a minute he stepped out into the hallway to the morgue. A few of the overhead lights were out, casting the hallway in shadows. Jason started walking, his shoes echoing off the walls. It was an eerie feeling, he thought to himself, while he moved further down the empty hallway.

When he'd finally reached the desk, it was empty. Wherever the person manning it was, they weren't where Jason needed them to be. Deciding he didn't want to wait, he walked around the desk and decided to search for where his mother was.

While he walked deeper into the labyrinth of the morgue's hallways, he caught the subtle smell of disinfectant, and something else. If death could be bottled up and sold, he thought he had found the fragrance.

Turning a corner, he saw two doors in front of him, one on each side of the hallway. Noise was coming from the door on his right and he decided that one should be as good as any other. Moving forward the few steps, he reached out and pushed the door open. As he stepped inside the door, the noise grew louder. It reminded him of when he was at home and city-workers would be trimming some of the tree branches away from the power lines in front of his house, the high pitched chainsaw slicing through the wood like a hot knife through butter.

He stopped cold at the sight he was unfortunately privy to see.

His mother was lying on a steel gurney and a man was leaning over her. He had what Jason guessed was a bone saw. The man had just finished cutting his mother's skull cap open and was even now removing her brains. Her internal organs were spread out on an adjoining table as if the man was doing inventory.

His face mask was covered with blood spray and, when Jason stepped closer, he saw his mother's chest was cut open; her empty chest cavity open to the room.

While the man removed the brain from the skull and placed it on a scale, he looked up and his face filled with surprise when he saw Jason.

"Uh, excuse me sir, but you can't be in here. You need to leave right now."

Jason wasn't hearing any of it. Staring at his mother's body, now nothing more than a piece of meat for this jackal to carve up and examine, plus the shock of finding out she was dead, hit him like a ton of bricks.

Images of his father being killed and eaten by something from his nightmares flooded back into his mind. Long dormant thoughts, pushed to the bottom of his mind, now rushed to the surface and overwhelmed him.

While Jason never thought it would happen in a million years, he fainted.

His vision blurred and he felt light headed. And the next thing he sensed was his body falling to the cold cement floor…then nothing.

While he was unconscious, his mind continued working, trying to deal with everything happening to him, his subconscious working overtime to catch up.

Images of his mother floated to him, back to just after his father had disappeared. She was fine now, her body whole once again. Jason was in his childhood bed, the blankets tucked all around him as his mother put him to bed for the night.

His eyes glanced to the closet door and he knew he was afraid of it, but for the life of him, he couldn't remember why. All the psychiatry sessions and drugs he'd been fed had done their job well.

His mother looked down on him and smiled, her eyes reflecting the wan light in the bedroom.

"Now you go to sleep, honey, and I'll see you in the morning," she said.

"But I don't want to," he whined. "There's something in the closet, I'm scared."

She sighed and sat down on the side of the bed next to her son. "Now look, Jason, we've been over this. There's nothing in your closet, you just had a terrible nightmare. Do you remember what the doctors told you?"

"Yes, that there's no such thing as monsters and that no matter how hard I don't want to believe it, Dad just left us." Jason repeated back to her. It had become his doctrine, the doctors wanting him to say it every night before bed. Jason had recited it so many times he'd begun to believe it himself.

His mother smiled, nodding and closing her eyes as if in prayer. "That's right, honey. I know it's hard, but it's the truth. Now you go to sleep, we'll talk more in the morning."

"Okay, Mom, but can you check the closet before you go to bed, please?"

She nodded. "All right, honey, if it will let you sleep, but we need to stop this, the doctors said so."

Jason just nodded, agreeing with her. "I know, but just one more time…to make sure. Then I'll be fine."

His mother sighed and stood up. Walking over to the closet, she opened it as wide as it would go. Jason hid under the covers of his bed, only his eyes peeking out, expecting his mom to be ripped apart and torn into little bite size pieces at any second.

But nothing happened.

"See, its empty, nothing in here but your clothes." Then she started to close the door.

Jason was relaxing, realizing his fears were unfounded.

Just before his mom closed the door all the way, a clawed hand stuck out and wrapped itself around the edge of the door.

Jason's eyes grew wide when he saw the obsidian appendage, but his mother didn't seem to notice. His vocal cords were frozen, his mother turning to walk towards him to give him one more kiss good night.

The closet door swung open once more, a small creaking from the old hinges filling the room. His mom just stood there, totally unaware what was behind her.

Jason wanted to scream at her, tell her to run, to get away, but he was frozen in terror. The Soul Eater had returned for his mom and as it raised itself over her, its own bulbous head scraping the ceiling of his room, he let out one soft squeak.

His mother heard it and looked down at him, curious.

"What's the matter, dear, are you all right?" She asked.

Jason never got the chance to tell her.

In one smooth motion, the obsidian shape dove down and swallowed her head, the dark lips wrapping around her head just above the shoulders. His mother's limbs started to jerk, the beheading sending her body into massive death throes.

The creature never moved, but continued sucking the life's blood from her body, like she was nothing more than a silly straw. His voice finally became unfrozen and he called to her, one hand frantically reaching out to her dancing, jiggling corpse, but he knew it was too late.

The creature had finished and it removed its mouth from her neck with a wet pop. Before his mother's body could fall, she was picked up and thrown over its shoulder like a sack of wheat.

The creature hesitated then, staring at Jason, as if it was debating if it wanted to take him this dark night, as well. Its mouth slid into a grin, his mom's blood dripping from the corners of the scarlet slit.

Blackened teeth could be seen in the gloom of the room, the red plasma glistening on the filed points. Then when Jason thought he was next, the creature turned and jumped into the closet.

There was a flash of red and orange and it was gone, along with his mother.

Now he was truly alone. An orphan with no one to take care of him in a big old empty house.

He started crying and something strong assailed his olfactory senses, causing him to shake his head.

He opened his eyes to see two men standing over him. One was the man who had been cutting his mother into little bite size pieces. The other was a tall man in an overcoat. Jason saw a badge pinned to the man's lapel. The man smelled of cigar smoke and too many bottles of beer. When the man used his hands to help Jason up, Jason caught a glimpse of where a wedding band once resided, now nothing but a faded tan line from years of working outside in the sun.

The cop helped him sit up, and then lifted him to a standing position. On unsteady legs, Jason was ushered out of the coroner's room and into the hall. There was a chair there now and he gratefully sat in it.

There was another person waiting in the hallway now, too. From the uniform, Jason deduced it was probably the absentee security guard from the desk down at the end of the hall.

Detective Finnegan helped him to the chair and grinned.

"There you go, fella, take it easy. You whacked your head pretty good on the way down, too," he said.

Groggily, Jason felt the back of his head. There was a small lump there now, confirming what the man just said.

"Wow, what happened?" He asked.

"What happened," the man in the white lab coat told him, "was that Stan here wasn't at his post and you waltzed right in here. I'm so sorry; you should never have had to see what I was doing in there." He had a small pen light in his hand and he flashed it into Jason's eyes, one after the other. "It appears that you fainted."

"Well, you seem okay now, no signs of a concussion," the coroner said.

Stan stood a little straighter, offended by the coroner's remark. "Now wait a minute there, Jim. I had to go to the bathroom. It's not like you would have watched the desk when I went," the security guard protested.

"I'm sorry, Stan, but that's not my problem. You need to take it up with your supervisor."

The two men continued bickering until Detective Finnegan held up his hands.

"Enough, you two. Christ, this man just saw his mother dissected and you two are bickering like a couple of school girls. Save it for later."

Both men stopped arguing, but by their appearances it looked like the subject was far from closed.

Jason looked up at Detective Finnegan. "Uhm, hi there, I'm Jason L..."

Before he could finish, Finnegan nodded. "Yes, I know who you are, Mr. Lawson. When you went down I was just walking in. I checked your wallet for your ID. I'm very sorry you had to see that. It's not usually like this in here. It's usually very professional." At that last word he looked at Jim.

"What, it's not my fault. I was just doing what I always do," Jim said offended.

Finnegan held his hand up again, calming the man down.

"All right, Jim, still, this shouldn't have happened." Finnegan looked to Jason again. "Look, Mr. Lawson, I don't want to sound callous, but I take it you identified your mother in there. Am I correct?"

Jason nodded. "Yeah, I guess so, at least of what you butcher's left of her," he spit.

"Like I said, Mr. Lawson, I'm really, really sorry. You should never have gotten down this far. I was doing the autopsy to see how your mother passed," the coroner said.

Finnegan's eyes lit up a little. "And did you?"

Jim nodded. "Actually, yeah, I did. Mr. Lawson, according to your mother's medical records, she was taking high blood pressure medicine, correct."

Jason nodded. "Yes, she was, why?"

"Well, because I did a tox screen and her blood has no chemicals in it what so ever. She wasn't taking her medicine and that's what resulted in the heart attack that killed her." He hesitated for the briefest moment. "I'm so sorry."

"That's okay, Doctor, it's not your fault." Jason looked up at Finnegan. "Look, I think I did what you wanted me to do, so if you don't mind, I'll be leaving now."

"Of course, Mr. Lawson. I tell you what. Because of all this, I'll bring the paperwork to you tomorrow. How about at noon?"

"Yeah, that's fine." He looked at the coroner. "When will my mother be released to the funeral home? You know, for the wake and stuff?"

"I'd say by tomorrow afternoon. Two the latest. Just have the funeral home call me and we'll work it out. You don't need to be a part of that."

Jason just nodded. On top of the way he felt, he had to do all the funeral arrangements on his own, although he was sure Emma would help.

"That's fine, bye then," he said, turning and walking away. He felt like he was in a daze, like he was watching someone else control his body.

"Oh, Mr. Lawson, wait a sec' won't you?" Finnegan asked while catching up to him.

He handed Jason a business card. "Here, take this. If you need anything that I can help with, give me a call."

Jason took it without seeing it. "Yeah, thanks, Detective, see you."

Then he left the morgue and his mother behind. He was pretty shaken up and he was looking forward to crawling back into bed and burying himself in the blankets for a few more hours.

Hopefully, he could put this horrible morning out of his memory. After all, it wouldn't be the first time he'd managed to push down terrible memories.

# CHAPTER FIVE

R J WAS PEDALING his bike as fast as he could, trying to make it home before he was seen by Ronnie. Almost everyday Ronnie and his two sidekicks would try to catch him and take his money and usually beat him up. He had managed to escape his grasp the other day thanks to his dad and he knew Ronnie and his goons would be looking for some payback

When they did, they never did it the easy way, like wedgies or wet willies. Oh, no, these bullies were serious, with punches to the stomach and face. One time, RJ got himself a split lip when he wasn't fast enough to escape. He'd told his mother he'd fallen off his bike and his face had hit the pavement.

She had hugged him and had then put peroxide on it, telling him he would be okay.

Now, as he turned onto one of the last street corners before his house, he could still remember the sting of the analgesic before it had started working, despite her soothing words.

His heartbeat was beating fast from both fear and pedaling. Once he turned the next corner, his pulse slowed a little. At least today he would make it to his house unscathed.

Without warning, Ronnie shot out from behind a parked minivan and crashed his bike into RJ's rear wheel. RJ struggled with the steering, and for a moment really thought he was going down, but at the last second managed to regain control.

He hit the brakes and fell a little to the side. Not the best stop, but still not the worst.

Kyle and Chris came up behind him, an evil smile on their lips. They knew what was coming and so did RJ.

"Hey, dork, where ya goin' so fast? You scared of somethin'?" Ronnie sneered.

Inside RJ's chest, his heart felt like it was going to explode, the fear was so strong. His legs felt like spaghetti, barely strong enough to hold him upright.

It took all of his strength to just keep from falling down. He looked around the street, hoping some grown-up would see what was happening and help him, but the street was deserted.

It was a little past three in the afternoon and most people were either greeting their children when they came home from school or still working.

He turned back to Ronnie while both Kyle and Chris started chuckling.

RJ swallowed the lump in his throat, and when he was sure his voice was steady, he looked into Ronnie's eyes.

"Hey, Ronnie, what's up? I was just goin' home, that's all. Can I help you with something?"

Ronnie laughed at that. "Help me? That's good, Lawson. The only thing you can help me with is to pretend you're my punching bag for a little while."

Ronnie looked to his two goons. "You guys get on both sides of him, and if he tries to run, you know what to do," he told them.

They both nodded and pulled their bikes to either side of RJ. Now he was stuck in the middle. For the briefest of flashes, he wondered if he could make a break for it. His house was just around the corner, and once he made it to his front lawn, he knew Ronnie and the others would give up; at least for this chase.

Tomorrow would be another day with more running and hiding.

Ronnie turned his bike around and started to pedal away from RJ's house. RJ had no choice but to follow him or risk getting a pounding right there in the middle of the street.

As he rode, the terror was building to the point he could barely pedal. His arms and legs were shaking and he couldn't remember the last time he'd been so scared. Evidently, it must have showed on his face, because when Ronnie turned around to check on him, his teeth flashed in a feral grin.

RJ had a vision of a car flying down the street and striking Ronnie at that exact moment. He could picture the front bumper of the car hitting Ronnie and his bike. He imagined Ronnie's body crumpling over the hood like a rag doll before his fractured and bruised body was thrown twenty feet into the air. His head would land first, hitting the pavement hard enough to crack his skull wide open. People would come running out of their houses to see what had happened, only to find the shattered remains of Ronnie's corpse. His blood would be pooling under him, his eyes showing a dead glassy stare.

That image gave RJ hope, but when they drove two streets over and went into a shadow enshrouded alley, he knew it would not be happening today.

Ronnie pulled up with his bike and climbed off it, the bicycle falling to the cement with a clatter. RJ waited, too scared to move until Ronnie pointed to the wall that lined one side of the alley.

"Get off your bike, squirt, and stand over there," he ordered RJ.

RJ did as he was instructed, a million scenarios going through his head. He could see himself being as strong and brave as Anakin Skywalker, using the Force to distract Ronnie and the others, then throwing punches at Ronnie and then blocking some from Kyle and Chris. Then he'd punch each one in their stomachs, and while they were down, he would hop on his bike and with a "so long suckers," ride out of the alley, leaving the three older boys licking their wounds.

But it was just wishful thinking. The truth was, he just couldn't muster up the courage. He was firmly intimidated by Ronnie and his two fellow bullies.

He went to the alley wall and stood there, hoping if he cooperated, maybe they'd just take his money and his bike so he would have to walk home. When that happened, he would usually find his bike just lying on the sidewalk somewhere along the route back to his house.

Ronnie knew if he took it for real, then RJ would have no choice but to tell his mom when she wanted to know where it was. So he would just take it a little and leave RJ with no choice but to pick it up and go home with his tail between his legs…again.

RJ stood perfectly still, waiting for his punishment, whatever it might be today.

Ronnie moved closer, until he was standing directly in front of RJ. He was a good four inches taller than him, and as he stood there with a malevolent grin on his face, RJ thought he looked ten feet tall.

His breath smelled like beef jerky and his shirt had a small yellow stain on it. If RJ had to guess, it was probably mustard. He knew they'd had hotdogs in the school cafeteria for lunch and knowing Ronnie, that was all he could afford, despite the fact RJ seemed to be supporting him single handedly.

Ronnie sucked in a big gulp of air and  let out a burp directly in RJ's face. Both Kyle and Chris liked that and they laughed from RJ's side. They were set up in a position in the alley so if someone walked by, they would be hard pressed to see what was happening to him, not to mention, from where they had stationed themselves, RJ couldn't get too far if he tried to make a break for it.

Ronnie enjoyed the laughter from his two friends; he liked to be the center of attention. That's why he was always doing bad stuff, RJ's dad had told him. Some kids will be either good or bad, just as long as it gets them attention. Unfortunately for RJ, Ronnie seemed to lean towards the bad stuff.

Ronnie leaned forward so his face was no more than an inch from RJ's.

"Listen up, squirt, do what I say and you'll be out of here in no time, got it?"

RJ nodded, too fearful to say anything. His heart felt like a jack rabbit was running back and forth in his chest and he was really starting to wonder if someone could die from fear alone.

"Put your hands up in the air, over your head," Ronnie told him.

RJ did as he was told, wondering what was going on. This was all new to him, which was giving him just the slightest bit of hope that maybe he'd be okay.

Then, without warning, Ronnie sent a punch straight into RJ's stomach. The breath flew out of his lungs and he bent over. He thought he was going to puke, but used all his willpower to keep it in. If Ronnie saw him throw up, then it would be just one more form of humiliation he'd use in the future.

The three bullies were laughing, thinking the entire episode was hilarious. RJ had gathered enough wind to stand back up, only now he had to lean against the wall or risk toppling over. He saw small white lights, like tiny stars, dancing across his vision.

There was a small voice in the back of RJ's head that was screaming at him to fight back. In front of him, Ronnie was just standing there, relaxed, his hands by his sides. RJ could send an uppercut into his chin that would probably have the bully biting his tongue in half, but the fear was too strong and he pushed the voice back down where it had stayed for so many years.

Before RJ realized it, Ronnie was punching him in the cheek. RJ's head rolled with the punch, only the inside of his cheek receiving a cut from his teeth.

Considering some of the punches RJ had received from his bully, that one actually wasn't that bad. Ronnie was rubbing his knuckles, preparing for another blow when a voice sounded from the end of the alley way.

"Hey, you kids, leave that child alone!" A woman's voice screeched. "Get out of here or I'll call the cops!" She screeched, her head looking this way and that for help.

"Shit, come on, guys, I don't need trouble from the cops, let's get out of here before the old bat finds one," Ronnie said, climbing onto his bike and pedaling the opposite way out of the alley.

Ronnie stopped and looked at RJ, a sneer on his face. "Keep your big trap shut if you know what's good for you, Lawson," Ronnie said and rode away.

Kyle and Chris, like the good lapdogs they were soon followed, leaving RJ alone in the alley.

When the woman saw it was safe, she walked down and looked at RJ. With the exception of a thin ribbon of blood dripping from the side of his mouth, he appeared fine.

"Are you all right, honey? I saw what those boys were doing to you. Do you need me to call your parents for you, so they can come get you?"

RJ shook his head, the movement causing him some pain. "No thank you, ma'am, I'll be okay."

He climbed onto his bike and pointed it to the end of the alley. "Thanks again ma'am, I don't know what those jerks might have done if you hadn't yelled at them."

She smiled at that. "Well, I'm just glad you're all right."

"Yeah, I'll be fine. Well I better get home, my mom's gonna be wondering where I am." Then he started off, leaving the woman behind.

As he pulled out onto the street, the woman shook her head, wondering why boys had to be so mean to each other when they were young. But then, as she thought of all the wars that had been fought over the decades, she figured no matter what their age, boys were always mean to other boys, even when they became men.

RJ rode his bike into his driveway and let it fall to the green grass at his feet on the side of the house. He took a few deep breaths to try to regain his composure, then wiped the few tears from his cheeks.

Though he'd done his best not to cry, eventually they came, as they always did. He would always chastise himself for being such a coward, knowing he would never break out from under Ronnie's thumb if he didn't stand up to him, but he just wasn't a fighter.

Luckily this time, his bruises were under his clothes, so there would be no explanations today to his mom. He noticed his dad's car was in the driveway, which was unusual for this time of day.

Probably just took some time off. His dad did that every now and again. RJ liked when he did, it usually meant they would go out to dinner for a change, so his mom didn't have to cook.

When he was sure he looked okay, he put on his best smile and started for the back door. As usual, it was unlocked and he stepped into the kitchen expecting his mom to be there, but instead the room was empty.

"Mom, you here? I'm home," he called from the kitchen table. He set his book bag down and opened the fridge, grabbing a grape soda.

"We're in the living room, RJ, would you come in here, please? Your father and I have something to talk to you about," his mom called.

Nervousness flooded through him as he tried to think back on the past two days or so. Had he done something wrong that they'd found out about? The more he racked his brain, the more he couldn't remember doing anything that would require him to be worried. So putting on his best game face he strode into the living room.

Both his parents were sitting on the couch, but his father's face looked sad. His dad reminded him of one of those Basset hounds he saw when they went to the park to play catch together last week.

Jason looked up at his son and gestured for him to have a seat on the nearby chair.

"Have a seat, son, something's happened you should know about."

RJ swallowed the soda in his mouth and sat down, for the life of him having no idea what was going on.

Jason filled him in on his grandmother's death and about what would happen next. RJ sat quietly through the entire speech, not really knowing what to say.

He had loved his grandmother, but had never really been that close to her. Her death was more like when a close friend dies. Someone you see all the time, but don't talk to a lot. A lot of the reasons for that fell onto Jason's shoulders.

Because what had happened to Jason had so traumatized him, once he'd turned eighteen, he had left his house and never stepped foot inside it again. So whenever RJ saw his grandmother, it was when she came to their house to visit or sometimes during the holidays. There were never the memories of walking into grandma's house and smelling fresh baked cookies or sleeping over on the weekends.

RJ just sat there quietly until Jason was finished.

"Well, that's it, son, are there any questions you want to ask me or your mom?" Jason asked.

RJ just shrugged. "Do I have to wear a suit for the funeral?"

Jason chuckled a little and looked to Emma, she smiled back. "Yes, honey, I'm afraid you do. The funeral is the day after tomorrow. It's in the late afternoon so the funeral home has enough time to get things ready and then there'll be a get together here at the house, afterward. Everything should be over by nine or so."

Inside RJ was moaning. That night was when most of his favorite TV shows were on and he didn't have a VCR in his room. He knew what his dad would say if he asked him to tape his shows, so he just sighed and stood up from his chair.

"May I be excused, please?" He asked, with a downtrodden look on his face.

Both his parents nodded and he went up to his room.

Jason looked to Emma and sighed. "Wow, Em' did you see his face? He took it pretty hard."

"Yeah, but he's a tough kid, he'll get through it. You did when your father left and so will he."

That caused a pang of sadness as he remembered his father, at what had happened that night. He told everybody, including the psychiatrist's, that he'd imagined the whole thing, that no shadow-shaped monster had come out of his closet to kill and take his father way. But inside where no one could go but him, he knew the truth.

That monster's did exist, and one of them had killed his father in front of him.

Jason stood up and stretched. "I'm going to go lay down for a while, I didn't get much sleep when I came back this morning."

Emma rubbed his leg. "Sure, honey, you go 'head."

Jason gave her a kiss on the cheek and went up to his room. As he walked by RJ's room, he paused, listening to his son's choice in music.

Motley Crue wailed through the door and Jason chuckled. After all these years, his bands were making a small comeback. It felt weird having his son listening to the same music he had listened to growing up.

Walking into his room, he closed the door and lay down on his bed. Visions of dark shapes and bloody teeth flew through his mind. It was another hour before he finally relaxed enough for sleep to even attempt to approach him.

When he actually drifted off to sleep, he ended up dreaming about his own father, and all the fun times they had enjoyed together, while he snored softly into his pillow.

# CHAPTER SIX


T HE FUNERAL CAME quick for the Lawson family. The church was the family's local parish, although Jason hadn't set foot inside the hallowed walls in years. If he'd ever had any faith in God, it disappeared the night his father was taken from him.

RJ sat in the front pew of the church, trying to look sad, but really not that broken up. He felt unhappy for his father, who seemed to be taking it pretty hard, though. RJ couldn't blame him. If his mom died, he knew he'd be crying all the time.

He looked at his mother, standing solemnly next to Jason, and she caught his glance.

She smiled wanly at him, sending her love across the room. He grinned back and then stood up, deciding he was feeling restless. He walked around a little. Strangers who he had never met him continually began telling him how sorry they were for his loss.

He ended up by his grandmother's casket, the top open to display the body. He looked down at her, his eyes scanning every detail. She looked so phony, like a statue.

As he looked at his first dead body, (with the exception of what he saw in the movies and on TV), he was the most surprised at how sanitized she looked.

Not a hair was out of place and her makeup looked like she had been to Hollywood and had a makeover by one of those shows his mom liked to watch.

He reached out to touch her hand, but chickened out at the last second.

"They did a nice job, didn't they, son? It looks like she's just sleeping," Jason said from his side. His cheeks were wet from crying.

He had been so absorbed looking at the cadaver, he hadn't heard his father come up to him. He didn't know what to say, so he just remained silent.

"She was a good mother to me, RJ, just like your mom is to you. I'm gonna miss her," Jason said quietly.

"Yeah, I'll miss her, too," RJ said, thinking that was the right thing to say. The truth was; he really didn't know what he felt. If anything, just a little creeped out by the whole thing. If he died, the last thing he would want is a bunch of people staring at his lifeless body. The whole thing gave him the creeps.

Jason became distracted when some more mourners gave their condolences, then some of them told RJ the same thing.

He thanked them and then continued on to the back of the church. He stopped in his tracks when he saw who had just walked inside the large theatre.

A young girl, looking to be the same age as RJ, had just entered with her parents.

She was pretty with high cheekbones, and had light, natural blonde hair that seemed to glow from the sun washing into the church from the open doors behind her. She spotted RJ and walked over to him, after a quick look at her mother to make sure it was all right.

Walking up to RJ, she seemed to glide across the floor. RJ stood transfixed. This was the girl he had an unrequited love for, the girl next door he'd always cared for.

Her name was Nancy May Masters and they had lived a few houses down from one other for their whole lives and he thought her blue eyes were the most beautiful thing he had ever seen.

Now that he was turning twelve, he'd begun to have feelings for her that he didn't quite understand. Jason had given him the sex talk, but there was still so much more that a simple talk could explain.

She had been his first kiss.

He was seven at the time and they had been playing house. He'd just come through the cardboard box that was supposed to be their home. He had kissed her on the cheek and she had smiled at him. He knew from that moment on that he loved her. At least in that puppy dog way of a school yard crush.

Like the way his heart beat faster and wanted to explode out of his chest whenever he saw her. It felt a lot like when Ronnie was ready to start pounding on him, but this time it was a little more pleasurable.

When she was only a few feet away, she smiled at him. "Hey, RJ, I'm really sorry about your grandma," she said quietly.

"Thanks, Nancy. I didn't know you were coming today."

"Yeah, well, our parents have been friends for like, forever, so they said they would come. I figured I'd come, too. You know, to see how you are."

He smiled at that, his heart beating like a drum solo. "Thanks, Nancy, that's really nice of you." RJ looked to the front of the church where the priest was getting ready for his sermon.

"So, ah, ww…would you like to come sit in ff…front with me and my pp…parents?" He stammered out.

"Sure, RJ, let me just make sure it's okay with my folks. Wait here, okay?" She walked away then, gliding through the other attendees in search of her parents.

He nodded, not knowing what else to say; feeling stupid from his bout of stuttering.

His suit was getting clammy and he began sweating from every pore on his skin. His mouth felt like a desert and he wished he could get a glass of water.

Slipping between two black-suited bodies in the crowd of mourners, Nancy reappeared. She was smiling, her face making his heart skip a beat.

"My dad said it's all right," she told him.

He was about to answer her when the priest starting speaking into a microphone, telling everyone to: "Please take their seats so they could begin."

RJ moved up the aisle with Nancy next to him. For the briefest moment, it felt like they were a couple, moving down the center aisle to be married. He liked the thought.

Once they had made it to the front, Jason gestured for him to sit down with a brief acknowledgement to Nancy.

The funeral began, the priest droning on about living in God's land forever and other similar sounding lines. RJ barely heard any of it. Nancy had to sit close to him to make room for the other mourners, so her body was touching his left side. He could feel her warmth and every time she moved or squirmed in her seat, he felt tingles up his legs and arms.

Despite the unhappy reason he was in the church, it was one of the happiest days of his life. Eventually the sermon ended and the priest gave instructions for how they would be getting to the cemetery.

Everyone stood up, getting ready to leave and Nancy turned to RJ.

"That was a nice sermon, I'm sure your grandma would have liked it," she said.

"Uh-huh, I guess so," RJ answered.

"Well, I better get back to my parents; they said they wanted me in our car when we went to the cemetery. I'll see you later at your house?"

His eyes lit up. "Sure, you bet!" He said enthusiastically and maybe a little too loud.

She chuckled at that and then she did the one thing RJ would never have expected. She leaned over and kissed him on the cheek.

"Hope you feel better, I'll see you in a little while." Then like an apparition, she disappeared into the crowd and was gone.

RJ stood in the pew with his hand on his cheek, dumbfounded. His parents were getting ready to go so he knew he had to leave, too.

"Wow," he said. "I'm never going to wash this cheek again." Then he ran after his parents so they could go to the cemetery.

RJ barely paid attention to the time at the cemetery, only looking forward to when they could leave and get to his house again for the gathering after the funeral. The priest went through the motions and in time they laid his grandmother to rest.

Then everyone climbed back into their vehicles and some followed them home while others just went their own way. Upon reaching his house, RJ had jumped out and waited on the curb for Nancy. Time went by, but her car never appeared.

After more than an hour had gone by, he decided her parents must have changed their minds and decided not to come.

He decided to go back inside, his heavy heart fitting the atmosphere perfectly.

He wandered into the living room and saw his dad in the corner of the living room. Jason was talking with a man that RJ had never seen before. With nothing better to do, RJ grabbed a finger sandwich from the buffet his mother had set up thanks to the caterer she'd hired and went over to hear what they were saying.

"But, Mr. Lawson, the house is yours now. Surely you at least want to think it over for a little while. I mean, the house is almost twice the size of the one you presently own and it's only a few streets over. Don't you at least want to talk it over with your wife?" The strange man said.

"No, I already told you my answer," Jason said. "My father died in that house and I swore I'd never step foot in it again. With my mother gone, you can just put it on the market and sell it. And God help whoever buys it."

"Really, Mr. Lawson, don't you think you're being a little melodramatic? I knew your mother for more than twenty years and have spent many an afternoon with her in that house going over her affairs. I never got even the slightest impression that there was something out of place about that house."

Jason took a sip of his drink and then pointed his finger at the man. "Look, I don't really give a shit what you think. With my mother gone, its mine now, and I'm telling you to sell that house, now if you can't handle it, then there's about a thousand other people in the phone book who can!" Jason's voice had slowly been going up in pitch as he became more agitated. All around him, people were stopping their conversations to hear what was going on.

Emma moved through the crowd and took her husband's arm.

"I think that's enough business for now, Mr. Reilly. Why don't we deal with this stuff in a few days when things have calmed down a little?" She suggested.

Mr. Reilly nodded. "Of course, how unsympathetic of me. Of course this is neither the time nor the place. Why don't I take my leave and let you mourn in peace. Once again, I'm so sorry for your loss. She was a great client and an even greater friend. She will be missed." Then he turned and moved away from Jason and Emma.

Jason watched him go, his hands forming into fists. Emma rubbed his arm, calming him down. After a few moments went by, the rest of the gatherers went back to their own conversations. It wasn't like they hadn't seen emotional outbursts at a funeral before.

"I'm okay, honey, it's just thinking about that house, you know?" Jason said quietly.

Emma nodded. "That's okay, Jason, whatever you want to do is fine with me. Now what do you say we go see some more of our friends, after all, they did take the time to pay their respects."

Jason nodded and as a couple they moved off across the living room and into the front foyer where a few people were gathered.

RJ sat quiet on the couch. With all the emotions flying, no one had noticed him.

What was his dad talking about? What was wrong with Grandma's house?

How did all that figure in to what had happened to his Grandpa?

Everyone in his family had always said his Grandpa had run off, probably with some stripper. At least that's what his grandmother had always said. Could it be that wasn't the truth?

Deciding it would keep for another day, he went off to get some more food. Those finger sandwiches were good.

# CHAPTER SEVEN

THE MORNING AFTER funeral was a Saturday.

RJ was in his living room, still in his Spiderman pajamas, despite the clock on the wall declaring it was well past eleven in the morning.

Sitting on his lap was a bowl of plain cornflakes. His mom usually got good cereal like Cocoa Puffs or Apple Jacks for him, but she'd been occupied with the funeral and now had to deal with the affairs of his dead grandmother.

That was all right with RJ, he knew how to make a bad situation better. Sitting next to him was the empty, ceramic cup of sugar. When he had started to eat his cornflakes, the jar had been half full, now thanks to him, it was empty and his milk was a sweet, sugary concoction that would make any dentist cry.

He was just in the process of finishing the milk when the doorbell rang. He knew his parents were both still in bed, after a long night of cleaning up the mess from all their guests, so he got out of his chair and went to the door. Peeking through the long piece of leaded glass that ran parallel with the door, he nearly dropped his cereal bowl when he saw who it was.

As fast as he could, he set the bowl on a nearby side table and then, realizing he was still in his pajamas, nearly freaked. He was about to run upstairs and change into some real clothes when the doorbell rang again.

"Will someone get the damn door?" Jason yelled from upstairs. By that he meant RJ, because Jason knew his wife was still next to him in bed.

Cursing his luck, he opened the door to see Nancy's beaming face looking back at him.

"Hi," she said, smiling prettily.

"Ah, hi. It's nice to see you, but what are you doing here?" He asked, nervous, but puzzled.

"Well, I thought that since I stood you up yesterday maybe we could go somewhere today instead. I've got the perfect place to show you." She looked down at her feet, a little shyly. "That is, if you want too."

His eyes opened wide, and his pulsed started racing. "Do I? Hell yes. Just give me a few minutes to get dressed."

She nodded. "Okay, by the way, I like your pajamas."

His face turned beet red and he turned to run upstairs. "Uh, thanks, look, stay right here, I'll be right back." Then he took the stairs two at a time and plowed into his room. As fast as he could, he tried to put on something that looked good on him, finally settling on a pair of Levis and a sweatshirt. Just right for the cool October air.

Running back down the stairs and jumping the last three steps, he slowed to a stop at the door. Nancy was still there, waiting patiently.

As an afterthought, RJ turned and yelled up the stairs to his parents.

"Hey, Mom, I'm going out for a little while, but I'll be back soon!"

"Wear a jacket, it's cold out," his mother's voice drifted down the stairs.

"Will everyone shut the hell up!" Jason yelled from the bedroom.

Nancy chuckled at this. "Sounds just like my house. Come on, let's go. Grab your bike; we have to go for a ride to get there."

"Okay. I'll meet you on the side of the house," RJ told her and then ran out through the back door where his bike was laying in the yard. Less than a minute later, he was pulling up beside her on the street in front of his house.

His eyes scanned her quickly as he stopped his bike. She was wearing a blue sweatshirt and a pair of tight jeans that made his stomach flutter every time he looked at her from the back.

He was already looking forward to following her wherever she wanted to go.

"Okay, you ready?" She asked with a mischievous grin.

RJ nodded. "You lead and I'll follow."

With a nod, she started up the street. RJ followed her, admiring the way her backside conformed to the bike seat. They rode for almost a half hour and RJ was really starting to get a little nervous. Just when he was about to ask her where exactly they were going, she turned off the main street they were on and started up a quiet side street.

RJ noticed a sign nailed to a telephone pole. He read it out loud for her to hear.

"Mount Hood golf course? Why are we going there?"

"You'll see," she said, breathing a little heavier as they began riding up a steep hill.

The road peaked at the top and then leveled out for a good quarter mile. They were now in Melrose, the city next to his small town of Malden. He had heard of this particular golf course before. Some of the older kids would come here and slide down the large hills with their sleds and snowboards in the winter. There was even a story, more of a myth actually, about something that had happened many years ago. While the story would change from kid to kid, depending on who was telling it, the main gist of the story would always stay the same.

"Hey, Nancy, did you ever hear the story of the kid with the severed fingers?" He asked her, pedaling to get next to her.

She made a frown. "Well, sort of, why, do you know it?"

"Uh-huh, you want to hear it?"

"Okay, what really happened?"

"Well, it seems one of the far hills on the course bordered a set of train tracks and one day a bunch of kids were sledding. Every time the train would come through, all the kids would sit up on top of the hill and wait for the train to pass. Sometimes for fun, they'd put rocks or nickels on the tracks and watch them get flattened.

One day while the train was approaching, one of the kids slipped and started sliding down the hill. He tried to stop, but the ice and flattened snow gave him no purchase. He slid right onto the tracks just as the train was ready to run him over. Another kid who was waiting down by the tracks saw all this happen and he ran over and pulled the boy off the tracks, the kid's hands dragging behind him.

He was just a little to slow, though, and just as his right hand was dragging over the tracks, the train ran them over, severing the digits like a knife through butter.

When the train was gone, the kids on the other side of the tracks got an eyeful. The boy was running around screaming, two of his fingers missing, the other two hanging by a thin layer of skin. While the boy ran around, the severed fingers were flapping around, blood spurting everywhere.

He was brought to the hospital by a parent who was there with a younger child.

But the story goes they didn't find all of his fingers and there's still at least one lying around the tracks somewhere, just waiting to be found."

"Ewwww, that's gross, why would you tell me a story like that?" She asked.

He shrugged, his legs pumping away.

"No reason, I just think it's kind of cool. Sorry if I grossed you out."

She smiled at him, the wind whipping her hair behind her.

God, she looks beautiful, RJ thought.

"That's okay, I can see why everybody tells it and now I know it, too."

They were now deep in the golf course, the winding road only large enough for one car at a time. Mostly it was just used by golf carts so lazy people who still wanted to play golf didn't have to walk so much.

They came out into a wide open area, and a small parking lot appeared in front of them. It was abandoned, RJ could tell. The asphalt was cracked and in serious disrepair, and there was a small amount of litter blowing around, which was unusual because the golf course was immaculate everywhere else.

But it was what was in front of him that really impressed him.

Sitting at the end of the lot was what looked like a small medieval castle, or better yet, a rook from a chess set. It was round and made of stone and was three stories tall. At the top, there was a stone border with breaks every two feet so an archer would have a place to fire from if the castle was under attack.

Nancy stopped at the entrance and climbed off her bike, gently leaning it against a ring of boulders that surrounded the parking lot.

"Come on, this is what I wanted to show you. Have you ever been here before?"

He shook his head; he had never known this piece of coolness existed.

She entered the large open entrance and held out her hand to him.

"I want to go to the top. That's why I brought you here." Then she pulled him behind her. The two of them started up the carved stone stairway. The structure had a landing and a small open area at each floor so they could look out through a small one foot square window. At their feet was the refuse from a thousand nights of teenage partying. Beer bottles and newspaper covered the floor from one end to the other, some shattered into a glittering carpet of slivers. Graffiti marred the walls, some looking to be years old.

Nancy kept pulling him, her touch sending tingles down his back. But the more he held her hand, the more he grew comfortable. The worst thing any boy had to worry about is if the girl he likes, likes him back. Well, he was pretty sure Nancy wouldn't have dragged him all the way here and then took his hand if she didn't like him. Still, his stomach felt like a thousand butterflies were trying to fight their way out.

Making it to the top, Nancy let go of his hand and walked over to the edge. The edge was at neck height and you had to stick your head in between the large stones mounted every two feet to see out of the top. The stones surrounded the entire top, making the circle complete.

She pointed out across the golf course to the horizon.

"There," she said, "that's what I wanted to show you."

RJ looked out across the open area and gazed out on the horizon. From where they stood, the city of Boston was clearly visible. The glass surface of the John Hancock building reflected the light like a giant mirror. He looked to his left and he could see the control tower for Logan Airport in East Boston, and as he continued to watch, he realized you could see one of the runways clearly, even now a plane was getting ready to take off.

"Wow," he said, "this is so cool."

She smiled. "I thought you'd like it."

The two stayed there for almost an hour, talking about movies and stuff from school. Down below them, they could see a few golfers driving by on their carts, oblivious to the two kids in the tower.

Standing up on the top, with the wind blowing his hair, RJ felt like a king. It was wonderful. He looked over at Nancy to see she was also gazing into the distance.

She must have felt him looking at her because she turned and stared right at him, her blue eyes never wavering. When their eyes met, time seemed to stop, and for just a few seconds they just stood there, gazing into each others eyes.

Then Nancy leaned forward just a little. RJ knew what was going to happen next and with his blood racing in his ears, he prayed he wouldn't screw it up.

He leaned in a little too, and when she didn't pull away, he leaned in some more. Then he decided if he didn't go for it, he'd chicken out, so he stuck his head in and gave her a firm kiss on the lips.

He closed his eyes and for just a moment felt like this must be what Heaven feels like. Her lips were cool and soft and he could feel her hair hitting his face gently as the wind continued blowing all around them.

Then he pulled away.

She opened her eyes and smiled.

"That was nice," she said.

He nodded, still a little too shocked to answer.

"Uh-huh," he managed. She chuckled at that, her smile growing a little larger. Then she checked her watch.

"Wow, look at the time, we've been up here all day. We should go," she told him.

"Okay, that's probably a good idea; if I don't check in every now and then my mom freaks," RJ agreed.

"Tell me about it. My mom's so over protective of me it's amazing I get to leave the house at all."

The two of them walked down the stone steps, kicking beer bottles out of their path as they went. Once at the bottom, they climbed on their bikes and then started the long ride home.

While RJ rode beside her, his stomach was a little calmer. Something had changed in the time since they had left his house. Now he was more confident with her, more relaxed. They rode in peace for the first half of the trip, and by the second half, they were both chatting up a storm again, talking about the newest movies and the teachers at school who were the biggest jerks.

They were about three blocks away from RJ's house when everything fell apart.

RJ was slightly in the lead, and when he turned a corner, he slammed on his breaks.

Nancy stopped too and was about to ask what the problem was, when the problem made itself very clear to her. Coming down the street in the middle of the road was Ronnie and his two goons, Kyle and Chris.

"Come on, RJ, let's go, they won't bother us," Nancy told him.

But RJ knew they would.

He turned to her then, his face was hard, his jaw tight. "Look, Nancy, I had a great time today, really. But I need to get going. You need to go the other way. I'll see you later; maybe we can go for a ride tomorrow again if you're not doing anything." He turned his bike around and started to pedal back the way they'd come. Nancy never had a chance to say good-bye, before RJ was shooting back down the street, his legs pumping like he was riding in a marathon.

She was puzzled for only a moment, though, until she saw Ronnie and the other two boys fly by her in a blur, going in the same direction RJ had been riding in only seconds before. All she could do is hope RJ would be all right and head for home herself.

She started pedaling again, hugging the cars on her right. She thought back to the kiss with RJ and smiled. It had been nice and she was pretty sure he liked it too.

Thinking of what would come next made her giggle to herself a little and she looked around to make sure she was alone, not wanting someone to see her and think she was weird or anything for talking to herself.

With one more glance behind her, the boys now long gone, she headed up the road; her heart going out to RJ, hoping he would be safe.

# Chapter Eight

R J PEDALED AS fast as he could, sparing glimpses over his shoulder whenever possible while his haggard breath slipped from trembling lips in small gasps of fright. They were right behind him and getting closer with every passing second.

He turned a street corner and realized he was on his grandma's street. Pedaling faster, he made a beeline for her house. Maybe he could find safety there.

Jumping the curb with his bike, he hit the brakes, the rear tire sliding on the grass lining the sidewalk. He pedaled harder and then his grandma's house came into view. He put on one last burst of speed, his legs feeling like they were going to fall off after riding all day with Nancy, and now having to run away from Ronnie, too, was pushing him to his limit.

He pulled up in front of his grandma's house and dropped his bike on the sidewalk. He ran up the stairs and squeezed the door handle.

Luck was with him, the door was unlocked, the handyman working inside having just left moments ago on his way to the hardware store for supplies. RJ charged inside, realizing the door was unlocked because there was no lock on the door. A set of tools lay on the floor as if someone had left in mid-work. RJ barely noticed. Ignoring the door, he ran through the house, seeing most of the furniture was already covered with white sheets. He ran into the kitchen and hid under the kitchen table, hoping he'd be safe there; the tablecloth draping over the sides and hiding him from view.

A minute later the front door opened wide, Ronnie and his two cronies stepping inside.

"I don't know about this, Ronnie. What if someone's home. We could get into a lot of trouble," Chris said.

"Shut up, dipshit, no one's here. This is Lawson's grandma's house and the old bat kicked it the other day. In fact, this is even better. We can pound him for as long as we want and no one will hear a thing."

Ronnie stood in the foyer, his head twitching back and forth like he could pick up RJ's hiding place by smell alone.

"You two, go upstairs and check around, I'll check down here," Ronnie ordered them.

Mumbling to themselves about how it wasn't a good idea, the two still gave in to Ronnie's stronger personality.

RJ heard this and decided he better get out of there and quick. As quietly as he could, he crawled to the back door that led to the backyard and opened it. He slipped through silently then closed it slowly with a soft click. Then he ran around the house and picked up his bike, pedaling for all he was worth to make it back home. His house was only a few streets over and with the head start he had, even if Ronnie found out he'd left, he knew he would be home free.

Back inside the house, Ronnie continued checking the first floor and then went down into the basement. After finding it empty, he returned to the first floor. Seems he was here, he decided to see if there was anything worth stealing.

While he dug around the first floor looking for both valuables and RJ, the other two boys went up stairs.

Stopping at the top of the landing, Kyle looked down the small hallway.

"Why don't you check down there and I'll check these rooms," Kyle suggested.

Chris shrugged. "Whatever, man, I don't even care if we find Lawson anymore, this sucks." With a look of boredom, he headed off down the hallway.

Kyle crept into the room which once belonged to Jason Lawson, the room where Roger Lawson had been killed and taken by something dark and evil twenty years ago.

Outside the house, dusk was falling with the shorter days of the autumn season. The room was shrouded in shadows when Kyle crept into the room. He looked around, almost all of Jason Lawson's belongings exactly where he'd left them all those years ago, when he'd left on his eighteenth birthday.

Kyle knelt down on the floor and pulled the bedspread back, expecting to see RJ's frightened face staring back at him. Instead, all he saw were a bunch of old comics and a few empty Lego boxes.

Letting the bedspread drop, he sat down on the bed. The little runt wasn't in here, he thought.

Then he looked over at the closet door.

As he watched the door, glancing down to the crack where the door met the floor, he noticed a dull and glowing luminance. Standing up, he figured RJ was hiding in the closet with a flashlight to keep him company.

"Pussy," he mumbled, "scared of the dark."

He walked to the door and grabbed the knob. Pulling it open, his breath caught in his throat and he almost fell down, his knees wanting to give out on him.

Where the back of the closet should have been, there was now a glowing, swirling light, which reminded him of that movie The Black Hole. The light seemed to swirl in a circle until it met in the center, then it would start all over again.

For the moment, he was in shock, not thinking to call his fellow friends in to see what he'd found. He stepped a little closer, and picking up a football on the closet floor, he tossed it into the portal. The ball disappeared with the sound like a plastic bag being popped after being filled with air.

"Whoa, this is friggin' awesome," he said to himself. He was about to call the others when there was a flash of light and something came out of the portal. Before he could so much as blink, a black arm with a hand that was all claws swiped out at his throat, severing his vocal cords and jugular in one razor like sweep of its arm. He tried to scream, but nothing came out of his mouth but a soft gargle.

Blood shot forth from the wound, the void pulling the bright red fluid into itself. Kyle stood perfectly still, his mouth opening and closing. He still didn't realize he was dead, despite the fact he was still standing.

With his mouth opening and closing like a fish and his eyes as wide as they would go, he watched something from his worst nightmares step out of the void. It towered over him, the face barely recognizable as humanoid. Where the mouth should be, a slit appeared and he could distinctly see sharp, fang-like teeth glinting in the darkness.

He tried to back away, but his muscles wouldn't cooperate. Already his vision was starting to blur, his nervous system collapsing while his brain cried out for blood and oxygen.

The creature leaned down and picked Kyle up like he was nothing but an infant and curled him to its breast like a weightlifter doing curls.

Its mouth-like orifice came down on his throat, and inhaled, sucking what was left of Kyle's blood into the slurping maw, feeling the dying boy's essence, his soul, fill him.

Kyle died then, mercifully falling unconscious from blood loss. And moments later succumbed to death. He never felt pain; the slice to his throat was so fast and quick it was more like a bee sting to his body's senses than a mortal wound.

Only seconds had passed since Kyle had discovered the void, and the creature now turned and closed the door to the closet.

The last time it had been here, years before, it had fed well, and with the portal once again opened, he knew he would return to this location, one of dozens across this new world.

By the lifeless corpse in his hands, the Soul Eater knew he'd been correct. Since the last time he'd been here, he had learned to keep the portal open longer. He planned on hunting for another three days before the portal would finally close for yet another twenty years.

The Soul Eater stepped back through the portal; there was much to do and little time. If his plans went right, he would capture some of the prey alive and take them back to the home dimension, there he would breed them. Then he would have an unlimited supply of food and wouldn't have to rely on the portal for sustenance.

But for now this corpse would satisfy him.

As the shadowy form returned through the portal, the light flashed out, leaving nothing of the slaughter that had occurred but a few ribbons of blood on the wall and wood floor of the closet.

Chris walked into the room, having come up empty in his search for RJ.

"Hey, Kyle, you in here?" He asked while looking around the room. When no answer was given and he could plainly see the room was empty, he turned around and headed back downstairs, thinking Kyle must already be down there with Ronnie, the two boys probably waiting on him.

Ronnie climbed up the basement stairs, checking the cellar yet again, pissed off at not finding RJ or anything worth taking.

He saw Chris waiting for him in the foyer and called to him.

"Well, did you find the little shit?"

Chris shook his head. "Nope, nothin's up there. He's not down here either?"

Ronnie made a face as if he was surrounded by idiots.

"If he was down here don't you think I'd be holding him?"

Chris just shrugged. Then he looked out the front window.

"Hey, Ronnie, Lawson's bike isn't out front where he left it when he came inside."

Ronnie charged to the window, throwing the curtain aside.

"Shit, the little bastard somehow got around us!" He spit.

Then the front door opened and a man stepped into the foyer. He was wearing a tool belt and Ronnie was able to see out the door at the van parked in front of the house. On the side of the van was a sign that read. "Vinnie Pascolli, Handyman. No Job Too Small."

Ronnie noticed the man had a plastic bag in his hand that had the local hardware store's name on it. This guy must have slipped out to get some parts for the door or something, and that's why Lawson had been able to get inside.

"Who the hell are you kids? What are you doing in here?" The man asked.

Ronnie barely gave the man a glance. "Come on, Chris, we're out of here."

Then he walked by the dumbfounded man and out into the darkening night.

Picking up their bikes, Ronnie looked around the area.

"Hey, where's Kyle?" Ronnie asked.

Chris looked around also. "I thought he was with you. I couldn't find him upstairs."

Ronnie spit onto the grass and decided to leave when the handyman came out onto the porch and began watching him and Chris.

"Screw him. He probably just left his bike and ran when that asshole pulled up. Get it for him and we'll give it to him later. Can't believe he bailed on us though. I'm likely to kick his ass for it, too."

Chris just nodded. He knew better to say anything when Ronnie acted like this. He could just as easily start messing with him, being that he was the only thing around for Ronnie to vent his wrath on. Balancing the empty bike while he rode his own, Chris got a rough start, but then rode down the street, Ronnie at his side.

Behind them, the house receded and the handyman went back inside to finish his work.

Ronnie spit into the street and looked at Chris.

"Don't you worry about Lawson giving us the slip. I've got something planned tonight for him that's gonna put that little shit in his place…his family too, bunch of squares, think they're so much better then the rest of us with their family dinners and TV time together. Bunch of faggots, that's what they are."

Chris had no idea what Ronnie was talking about and frankly, he didn't want to. He just kept riding in silence, hoping Ronnie would just forget he was there.

"Oh, yeah, man. I've got a surprise for Lawson that's gonna blow his mind."

The moon was starting to rise in the October sky, only a few clouds marring the horizon. If Ronnie had studied the sky a little more closely, he would have noticed just a hint of red, the moonlight reflecting off the clouds and casting a pallid glow down on the city.

But he didn't. So he continued pedaling, his mind swirling in anticipation of the coming night.

## CHAPTER NINE

WHEN RONNIE RETURNED home, his father was in the kitchen. He'd just finished frying up a couple of pork chops and he placed one on a plate for Ronnie. He looked up when his son stepped into the kitchen.

"Well, look whose here, decided to grace me with your presence, did ya?" His father said. Next to him on the countertop was a bottle of Jack Daniels, his chosen poison. Ronnie sat down at the table, keeping his mouth shut. While he was one of the toughest kids in the neighborhood, he was nothing in his own home. His father was a big man, just shy of six feet. His shoulders were wide thanks to the work he did as a brick layer, at least before he was fired for drinking on the job. His father tossed a plate with one lone pork chop in front of him and then sat down with the other plate in front of him. Reaching over his back, Ronnie grabbed the lonely loaf of bread sitting on the counter. Pork chops and bread was considered a grand feast in his house.

For just a moment, he wondered what Lawson was eating for supper at his house tonight and decided he didn't want to know. A few years ago, he had been friends with RJ. He'd spent many dinners over his house, eating home cooked meals and playing video games while joking with RJ's dad. RJ's father was nothing like Ronnie's father. RJ's dad listened to him when he talked and would play catch with him when he went over to RJ's house.

It was only when Ronnie's father began getting worse at home that made Ronnie begin lashing out. RJ had been the closest person to him, so had received the brunt of Ronnie's wrath. Mrs. Lawson had found out about the beatings and had banned Ronnie from visiting anymore.

While he ate his dry pork chop, Ronnie thought about how he'd really screwed it all up. And the reason sat across from him at the kitchen table, nibbling on a pork chop.

His father looked up from his plate, seeing the look on Ronnie's face.

"What's your problem, not good enough for you?" He asked, referring to the meal.

Ronnie just shrugged.

His father reached over and grabbed his bottle of Jack Daniels from the counter and took a swig right from the bottle. Slamming it down on the table, he started to eat again, mumbling under his breath.

"So, Dad, a glass too slow for you now? Figure why bother?" Ronnie jibed, knowing he was poking a sleeping bear.

"Mind your own damn business, Ronnie," he spit, taking another swig. "Damn, kid, thinks he's better than me, just like his mother," he mumbled the last bit.

Ronnie heard him, though, and couldn't hold it in.

"You shut up about Mom, she was a good woman, and if she was here now, she would never let you treat me like you do. In fact, she probably would have left your drunken ass and took me with her along time ago!"

His father looked up, rage filling his eyes, some real, some from the alcohol. Even on a good day, his dad was a mean drunk.

"Why you little, snot-nosed bastard. How dare you talk that shit in my house. If it wasn't for me, you'd be living on the street!"

"Yeah, well, sometimes I wonder if I'd be better off. I'd probably eat better than this shit," Ronnie snapped while pushing the pork chop away from him.

Before Ronnie knew it, his father had backhanded him across the face, his knuckles hitting Ronnie in the nose.

"Why you ungrateful bastard, I ought to teach you a few manners right now, but the games on and I'm not gonna miss it because of you. So, I suggest you get your ass out of my face or I swear you won't be able to go to school Monday, I'll give you so many bruises.

Ronnie stood up. "Fine, I'm out of here, and maybe this time I won't come back!" He yelled, heading for the front door, blood dripping from his crushed nose, courtesy of his father's backhand.

His father's laughter followed him from the kitchen. "You'll be back; you're not fooling anybody, and while you're out there, take out the damn trash."

"Fuck you!" Ronnie yelled from the front door. He heard his father getting up, the kitchen chair scraping on the old linoleum.

"Why you little…when I get my hands on you!"

Ronnie didn't hear the rest; he was already running to his bike and jumping on it. He would never have said that to his father if he'd been in arms reach of the man, but the sudden burst of courage came easily when you had half a house separating you.

He pedaled away from his house, his father yelling at him from the front porch.

Ronnie stopped at the end of the street and looked back.

One of his neighbors had come out of their house, curious what all the yelling was about. He saw his father forget about him and turn to his neighbor.

"What the fuck are you looking at, Macaroy? Mind your own goddamn business!"

Ronnie saw the neighbor flip his father off and return back inside, the sound of the front door carrying to Ronnie, even way down at the end of the street.

His father seemed to stop for a minute, as if he'd forgotten what he was doing outside, then he went back in and closed the door.

Ronnie sat on his bike in the middle of the road, the few cars just driving around him, their headlights bathing him with their luminance. The only advantage to having a drunk for a father was in an hour or so, he could go back home and his father wouldn't remember what they had fought about.

Ronnie turned his bike around and pedaled up the street. He figured he'd go see Chris or Kyle until he was ready to go back home. He had all the stuff he needed for tonight in his ratty, falling apart garage.

He just had to wait a few more hours until he knew the neighborhood was asleep.

Then it would be party time.

When RJ had made it home, he stepped in the back door and breathed a sigh of relief. He'd made it. He had gotten away from Ronnie.

His mother turned to look at him, her body facing the kitchen sink where she was washing some vegetables for dinner.

"Hi, honey, where were you all day?"

RJ shrugged. "Around, Mom, gees what's with the twenty questions, can't a guy have some privacy?"

She turned and walked over to him, her wet hands grabbing his cheeks. She pulled him toward her and then gave him a big kiss on the cheek.

"Not as long as you're my son, and I love you," she teased. "Now go get washed up for dinner. I'm making lasagna. I figured with everything your father's gone through in the past few days he could use a good comfort meal."

RJ pulled away, wiping his face. "Gross me out, Mom, your hands are all wet. Thanks a lot." RJ left the kitchen, moving off to the bathroom, mumbling about mothers and what he would do once he turned eighteen.

Emma chuckled to herself. They never knew how good they had it until it was too late.

RJ went to the bathroom to wash up. Despite all the action thanks to Ronnie at the end of the day, he was still feeling pretty great.

His exuberance showed through by his humming a catchy song he'd heard on the television, something about a phone commercial. He thought back to his day with Nancy, thinking about the way she smelled and how her eyes had sparkled in the sunshine while they had stood on top of the tower.

He remembered how her hair had flown around her while they were riding their bikes, looking like a golden halo.

He sighed, sitting down on the toilet, the lid still down. He found he was starting to sweat and he wondered if this was what it was like to be in love. He couldn't stop thinking about her and wondered if he'd be pushing it if he called her later.

Shaking his head, he decided he needed to play it cool. He'd call her tomorrow, that way almost an entire day would have gone by.

Finishing up in the bathroom, he got his hands wet quickly and wiped them on the towel hanging next to the sink. Because he had used no soap, and hadn't so much as rubbed his hands together to wash them under the water spray, the towel looked like it had been tossed in a mud hole.

With a song still on his lips, he went back to the kitchen for dinner. He just realized he was starving and a hot meal would hit the spot nicely.

With a bounce in his step and love on his mind, he went to join his family, looking forward to his mom's famous lasagna.

# CHAPTER TEN

IT WAS A little past two in the morning, when Ronnie rode his bike down the dark, quiet street, only the moonlight and a few streetlamps keeping the darkness at bay.

After leaving his house earlier in the night after his argument with his father, he'd gone to see Kyle, but his friend wasn't home. His mother seemed worried and Ronnie promised to let her know if he saw him. Wondering where his friend had gotten to, Ronnie went to Chris' house and had stayed there the rest of the night. Chris' mom was divorced and worked second shift, so she hadn't come home till just before twelve. That had given Ronnie plenty of time to relax and then sneak out Chris' bedroom window when his mom's car pulled into the driveway.

He had ridden his bike home to find his father passed out on the living room couch. From there he had gone to his room and hung out for another hour until he was ready for what he'd planned that night.

After grabbing the supplies stockpiled in the garage, he rode his bike towards RJ's house.

His nose still hurt from where his dad had slapped him, but he brushed it off. Compared to some of the beatings he'd received in the past, the punch in the nose was nothing more than a love tap. The spokes of his tires reflected the ambient moonlight, sending little sparks of reflected luminance across the asphalt. He slowed down when he reached the beginning of RJ's block, figuring he'd stash his bike in someone's shrubs and then creep up to the house by using the bushes of the nearby homes.

Taking everything he'd brought with him in an old paperboy's sack, he laid his bike in between a few bushes and started down the street. The night was cool and he could see the fog of his breath every time he exhaled, but it was still warmer than usual for an October night.

A dog yowled in the distance, causing him to stop and survey his surroundings. After a moment, he started moving again. Looking at the houses on his left, he noticed a few still had lights on, the soft glow of illumination seeping around the closed shades and curtains in the windows.

When RJ's house was directly in front of him, he checked one more time to make sure no one was around to see him, and then ducked into the side yard. In seconds he was absorbed in the shadows of the house, and he walked to the backyard.

Then in the darkness of the night, he took out his supplies and laid them out in front of him. Once he was done, he stood up one last time to make sure he wasn't spotted, then leaned forward and got to work.

*    *    *

Inside the Lawson house, Jason tossed and turned in his bed. It had been a rough couple of days and his stress level was through the roof. Emma had given him a valium to help him sleep and he'd accepted one gladly. He almost never took sleep aids, figuring if he couldn't sleep, than he just wasn't tired enough.

But tonight was different and he had accepted the small pill gladly.

Now he was half into a deep sleep and half still on that horizon that every person balances on before succumbing to sleep every night.

Visions of the funeral flashed into his mind, then pictures of his father's face before he was killed and devoured in front of his eyes. His mother's face flashed by, the pale make-up she was wearing giving her the look of a cheap harlequin.

He found himself standing at her casket again, looking down on her lifeless body. Emma was next to him and she looked down at the prone corpse, too, and his wife's black dress seemed to shimmer in his dream, like it had a life of its own.

"You know, Jason, the mortician really did a good job; it looks like she's just sleeping," she said, trying to be comforting. "It looks like she could just wake up and say hi to us all."

Jason snorted. "Bullshit, Em', she looks dead and her face looks dead. Shit, I wonder if I open up the bottom half of the casket if she's even wearing pants. This is all just a show, it's phony. This isn't what she looked like when she was alive. This is like a store mannequin that's been made up to look like her and then shoved into this coffin."

He looked at Emma, his face set into a grimace. "It's nothing but a lie."

Emma threw her hands into the air in an I give up, gesture.

"Whatever, honey, I was just trying to be supportive. I'm going to go over there for a while and leave you alone." Then she moved away, frustrated with him.

Jason let her go, ignoring her.

He looked down at his mother's corpse and sighed. So many things left unsaid, so many things he would have told her if he'd known she was going to die so soon. If only she had believed him when he'd told her what had really happened to his father and not have to let her think he left her for another woman all those years ago.

She had never recovered from the betrayal she'd thought she had suffered. She had never dated and had never even considered it. Roger Lawson was the man she had loved and he was the only man she would ever love.

A single tear dripped down Jason's cheek to land on his mother's neck. He reached down with his finger, wanting to wipe it away when her eyes snapped open.

He froze in surprise and shock, not believing what he was seeing. How could this be? She was stuffed with embalming fluid and he'd seen first hand her insides being torn apart one organ at a time by the coroner.

Her head turned to look up at him and her mouth opened to say something. A dull rasping sound came from her mouth, and she blinked her eyes, trying to focus them.

Jason looked around him at the other people nearby, wanting to tell them this was all a mistake, that his mother was alive, when her hand reached up and wrapped itself around his wrist like a steel clamp. The nails were sharp and they dug into his flesh, tiny red rivulets running down his arm to drip onto her white funeral dress.

He winced when her grip become stronger and tried to pull away, frightened.

When he backed up, he pulled her to a sitting position. His wife ran over to him and saw his mother awake. She moved closer, her arm going behind his mother to help the woman sit up, when the supposedly dead woman snapped her head down and ripped a mouth size chunk of flesh from Emma's arm.

Emma screamed and pulled away, blood shooting from the wound and striking Jason in the face. For a moment he was blinded and he tried to wipe his eyes clear with his one free hand, his other still trapped in his mother's deadly embrace.

Emma fell back, screaming, while she cupped her arm against her chest, scarlet ribbons of plasma shooting out between her hands to stain her black dress an even darker shade of obsidian. Jason saw her stagger away and then he turned to look back at his mother.

Her face was only inches from him now, and to Jason it seemed she was going to lean forward and kiss him on the forehead like she used to do when he was a child, but instead, her face darted to the side and her already bloody teeth sank into his throat, tearing at the flesh and tendons like a rabid dog.

He screamed, the pain blinding him and he tried to pull away from her, but her teeth were fully entrenched in his neck.

With out thinking, he swung his fist at her, panicking, and her mouth separated from him by the force of the blow. She fell back into the coffin and Jason slammed the lid closed. His blood was pumping out of his neck wound and he tried to staunch the viscous fluid with his hand, but he knew it was no use.

In front of him, the coffin rattled on its pedestal as his mother banged against the inside trying to escape. It was like a dozen rabid dogs were fighting to break loose, the coffin lid bouncing up and down, and only Jason's waning strength keeping it closed.

Dazed and losing blood fast, Jason backed up and struck a candelabrum with his arm, knocking the lit candles to the floor. The small flames caught on the cotton draperies that covered the coffin and nearby tables, the material blazing to an orange and red life of its own.

A black acrid smoke filled the church and he stumbled to his knees. The edges of his vision were blurring, like he had a serious case of tunnel vision, and his breath came in gasps while he tried to filter oxygen from the smoke. He fell to his knees to see his wife already on the floor, her supine body not moving, and a large pool of blood cascading around her.

Her eyes stared up at nothing, as if she was looking to the ceiling of the church, asking God why this horrible thing had happened.

Jason reached out to her with his hand, but his strength was waning and his arm sagged to the floor, with the rest of him following. He laid flat on his back, staring up at the ornate ceiling of the church, the coffin still shuddering on its pedestal as the ghoul that was once his mother tried valiantly to escape.

Then from the blackness, a shrouded figure in black stepped out, the waves of smoke parting as the form drifted closer to him, like the ripples in a lake flowing away from a tossed pebble.

It was humanoid in shape, but that was where the resemblance ended to anything that might have ever been human. It had black hair coming from its shoulders, billowing behind it like a large cape, and its ebony flesh seemed to absorb the light.

Jason looked up and knew what he was seeing in an instant. This was what had killed his father. This was the creature from his closet

He tried to raise his hand to it, as if he could somehow fend it away, but then it stepped back into the smoke and was swallowed whole. His hand fell to the red rug that adorned the church floor and he knew he wouldn't have the strength to lift it again, no matter how hard he tried.

Then the coffin above him shook one final time, and became dislodged from the pedestal. It seemed to balance for a heartbeat, almost like it might not fall, but then his mother banged once more and the coffin tipped over.

Jason looked up at the falling coffin coming straight for him and knew he'd be crushed to death. He let out one final scream before the smoke of the church caused him to cough uncontrollably, then he fell into unconsciousness and darkness.

*    *    *

Ronnie tossed the red, two gallon gas tank to the grass and reached into his pocket for the disposable lighter he'd placed there less than three hours ago. The smell of gasoline suffused the area and he pulled the lighter free with an evil grin. With no hesitation on his part, he flicked the steel wheel on the tip of the lighter, the small flame igniting immediately. Holding the lighter and relishing what was to come next, the small flame danced in the light breeze. The breeze was enough to move the flame, but was far from strong enough to extinguish it.

He pulled a rolled up piece of newspaper from his back pocket and lit the end. The paper caught at once, a small torch now in his hand. With one last look to make sure he was unseen, he tossed the torch into the gas covered bushes.

Ronnie had made sure to spray the side of the house, as well as the surrounding foundation. When he tossed the flaming paper to the gas soaked ground, a blossoming fireball erupted.

The blaze came so fast, Ronnie had to jump back, feeling the heat on his face. For a second or two, he stood mesmerized by what he'd wrought, then he came to his senses and gathered his paper bag and loose items.

Running out of the yard, he sprinted to where his bike was hidden in the shrubs, then without a backward glance to the small conflagration, he hopped on his bike and pedaled away. The cool breeze felt good on his face, and once he had made it to the end of the street, he slowed the bike and turned around to look back at RJ's house.

The flames were just starting to peek out from the back, the glare illuminating the top of the house.

Ronnie grinned. That'll teach the little bastard to run away from him. By the morning, Lawson and his family will be in the same boat as him.

So far the flames had gone unnoticed, the neighborhood fast asleep. Ronnie turned away and began pedaling for home. He felt no guilt in what he'd just done, his own internal suffering masking the realization of what he'd just set into motion. With the flames growing higher, he pedaled away, whistling a tune from the rock group, Kiss.

"Hot, hot, hotter than hell," he sang to himself while he pedaled away, swaying back and forth with each pump of his legs.

His conscious was clear, in fact, when he thought about what it had been like when the fire had surged upward over the house and how it had made him feel, forgetting all his problems for the time being, he thought to himself that he might just not be done setting fires.

In fact, it might just become his new hobby.

# Chapter Eleven

WHILE RJ HAD been ready for bed that night, he entered his bedroom and stopped at the door. He took a quick look around the floor near his bed, and when he was satisfied it was clear, he ran across the bedroom floor as fast as he could and jumped the last three feet onto his bed, careful to keep his feet well clear of the opening underneath the box spring. He did this for a very important reason. A reason children all over the world did the same thing every night before going to bed. He knew under his bed was where the monsters hid. Well, there and in your closets.

He dove under the covers, making sure every limb was underneath the blankets. Every kid who ever lived knew it was a rule that the monsters couldn't get you if you were under the covers. He lay in his bed, his breathing heavy from the exertion of vaulting to the bed and making it safe to his haven, untouched by inhuman hands.

He didn't move, letting his ears hear every nuance of the room.

He knew he was probably getting a little old to believe in monsters, but some things were hard to shake when you were a kid, like the first time his parents told him Santa Claus wasn't real. Now he knew that the only fat guy who brought them presents on Christmas Eve was his mom's brother, Uncle Bob.

Uncle Bob weighed a good two-fifty and smoked like a chimney, but he'd always treated RJ well, so he liked him.

RJ lay perfectly still, the sound of a stray branch scraping the window of his room. Images flooded his mind of strange creatures sneaking into his room when he was asleep, only his blankets keeping him safe.

The minutes rolled by and RJ peeked out from under the covers. The room was dark, filled with shadows caused by the light from the street lamp on the sidewalk in front of the house, the thin rays sneaking past his shade and the curtain covering his window.

His eyes glanced to his closet, still open about an inch. He realized there could be something sitting in its confines even now, just patiently waiting for an unsuspecting RJ to go to sleep so it could strike. His eyes stared at the closet for five minutes straight, hoping nothing would appear and jump out at him, and yet something deep inside him hoping that something did.

Reaching under his head, he pulled out the extra pillow that resided there and threw it at the closet door. The door slammed shut, the pillow falling to the floor. RJ left it there.

Better to sleep with only one pillow than risk the wrath of the denizens under his bed.

More time passed and his breathing began to slow. All the jumbled images of his day slowly evaporated until he drifted off into a restful sleep, unaware that the monsters he was so afraid of were irrelevant and imaginary and it was the real monsters he dealt with every day who were the true threat.

RJ opened his eyes to see his room was filled with smoke. Coughing from the toxic fumes, he did what he had learned in school and rolled off the bed and landed on the floor. He breathed a little easier, the air not as bad near the floor.

Smoke detectors wailed from the hallway outside his bedroom door and his heart started to beat faster.

The house was on fire!

Crawling towards the door, he opened it to see the darkened hallway filled with smoke. He immediately started coughing uncontrollably, the air near the floor just as bad here as the rest of his house.

Trying to control his coughing, but failing miserably, he crawled towards his parents' bedroom.

He reached up with his right hand and turned the knob, the door opening inward.

"Dad, we're on fire! What do we do?" He called into the bedroom. No one answered. He crawled closer, the bed and the entire room shrouded in smoke.

Once he reached the bed, he pulled on his father's arm, trying to get him to wake up. Jason groaned in his sleep, but otherwise remained still.

RJ had no way of knowing that Jason had medicated before falling asleep, the valium plus the smoke keeping him unconscious. RJ crawled around to the other side of the bed to try and wake his mother. He shook her violently, but she was unconscious, smoke inhalation causing her to fall into unconsciousness, one in which she could possibly never wake up from.

RJ looked around the room, panicking. He was in a burning house with both his parents immobile! What could he do?

His eyes caught the window and he crawled over to it. Holding his breath, he reached up and unlocked it, then pushed it up, letting in the cool clean air. He stuck his head through the window, the cobwebs from his head and his coughing disappearing. When he thought he was better, he dropped to the floor and went to his mom again. She wasn't that much bigger than RJ; the boy having had a growth spurt this past summer.

With a moan from the weight of her unmoving body, he pulled her off the bed. Then he dragged her into the hallway and down the stairs. Never once did he think to pick up the phone and call for help. He was in his own world, where his parents were in trouble, and if he didn't do something, they would be lost to him forever.

The first floor was even worse than upstairs. Flames could be seen at the back of the house, the living room burning brightly.

RJ tried to ignore the inferno and keep his mind on the task at hand, namely, getting his mom out of the house and then returning for his dad.

As he dragged her down the stairs, her head would make a dull thump every time she went down another step. RJ would pull her and be rewarded with a thump. Pull, thump, pull, thump. All the way to the bottom.

When he reached the bottom floor, his own coughing was almost uncontrollable. Tears filled his eyes and snot dripped from his nostrils to fall on his lip before landing on his pajama shirt.

He barely managed to reach the front door before passing out, but with his last ounce of willpower, he managed to unlock the door and let it swing open.

Just before he gave in to unconsciousness, he saw red flashing lights in front of the house and heard the wail of sirens. Then, with his mother next to him, he passed out, falling into a black abyss in which he had no control over.

Jason was still trapped in his nightmare, his mother's coffin falling on top of him. He couldn't breathe, the air seemed sour. No matter how hard he tried, his lungs couldn't take in the necessary oxygen. He felt himself being shaken and thrown around, like a little girl's rag doll.

He had no idea what was happening and tried to say something, the words coming out in gibberish. He felt himself bouncing up and down, a pressure on his chest.

Then a bright light was blasted onto his eyelids and he opened them just a little. Red lights were everywhere, and when his eyes opened more, he saw a masked man in a yellow fireproof coat leaning over him, with a flashlight mounted to his helmet. Before Jason could stop him, the man put a clear mask over his nose and mouth and cool oxygen flooded his lungs. He breathed in greedily, his mind clearing a little.

He turned his head to see his house was a blazing inferno. Men were on the roof, chopping into the shingles to try and release some of the heat.

He tried to sit up and felt strong hands under him, assisting him. He looked around his front yard, seeing his neighbors standing on the sidewalk in their pajamas and bathrobes. Everything he saw had an eerie quality to it thanks to the flashing emergency lights.

Then his mind came into focus and he realized what was happening. He ripped the mask from his face and tried to stand up.

"Oh my God, where's my family. Where's my wife and son?" He called to anyone who would listen.

"We're here, Jason, we're safe," Emma's voice said from behind him. Relief flooded through him and he rolled over onto his side to see his wife and son sitting on the bumper of a paramedic's van. Both wore oxygen masks, and when he looked at them, both Emma and RJ waved to him, the blanket they were both wrapped in sliding a little off their shoulders.

He lay back in the grass then, relieved his family was alive. His eyes glanced at the burning wood and vinyl of what was once his house and he felt a terrible blow hit him. His entire house was a blazing bonfire, the firemen only trying to keep it contained from spreading to the nearby homes.

His heart sank and he lay his head back down on the trampled grass. First his mother died, and now this. If there was a God, then

Jason was pretty sure he'd done something to piss him off royally.

Climbing to his feet on unsteady legs, he stumbled over to his wife and son, all of them hugging each other with the same sentiment.

Their house may be gone, but they still had each other.

*　　*　　*

The sun rose on the blackened husk of smoldering wood that was once RJ's home. He stood on the front lawn, now torn up and muddy from all the water and the emergency crew's boots.

Tears ran down his face as he thought about all his stuff, now nothing more than ash. The firemen hadn't been able to save anything. The entire house was destroyed, including the contents.

Everything they had ever owned was gone.

Next to him, on the denuded lawn, Jason stood quietly. He had large circles under his eyes and he gazed at the house with a blank, almost zombie-like stare.

The three of them had spent the night next door at their neighbor's house. None of them had slept, still in shock, none of them wanting to accept what had happened to them.

Emma walked across the lawn from the next door house with two cups of something hot, the steam drifting from the contents to float away on the light breeze.

When she was close enough to them, she handed one of the cups to Jason.

"Thanks, honey," he said, taking the cup from her. RJ caught the aroma of coffee beans and made a face. He hated the stuff and couldn't imagine why adults liked it so much. The same went for beer. One time when his dad was still sleeping in on Sunday with his mom, he had snuck a beer from the refrigerator. The click of the can opening made him jump in the silent kitchen. He had made sure his parents were still sleeping and had tried the fabled beer all his friends at school said was great.

He'd taken two sips and almost gagged. Then he'd poured the rest down the drain and tossed the empty beer can with the others in the recycle bin in the backyard. His father would save the empties to return for the deposit and he'd never notice one more can.

Since then, he'd never given beer a second thought. And the same went for coffee. Jason saw his son's face and smiled wanly. He put his arm around RJ and gave him a hug.

"I know it sucks, son, but we're all alive and safe and together. That's what really counts." He gestured towards the house with his coffee cup. "That stuff we had in there can be replaced, but you and your mother can't be. Thank God you're all right. That was a very brave thing you did last night. You saved your mother, you know."

RJ blushed, not used to the attention. "Gee, Dad, I just did what had to be done, just the way you always taught me to. I'm just glad the fire guys showed up when they did, 'cause I wasn't looking forward to trying to drag your big butt out of the house on my own."

Jason chuckled and turned to look at Emma. "Well, will ya look here, we got ourselves a comedian in the family," he joked.

Emma nodded with a grin, but then her face grew more serious. "Look, Jason, after I got my head around what's happened to us this morning, I started to think about where we're going to live. And then it came to me. Your mother's house is empty now and you own it. We could stay there while the homeowner's insurance figures out what's they're going to do. RJ won't even have to change schools because the house is so close."

Jason's face turned to stone. "You know how I feel about that house, Emma. I won't go back there," he said, his voice flat.

She nodded and smiled like she was trying to reason with an unruly child.

"I know that, honey, but we have to live somewhere and you're mother's house is the perfect place. RJ needs some normalcy in his life and lately it's just one thing after another. First your mother passing and now the house, what's next?"

Jason shook his head angrily. "Forget it, Emma, it's not happening."

Emma's face grew hard, her eyes flaring with anger. She stepped one foot closer to her husband and her voice grew low so RJ had to strain to hear her.

"Look, Jason, I'm going to go there and RJ is coming with me, now if you want to leave us there alone, that's your choice, but I can't believe deep in your heart, after everything that's happened, you're going to abandon us now." She reached for RJ's hand like he was still five, but the look in her eyes would brook no argument. RJ took her hand and they both walked back to the neighbor's house, Emma almost dragging him.

Jason stood on the lawn alone, staring at his shattered house. A hundred things floated through his head. The fire marshal was coming by later to try and discern the reason for the fire. His mother's lawyers had papers for him to sign. He needed to call his work and tell them what had happened to his house and take a few more days off, and now his wife wanted him to move back to the house where the single most traumatic event in his life occurred.

He sighed, his shoulders drooping as low as they would go.

As he walked back to the neighbor's house, he had a feeling it was going to be a long day.

<h1 style="text-align:center">CHAPTER TWELVE</h1>

THE DAY AFTER the fire, RJ was hanging around with one of the few people the same age as him that he would call a friend.

His name was Glen Higgins and RJ had known him for most of his young life. At the moment, the two were riding their bikes in the middle of the street. School had been over for almost an hour and they had to make up their mind quick on what they wanted to do. This late in the season, the daylight hours grew shorter with each passing day so playtime was at a premium.

"I don't know, what do you want to do?" RJ asked Glen.

Swerving his bike around a patch of sand, Glen shrugged. "I don't know, what do you want to do?"

"I just said that, dufus," RJ said.

"Oh, yeah, sorry."

They rode in silence for a few minutes and then Glen spoke up.

"So, you're gonna go live in your grandma's house?" Glen inquired.

RJ nodded with the rhythm of his pedaling. "Yeah, I guess so. That's what my mom said."

"What about your dad?" Glen asked.

"He's not too happy about it. All I can figure out is something happened to him when he was a kid, like around my age, but he won't talk about it."

"Do you think it was something bad?" Glen asked.

RJ shrugged. "Don't know." He concentrated pedaling for a few more minutes and then his face lit up with an idea.

"Hey, I know what we can do, let's go to the Highlands and get some tennis balls. The coach at the school said he'd give us a quarter for each one we give him."

Glen's head bounced up and down in approval. "Okay, that sounds cool, race ya," he said, then took off down the street.

"Oh, no, you don't," RJ replied and started pedaling for all he was worth.

The two boys weaved in and out of cars, working their way across town. Finally, they drove by a small building no bigger than a guard house. Next to it was a large sign that read: GRANADA HIGHLANDS, Luxury living at affordable prices.

The two boys blew by the sign, barely noticing it was there. They knew this route by heart, driving on the same streets in the summer until they reached the top of a long steep hill.

At the top were the luxury apartments the sign proclaimed. The two bikes weaved around the security shed, the guard inside barely flinching at their passage.

In the summer months, they would sometimes sneak into one of the pools the complex maintained. They would have a blast until someone would figure out they didn't live there and call security. Usually with a complimentary towel, the two boys would dash out of the gate and run for all they were worth, laughing the entire time.

Today they were going to the tennis courts, which were situated in the back lot of the complex.

Granada Highlands sat on top of a very large mountain, and on the side of the tennis courts dropped away to Route 60, a main thoroughfare through all the neighboring towns and cities. The boys would always climb around the steep slope, finding all the tennis balls that had accidentally been knocked over the tennis court's fences. Sometimes when picking was slim, they would crawl up to the fence and stick their hands under the fence, taking the yellow balls while people were still playing. Today wasn't one of those days and the two boys soon had a plastic bag filled with the bright yellow orbs.

RJ looked down at his pants, now covered in dirt and mud. "Oh, man, my mom is gonna kill me when she sees my clothes."

Glen waved the statement away. "So, just put them at the bottom of the hamper. Besides, I think your mom has more important things to worry about right now."

"Yeah, you're probably right," RJ said. He looked up at the sky, the sun starting its downward spiral.

"Hey, it's gonna be dark soon, we better go."

"Okay," Glen said. While the two boys were gliding back down the steep hill, Glenn called to RJ.

"So, did you really lose all your stuff in the fire?"

With a sad look on his face, RJ nodded. "Yeah. Everything I owned is gone."

"Shit that sucks. What happens now? Do you have to buy everything again?"

RJ slowed down a little so he could be closer to Glen. "No, my dad said we're gonna get a check from the insurance company for the house and all the stuff that was inside it. He said he'd be able to replace almost all of the stuff that got burned."

"What about the letter from Nancy? Did that get burned up, too?" Glen asked.

RJ knew exactly what he was talking about. Last year everyone in school had to write to a friend and Nancy had written to him. The letter was just silly stuff, like do you like candy and what do you want for Christmas, but it was in her handwriting. He'd kept it in a shoebox under his bed with a few other cherished things from his childhood.

But they were gone now.

"Yeah, 'fraid so. It's all charcoal now."

Glen gave him a big smile. "Guess you'll just have to have her write you another one. Maybe this time it'll be a love letter." Glen had stretched the word love out and had said it in a cute and mocking tone to tease RJ.

RJ grinned back, holding his tongue. He hadn't told his friend about him and Nancy the other day. That was private, between her and him.

Glen took his silence as a form of submission and grinned wider and started to sing the rhyme: "RJ and Nancy sitting in a tree, k...i...s...s...ing." Before he could finish, RJ threw a tennis ball at him, the small, yellow ball bouncing off his head.

"Hey, that hurt, ya jerk!" He snapped.

"Then quit giving me shit," he snapped back.

They rode in silence for another minute and then Glen spoke up again.

"Hey, did you hear about Kyle O'Malley?"

"No, what?" RJ asked.

"Well, he hasn't been in school for a few days and his mother doesn't know where he is, either. They think he ran away from home."

"Good, that's one less asshole to have to deal with," RJ said coldly.

"Gees, that's harsh. What if he's dead somewhere or someone took him, you know, like a molester or something?" Glen said.

RJ spit to the side of the road. "Harsh? That's easy for you to say. It's not you he likes to beat up on with Ronnie and Chris; frankly, I hope the jerk is dead," RJ said flatly.

Glen just nodded, not used to the venom in his friend's voice. They rode on in silence, and when they made it to Glen's street, he waved bye and turned onto it. RJ kept going. He was sleeping at the Miller's house for just one more night, and tomorrow when he left school, he was supposed to go to his grandmother's house.

A shiver went up his back when he thought about the last time he'd been there. Ronnie had almost got him that day. Warily he looked around the street to make sure his neighborhood bully wasn't around.

With a sigh of relief, he pedaled a little faster. His stomach was rumbling and he knew they'd be eating takeout, since they had no kitchen to call their own and Mrs. Miller wasn't much of a cook.

With the sky darkening, he coasted the rest of the way to his sort-of home; then let his bike fall on his old driveway, now a driveway that belonged to nothing but a burnt and blackened husk of a house. Ignoring the falling bike, he ran to the front door of his neighbor's house and rang the bell.

A second later his mother let him in and the door closed.

Up in the sky, the horizon gave off just a hint of red and orange as the sun began to set for another day.

# Chapter Thirteen

J ASON STOOD IN front of his childhood house, his face void of emotion. Emma sat in the car behind him, waiting for him to tell her he was ready. She was eager to go inside, but wanted to give her husband the space he so desperately seemed to need.

More than ten minutes had past and she was about to get out of the car and go inside whether he was ready or not, when he finally turned around and looked at her.

She was taken by surprise to see tears on his cheeks. He held out his hand to her and she climbed out of the car and walked the four feet separating them.

"Honey, are you all right?" She asked quietly.

He nodded and absently wiped his cheeks with the corner of his shirt sleeve. "Yeah, I'll be fine, just a lot of memories came back and hit me so hard and fast." He pointed to the side yard where there was a long strip of partly dead grass.

"Over there was where me and my father used to play catch together. We'd throw the football or the baseball around for hours. Then my mom would make us come in for supper." He then turned and gestured to the driveway on the right side of the house,

"I remember one time when we were washing his car. I sprayed him with the hose and at first he was so mad, but once he saw the smile on my face and how happy I was, he calmed down and laughed, too. Then he threw the bucket of soap at me. I got covered and ended up slipping on the grass. Then he ran over, picked up the hose, and kept squirting me until I said uncle."

Emma stood quietly next to him, listening to her husband reminiscing about days past. She rubbed his arm for support.

Then Jason looked up at the sky as if all the answers he'd wanted over the years were just up there waiting for him to ask.

"Maybe I did imagine everything I thought happened to my dad, but Jesus, it all seemed so real, but that would be impossible, right?" He asked Emma.

She nodded. "Of course, honey, monsters aren't real, they're just a part of all of us that we use in movies and books to get us scared. Personally, I don't like to be scared, but everyone else seems to love it." She shivered. "All those damn horror movies and slasher flicks, they're sick."

He chuckled at her. "Yes, honey, we all know your views on today's cinema. All right, I guess I'm ready to go in, but you have to give in to one concession. It's a deal breaker if you say no."

"All right, what is it then?" She asked, curious.

"I want a gun," he said flatly.

Her eyebrows went up and she was all set to protest when Jason put his hands up for her to stop.

"Now wait a sec, before you start arguing about having a gun in the house, hear me out. I'll buy a lock box for it that only I know the combination to and I promise never to tell RJ about it. It'll be safe. But if I'm going to live in that house again after all these years, then you have to let me have some form of a security blanket."

Her face was red as she thought about what he'd just said. She knew her own stance on guns. They were dangerous. How many children had accidentally been shot after finding a parents' gun?

But she also knew what a sacrifice Jason was making by returning to his childhood home.

After a few moments of thinking it over, she looked into her husband's eyes.

"All right, fine, you can have your gun, but the lock box better be bolted to the floor of our closet in our bedroom and RJ must never know."

He smiled at her and pulled her close, hugging her.

"You see? That's why I love you so much, you're always willing to negotiate."

She grinned back. "Well, my mother always said that marriage was a constant fight for dominance over each other and sometimes you had to know when to fight and when to give in. Besides, I know what you've been through lately and I've decided to cut you a little slack." She started toward the house, but stopped and turned back to look at him, her finger pointing in his direction.

"But only for a while, then its back to the way it's always been."

He laughed at her. "You mean you're in charge and I have to do whatever you say?" He joked.

"Exactly, because that's the secret to a healthy marriage…do whatever your wife tells you to do."

He laughed a little more, and with the house keys in his hand, followed her up the walkway.

*     *     *

The dismissal bell in the school had just rung and RJ was unlocking his bike to go home, his book bag lying next to him. Wrapping the chain lock around his shoulder, he looked up to see Nancy walking toward him.

He hadn't talked to her since the day they'd spent together in the castle. He'd seen her a few times in school, but she was always with her girl friends.

He stood and waited while she came closer.

When she was almost on top of him, he saw her smile.

"Hey, RJ, I'm so sorry I haven't talked to you. How're you doing? I heard about your house, that's terrible."

"Thanks, Nancy, but we moved into my grandma's house so at least we have a place to live. Actually, I was going to go there now, you want to walk with me, I don't have to ride my bike."

Her bottom lip curled down into a slight frown. "I really would, but my mom's picking me up out front of the school, we're going to get our hair done. You know, girl's day and all that. Look, I've got drama class for the next few days after school, but when it's over can we get together?" She asked hopefully.

RJ nodded so hard he thought his head was going to go flying off his neck and he quickly calmed down, not wanting to look to eager. "Ah, sure, that would be great, maybe we could walk home together?"

She smiled. "Yeah, okay, meet you here after the last bell on Friday?"

He smiled shyly. "Okay, that's fine with me."

She started to walk away with a wave of her hand. "Okay then, see you later," she said moving away.

RJ waved to her, and with his heart skipping an extra beat, climbed onto his bike and started pedaling to his new home.

*　　*　　*

It felt weird walking into his grandmother's house as if it was his. His father was in the kitchen on his cell phone, by the tone of the conversation, it sounded like he was talking to someone with the homeowner's insurance.

"You can't be serious, arson? Who the hell would want to burn my house down? I see, and how does that affect the claim we put in, okay, well at least that's good news, okay, I'll talk to you soon and thank you." He closed his phone, severing the connection. When he turned around, he was startled by the sight of RJ standing behind him.

"Jesus, RJ, don't sneak up on me like that, you know I'm jumpy as it is," Jason said.

"Sorry, Dad, but you were on the phone and I didn't want to interrupt you. I heard some of what you said; did you say something about arson?"

Jason nodded and sat down at the kitchen table. The same table he'd sat at for a thousand dinners growing up.

"Come here and sit down with me, will you, son," he said. RJ did as he was asked and pulled out one of the chairs. A tingle went through him when he remembered the last time he'd been at this table, or namely, under it.

His father crossed his hands in front of him on the table and let out a sigh.

"The fire marshal gave his findings to the insurance company. He said that the fire started outside on the side of the house and a chemical accelerant was used, probably gasoline. Son, someone set our house on fire with us sleeping inside. Now I'm not accusing you of anything, but if you think you might know anything about what happened, you can tell me. You know that, don't you?"

RJ nodded, a little surprised. "Wow, Dad, I don't know what to say to that. Do you really think I might have been involved with burning my own house down?"

Jason shook his head slowly. "No, of course not, but, I remember what it was like to be your age and I did stupid stuff, too, so I just had to ask, that's all. If you tell me you don't know, than that's good enough for me," Jason finished and then just looked at his son, waiting patiently for an answer.

"Well, I don't know and I can't believe you'd ask me. Where's Mom?" He asked, changing the subject and a little hurt inside that his father would even have to ask him the questions he just had.

"Your mother went out to get a few things like groceries and a few other items. When Grandma died, she pretty much left the house in move in condition, but your mother wants there to be at least a few things that are hers."

RJ nodded. "Uh-huh, so where do I sleep?" He asked, curious.

Jason stood up from the table, the chair legs scraping the floor when his legs pushed it backwards.

"Now that's a good question. There's only three rooms upstairs, your grandma's room, my old bedroom and a small room that's kind of like a sitting room. My mother used to use it as a sewing room. You want to come upstairs with me and check them out?" Jason asked.

RJ nodded and stood up. "Sure, let's go."

Jason turned and walked out of the kitchen, RJ following him into the living room and up the stairs. At the top of the landing, Jason went into the first room on his right, RJ close behind him.

"Well, son, this is my room," he said. His eyes darted for the closet and he repressed a shiver, telling himself it couldn't have happened.

RJ was looking everywhere at once, his eyes trying to take it all in. On the wall was a picture of Catherine Bach, the woman who had played Daisy Duke back in the 80's. She smiled down at the two people in the room in a pair of cut-off denim shorts and a red plaid shirt. Her shirt was missing a few buttons and her more than ample cleavage dominated the picture, as did her long legs.

RJ had seen the new Dukes of Hazzard movie and thought it was all right, but he had never gotten into the original series. Now, as his eyes glanced over the form of Daisy Duke, he thought he just might give the show another chance.

"So, what do you think, son, will this do?" Jason asked him.

RJ shrugged. "Guess so, I mean, it's not like I have a choice, right?"

Jason sat down on the twin bed. "Yeah, that's true, but the way I see it, we're all in it together. Your mom and I don't have much of a choice either."

RJ went and sat down next to his father, the bed creaking under their combined weight.

"Hey, Dad, you never talk about Grandpa that much, like where he went and why. How come?"

Jason grew quiet and his eyes seemed distant, like he was trying to see something a million miles away.

He let out a deep breath and turned to look at his son.

"Listen, RJ, some things happened when I was about your age that I thought happened, but couldn't have. I've spent twenty years running from them. That's one of the reasons why I never wanted to come back to this house again." He looked over at the closed closet door and he could feel the old fear creeping up inside him again. Real or not, it still scared the shit out of him.

"But circumstances made me come back, for you and Emma. In fact, that's the only thing that would ever have made me. So, we're here now and I've got a lot of stuff to work out." He paused for a second, as if debating if he should tell his son something, then he seemed to give in to it.

"Listen, RJ, I want to ask you to do something for me, no matter how crazy it sounds, will you do it?"

Not knowing what his father was talking about, RJ just nodded.

"Good, okay then. If you ever see something weird either in your room or somewhere else in this house, you have to promise me you'll tell me. No matter how crazy it sounds. Will you promise me that?"

RJ looked at his father and wondered if his dad had finally cracked, but his eyes glowed with such intensity he could never remember seeing them like that before.

He nodded yes. "Sure, Dad, whatever you want," he said quietly.

Jason patted his leg. "Good, all right then." He stood up, and moved to the bedroom door to leave. Then he turned and looked at his son.

"Remember what I said, no matter how crazy or weird, you can tell me. I'll believe you, I promise." Then he left the room, closing the door behind him.

RJ sat on his new bed and looked at all the alien belongings that were once his father's, and he guessed, were now his. He wondered what the hell his father had been talking about.

After a few minutes, he decided it probably didn't matter, in fact he wondered if his dad was trying to set him up for a Halloween prank. The holiday was only a few days away and he knew his dad always tried to have fun, despite the fact RJ had always thought his heart wasn't in it.

Still, he did it for his wife and RJ.

Pushing all the crazy thoughts out of his mind, he stood up from the bed and decided to start investigating his new room. He started with the bureau drawers and would continue checking all the new stuff until his mother would call him down for supper an hour later.

RJ ignored the closet for now, and when his mom called, he left his room and ran down the stairs as fast as he could. Jumping the last three steps, his feet striking the hardwood with a loud thump, he got a rebuke from Jason for his troubles.

Upstairs, in the darkened bedroom, a dull red glow could be seen from under the closet door, unbeknownst to RJ or his parents.

# CHAPTER FOURTEEN

A FEW DAYS later, RJ left his house for school like he always did.

The sun was high in the sky and it was a brisk, October morning.  He was in a good mood, he knew that for sure. The reason for his chipper disposition was he had been able to avoid Ronnie for three whole days straight.

With the exception of not seeing his local bully, the three days went quick, nothing special happening; except one wonderful event which had occurred yesterday.

He especially enjoyed yesterday because he'd spent his lunch with Nancy.

The two of them had been in the middle of the cafeteria surrounded by more than a hundred of their fellow classmates, but to RJ they were the only two in the room. After lunch he'd felt like he was walking on air, and barely remembered the rest of the day.

When the dismissal bell rang, ending the third school day, he'd unlocked his bicycle and ridden home; for a change, making it all the way home without Ronnie seeing him. That was the best part.

While he rolled into his new home's driveway, he wondered if the day could get any better.

Walking up the front walk, he squeezed the door handle and found it unlocked. Stepping into the front foyer, his eyes took in the grand wood carvings that covered all the moldings over the doors.

RJ had always fancied himself a carpenter. He enjoyed

woodworking in school and had even made his mother a table in wood shop. He thought about the table, realizing it was nothing more than burnt wood now. That made him sad, until he realized he could make another one for her, this time even better than the first one.

Closing the front door, he walked into the house. The television was on in the living room and he headed for the sound. Stepping into the room, he stopped short when he saw his father and what he was holding in his hand.

Jason looked up surprised to be interrupted, and with a startled look on his face, set the .38 Smith & Wesson revolver down with a muffled curse.

"Jesus, RJ, why the hell didn't you say you were home," Jason said, while trying to cover the weapon with a red, oily rag.

"I'm sorry, Dad; I didn't realize I had to announce myself every time I got home." He pointed to the gun now under the rag.

"Is that a real gun? Does Mom know about it, can I hold it?" He asked in a rush of words, excited.

Jason stood up, looking down at RJ from across the room.

"No you can't hold it, what the hell kind of question is that? Shit, if your mother finds out you know about this, then she's going to kill me." He stepped closer to RJ, and the boy bent back a little, not knowing what his father was going to do next.

"Listen, RJ, you've got to promise me you'll forget you ever saw that," he said, pointing to the gun. "It was never here. Do you understand me?" His father said with a touch of nervousness to his eyes that made RJ a little fearful.

RJ nodded slowly. "Yeah, Dad I get it, but what's the problem, a lot of people have guns?"

Jason nodded. "I know that, son, but the rules of me having this gun are that your mother didn't want you to ever find out it was here. So you have to promise me that you'll forget about it."

"Okay, Dad, you can trust me, but before I forget about it, can I see it?"

Jason looked at his son, as if he was debating the question.

"Please, Dad? What's it matter now. I just want to look at it a little closer, that's all."

Jason's posture relaxed slightly as he gave in to his son. "All right, fine, but your mother's going to be home soon so we need to make this fast."

"Cool," RJ said, running over to the couch and sitting down.

Jason went back and sat down next to him and took the rag off the weapon. RJ's eyes lit up when he saw the polished metal reflected in the light of the room. The pistol grip was also black, with ridges so the shooter could hold the weapon firmly.

Jason picked up the revolver and then held it closer for RJ to see it better.

"All right, RJ, this is the cylinder where the bullets go," he said, cracking it open and showing him the round wheel with six holes.

"And this is the safety, you flick this up or down depending on if you want to fire the weapon."

RJ's eyes were wide as he looked at the gun. "Well, which is which, Dad?"

Jason studied the weapon and frowned. "You know what, son? I'm really not sure. Let's put it this way. If you try to shoot and nothing happens then the safety's on."

RJ chuckled at that. "Fair enough, Dad. Are you going to use it, you know, like go to the gun range or go out to the woods and shoot cans?"

Jason nodded. "Sure, when I get a chance, but for now it'll just have to wait. Now you have to keep your word and promise me you'll forget you ever saw it."

RJ stood up and placed his hand on Jason's shoulder.

"Don't worry, Dad, your secret's safe with me," then he took off out of the room and up the stairs. Jason could hear the pounding of his son's footsteps and then it was quiet. A second later, he heard the upstairs toilet flush and then more footsteps as RJ walked to his room. A door opened and closed and then more silence.

Jason let out the breath he didn't realize he'd been holding. When his son had placed his hand on his shoulder and told him he could trust the boy, Jason realized how much his son was growing up. Reaching over the side of the couch, he picked up the lock box he'd bought when he had purchased the weapon.

After taking a second to load the .38, he placed it in the metal box with a small cardboard box of ammunition for the gun.

Then he closed it, making sure the lock had caught. Standing up, he walked up the stairs to his bedroom, and placed it inside his closet. Just knowing it was there gave him a modicum of security.

Closing the closet, he heard the booming bass of his old record player. RJ had found some of his old records and was giving some of them a try. As he stood outside his old room, he heard Aerosmith singing about toys in the attic.

Chuckling to himself, and feeling older than he should, he went back downstairs. It seemed his family was doing okay after his mother dying and then their house burning down. At least they still had a roof over their heads, and the more Jason spent in his old house, the more he realized his trepidations may have been unfounded.

Stepping into the kitchen and grabbing a beer from the fridge, he looked out on the backyard he used to play in. Apparitions conjured by his memories floated by the window, him and his dad playing catch or Frisbee, or a barbecue with him and his parents.

All the years he'd wasted when he could have been here with his mother, if it wasn't for his messed up memories. He shook his head. He didn't know what to believe anymore.

He heard the front door open and then Emma's keys jangling in her hand.

"Can someone help me with the groceries? I've got my hands full!" She called from the door.

Jason set his beer on the counter, his ruminations forgotten.

"Coming, honey, hold your horses," he said and went to help her.

Upstairs, coming from RJ's room, the song had changed. Now the Eagles were singing about a heartache tonight; the melody drifting down the stairs while Jason and Emma unloaded groceries together.

*　　*　　*

That night for supper they had eaten hamburgers and French fries.

When RJ finished off his second one, he leaned back in the chair and sighed, sliding his hands in his pants pockets.

"That was great, Mom, I'm stuffed. What's for dessert?"

Jason frowned. "Jesus, son, you just ate enough for two grown men, don't you think you've had enough? And you still need to do your homework, don't you?"

Emma set her glass down and smiled. "Oh, lighten up, Jason. He's a growing boy after all."

RJ sat up straighter and grinned from ear to ear. "Yeah, Jason, I'm a growing boy, lighten up."

Jason frowned at his son, and before he could say something in return, RJ pushed his chair back and stood up, getting ready to go do his homework.

"Relax, Dad, I was only kidding, I'm going," he said, taking his hands out of his pockets. When he did, something bright yellow fell out and fell to the kitchen floor. All eyes went to the small object as it bounced once and then landed at Jason's feet. He leaned over and picked it up, his mouth turning into a frown.

"What's this and why do you have it?" Jason asked firmly.

RJ barely flinched. "It's a lighter, duh. I found it on the way home. Why, what's the big deal?"

"Our house just burnt down and you ask me what the big deal is when I find my son has a lighter in his possession?"

"Well, yeah, Dad, it's not mine, I just picked it up, why are you getting so mad? Take it if you want it, gees." He looked to Emma. "Can I go now, Mom?"

Emma looked at her son. "Sure, honey, I'll talk with your father and we'll be up later to talk to you some more about this." RJ turned to leave and Emma called to him again.

"Oh, wait a sec, RJ; did you put all those clothes I got you into your closet yet?" She asked.

"Yeah, Mom, I'll get to it, what's the rush?"

Emma frowned. Boys, always so messy and lazy, she thought

"Fine, but I want them put away by tomorrow night or else," she threatened. "I didn't spend two hours in the clothing store today so you could leave them in bags on the floor of your room."

RJ waved an acknowledgement. "Okay, dully noted, it shall be done, my queen," he said, then bent over at the waist, bowing gracefully to his mom, with a flourish of his left hand. He popped back up, and with a quirky smile on his lips, ran away and up the stairs to his room.

Jason leaned back in his chair. "You know, that boy's starting to become a wise guy."

She chuckled. "So, and you weren't at that age?"

Jason grinned at that, thinking about all those years ago, before his father had disappeared and he'd been happy.

"Yeah, that's a good point. Next to me, he's a regular saint." Then he changed the subject. "And what about the lighter, Emma?"

Emma smiled at him softly. "Jason, did you see the boy's face when you confronted him? There was no guilt there. He didn't look as if he'd just been caught with something he shouldn't have. I know my son, and I believe him when he says he found it."

Jason sighed and nodded in agreement. "All right, fine, you win, the matter's closed." Then he slid the lighter into his pants pocket and forgot about it.

He stood up and kissed his wife on the cheek. "Dinner was great, honey, is it okay if I go outside for a walk?"

She nodded. "Sure, but be back in an hour, things are finally quieting down around here and I want to spend some time with you before bed."

"Okay, it's a date," then he kissed her again, and after grabbing his jacket from the coat rack by the front door, walked out into the cool evening air.

The sun was just starting to set, the oranges and reds lighting up the sky.

With a sigh, Jason closed the door and headed out into the night. A walk would do him good; at least to work off that burger and fries he just had, and at best, help him clear some of the cobwebs of memories that kept haunting him.

*     *     *

RJ entered his room and closed the door, falling onto his bed with a soft squeaking of old springs. He stretched out, feeling pretty good about life at the moment.

His stomach had a pleasing pressure on it thanks to all the food he'd eaten and as he lay there, he thought about Nancy. Her eyes, her hair, the way her chin would dimple when she smiled.

He glanced over at the bags of clothes his mom had bought for him, deciding he'd put them away tomorrow after school. Since he'd come to live in his new room, he hadn't even opened the closet door yet. What for? There was nothing in there he needed and he just hadn't been interested.

With a light sigh, he sat up on his arms and scanned his room. His book bag was lying on the floor and he figured he should just do his homework and get it out of the way. Then he could watch TV until it was time for bed.

There was a repeat of Smallville on the Family Channel tonight and he wanted to see it, having missed it when it had been on during primetime. He needed to talk to his dad about getting him a TV and a VCR for his room so he could just tape the shows he wanted to watch, but with so much happening at once, he thought it might have come off as a little selfish, so he was biding his time until the right moment.

Walking across the room, he picked up his book bag and pulled out his math book. With another sigh, he opened the book and started working on his algebra while sitting on his bed.

Behind him, underneath the closet, a dull red glow continued to throb as the portal continued to open, while across the room on the bed, RJ concentrated on his equations.

# Chapter Fifteen

JASON HAD JUST returned from his walk, feeling refreshed despite his weary legs. He'd been out for a little more than an hour and he went straight into the kitchen, wondering if Emma was still in there.

She was, and at the sound of his footsteps, she turned around to look at him.

"About time, I was just beginning to worry," she smiled.

"Sorry, I've just been thinking. There's still so much to do, you know? There's dealing with all the paperwork we lost in the fire and my mother's bank accounts. Then we have to change things over on this house from my mom's name to ours. I still need to get my mom a head stone." He slumped into one of the kitchen chairs, the clear head from his walk quickly filling up again.

She walked over to him and wrapped her arms around him, hugging him.

"Don't worry, everything will work itself out. It has so far. We should be homeless right now and instead we're living in this beautiful old house." She sighed. "I just wish your mother could be here with us. I enjoyed her company."

Jason rubbed her arms and hands. "Yeah, I miss her, too." Then he gently extricated himself from her embrace and stood up.

"I'm going upstairs. Figure I'll wash up. Then I'll come back down and we can spend some of that quality time you were talking about." His mouth curved up into the slightest hint of a devilish smile, his eye glinting knowingly.

Her eyebrows went up at that. "Why, Mr. Lawson, I do believe you're trying to seduce me. Does your wife know you act like this?"

He turned and wrapped his arms around her. "Does she, hell, it's one of the things she loves about me," then he kissed her again, and after giving her a slap on the butt that made her squeak with fun, he left the kitchen, walked through the living room, and headed up the stairs.

He paused by his son's room, debating if he should go in and say hello. He could hear one of his favorite old rock bands filtering through the door now. Whitesnake was screaming they were hungry for love while the guitar railed in the background.

He decided he'd talk to his son later and let him relax and enjoy his new room.

He went to the bathroom and washed his face and hands, deciding he'd take a shower later before bed. Walking into his bedroom, he sat down on the bed and lay back so his feet were still on the floor. He looked up at the cracked ceiling, telling himself he'd have to replaster and paint it one weekend, when a scream rang out from down the hall. For a moment, Jason lay still, wondering if he'd heard what he thought, or if his son was just singing to the music he was listening to.

But then the yell was louder and more intense.

"Dad, there's something in my room! It just came out of the closet! Ahhhh! Help me!" His son screamed, his voice never sounding so terrified.

A thousand thoughts struck him at once as he sat up in bed. All the memories he had pushed down inside him surged up and came to the forefront of his mind.

Could it really be happening again, after all these years?

Less than a second had ticked by on the clock on his nightstand, and he jumped to his feet, already running to his closet. With shaking hands, he unlocked his lock box, not believing he needed the gun only days after placing it on the floor of his closet.

Not really knowing what he'd need, he grabbed the box of ammunition and shoved the box into the front pocket of his pants. Then picked up the already loaded weapon and he ran as fast as he could to his son's bedroom.

Just before he opened the door, Emma had come halfway up the stairs.

"No! Stay there, I'll handle this!" He ordered her.

Not used to hearing that kind of tone in her husband's voice, she obeyed, stopping on the stairs and waiting, her eyes showing how worried she was about her son.

Jason turned the doorknob to RJ's room and charged in, his weapon leading the way. He stopped in shock and horror at what stood before him.

The same black shaped creature from his memories stood in the middle of his old room. RJ was across the bedroom against the far wall. The room was a disaster of loose items. In his panic, RJ had thrown everything he could think of at the creature to keep it at bay.

"Dad, what the hell is that thing and why does it want me?" His son called to him.

"Just stay there, RJ! I'll handle this, you're going to be all right," Jason yelled.

At the sound of his voice, the obsidian creature turned to face him, its hair-like cape fanning out around it.

Jason stood transfixed, for the moment paralyzed. He remembered what had happened to his father like it had happened only moments ago, and he felt like he was eleven again, hiding under his bedcovers while his father battled some demon from Hell.

The creature swiped a clawed hand at Jason, the limb striking him on the shoulder and sending him flying. Jason struck the wall hard, but bounced off and came to his feet, quickly; shaking his head to clear it.

That was when he realized he had a gun in his hand. With a shaking arm, he brought up the .38 and squeezed the trigger at the creature.

Nothing happened

"Dad, the safety, flick off the safety," his son called from the other side of the bed.

His son's voice cut through his fear and his thumb moved up and found the small lever on the side of the weapon. Flicking it with his thumb, he squeezed the trigger again, directly at the creature's torso.

The weapon barked and Jason felt the kick, as for the creature, it barely noticed the passage of the round. The bullet went through its form and then lodged in the wall behind it. A low hiss came from its mouth and it darted for Jason again. The head reared up and grazed the ceiling as it prepared to come down on top of Jason and take off his head like it had done to his father, twenty years earlier.

But Jason remembered and reacted to protect himself.

Some small spark of intuition told him to drop down onto his butt and then roll away just as the creature dove down like a striking snake. Black teeth snapped on empty air and Jason continued rolling away. His hand wrapped around something on the floor and he realized it was a baseball bat. Not the one his father had used all those years ago, but a newer, aluminum bat.

Picking it up, he held the bat in his left hand, the right still holding the revolver.

He aimed at the creature from less than four feet away and squeezed the trigger again. The sound of the gun firing in the small room sounding like an explosion. The creature didn't flinch, but hissed and came at Jason again.

He panicked and dropped the revolver to the floor and swung the bat as hard as he could; knowing what the result would be, but desperate.

He expected the bat to go through the form harmlessly, as the wooden bat had all those years ago when his father had tried to save him, but instead the aluminum bat seemed to hit something.

It was like striking Jell-o, the bat continuing its arc in a half circle, but seeming to slow in the air.

The creature reared up and hissed, its talons clawing the ceiling as it seemed to writhe in pain. Then it lashed out at Jason again. Jason held the bat like a sword and the talons struck it, sending Jason skidding across the room again. He landed in a pile of clothes, still in the paper and plastic bags Emma had brought them home in.

"Dad!" His son screamed as he watched his father being thrown around the room like a stuffed animal.

At the sound of RJ's voice, the creature turned again to look at the boy. Jason struggled to get back to his feet, already knowing in his mind he would sacrifice himself to save his son, just as his father had done for him so many years ago. But he never got the opportunity.

The creature bounded over the bed and scooped RJ in its arms like he was nothing more than a baby kitten. RJ screamed and tried to punch the muscular chest, but his blows did nothing.

"No! Put him down you bastard, take me instead!" Jason screamed. His eyes scanned the room and he jumped in front of the closet, knowing the creature had to go through there if it wanted to escape with his son. At the last second, Jason realized he was unarmed, the revolver and bat lost when he'd been tossed around the room like a rag doll.

The creature never hesitated. It bounded over the bed, the clawed feet hitting the floor with house-shattering force, and charged at Jason, RJ held tight in its grasp.

Jason was ready, he had his arms up, and he was prepared to grapple with the monster, if only to get it to drop his son.

The creature hit him like a bull, one arm swiping him aside like he was a child.

Jason rebounded off the wall, and as he jumped to his feet, he saw the back of the creature running into the closet and the portal beyond.

Jason saw his son's face looking over the creature's shoulder.

"Dad, help me, don't let it take me!" He screamed with tears rolling down his cheeks in terror.

Then he was gone, vanished through the portal.

"RJ, no!" He screamed to empty air. He stood immobile for less than half a second, then before he could even think of changing his mind, he bent over, grabbed the revolver and the aluminum baseball bat, and charged towards the glowing portal.

The portal was beginning to close and Jason thought he was just going to end up plowing head first into the closet wall, but just before it snapped shut, he dove through the swirling lights, his body almost horizontal from his leap.

He felt something tug at his right foot and terror hit him, making him think the portal had closed on his leg, severing the limb from his body. But when he landed in the dirt somewhere else, he saw the limb was still intact.

Unfortunately, however, he was alone.

There was no sign of his son or the creature that had taken him.

Looking down at his foot, he saw he was missing about half an inch from the sole of his shoe. It was cleanly severed as if a sharp knife had cut it off.

The portal flared closed and he was cast in darkness. He lay horizontal for another five seconds, catching his breath and trying to regain his faculties, not really knowing where he was or what he was doing.

Then it all flooded back to him in a rush and he rolled to his knees, standing up. He was able to see a little better now, his eyes adjusting to the gloom. He was in what appeared to be a cave. The earth under his shoes was a dark red, almost similar to blood, and the cave walls looked like they'd been carved by tools.

He moved closer to the nearest wall and noticed the sharp gouges in the rock. Thinking of the creature's claws, maybe tools hadn't excavated this cavern, instead, maybe it had been talons.

Repressing a shiver, he did a quick inspection of his body. With the exception of a few bruises, he seemed to be unhurt. He still had the bat and the gun, and while he moved around the cave, the box of ammunition rattled in his front pocket.

His foot struck something hard and the object rolled across the cavern floor. In the wan light, his mind brought up images of a severed head rolling across the dirt, a gaping maw staring at him with sightless eyes.

Deciding he needed to see what it was, too make sure it wasn't RJ's head; he walked across the cavern until he was standing over the dark shape. It appeared to be the size of a young boy's head, and with his heart in his throat, he bent over and picked it up. He expected to feel the hair of his son's head, the soft flesh of his cheeks, now pale white from lack of blood.

Instead, he picked up a football. He laughed with relief in the confines of the cave, his voice echoing off the walls; the feeling of happiness rushing through him to the point he thought his legs would give out.

He dropped the football and hope surged within him.

Maybe his son was still alive?

Walking back to where he'd landed upon arriving in the cave, he examined the wall where the portal had been. Strange carvings covered the sides of the wall. They seemed to glow faintly, their luminance clearly visible in the dull light.

Jason's eyes drifted to what looked like a handprint on the right side of the carvings. The imprint was three times the size of his and the fingers in the impression were long and tapered to fine points. Jason thought back to when he had seen the creature's hands, the talons for fingertips.

So this impression was for the creature, he thought. He had no idea what that might mean to him or his son, but he filed it away in the back of his mind. It might come in handy later.

Hitching up his fallen pants and fixing his shirt, he placed the revolver in the back of his pants. He didn't know if it would help him here, it didn't seem to do much good in RJ's room, but it was all he had.

Hefting the aluminum baseball bat like a sword, he started out of the cavern.

What looked like footprints covered the earthen floor and he decided to follow them. If he was correct, they were the spoor of the creature after it had returned to wherever he was now.

The cave turned into a tunnel. The ceiling about three feet above his head. He walked in silence, with only his pulse pounding in his temple for company. He was frightened out of his mind, but he knew if he didn't find RJ soon, it would probably be too late…if it wasn't already.

The tunnel dog-eared to the left and he followed it. Fifty yards from there he came to a fork in the tunnel. The tunnel now split off into both the left and right directions. Jason looked down on the dusty earth, trying to see the markings of the creature's passage, but it was nothing but smudges going in both directions.

Deciding to take the right tunnel out of some old saying he remembered as a child, he started off again. Less than twenty feet later, his foot kicked something across the floor, the tiny echo of the object rolling away drifting around the tunnel.

Jason stopped, waiting to see if he'd been discovered, but as the minutes moved by and nothing happened, he was confident he was safe.

Moving forward, his shoe landed on something brittle that crunched under his sole. Remembering he had a cigarette lighter in his pocket, he pulled it out, flicking the head of the small Bic lighter. The tiny flame burst to life, wreathing him in a small circle of light. He looked down with the lighter leading the way and saw the tunnel floor was covered in what seemed to be bones. They seemed very old, like the kind of bones someone might find in an animal pit after the meat has been stripped away. The bones were bleached white and were cracked and splintered as if the animal who had fed on them had gone for the sweet marrow within. Jason picked up one of them, if he was right; it was a human leg or thigh bone, or perhaps a femur if he was correct.

The bone had been cracked in half, reminding him of when his father used to crack the pork chop bone at dinner to get the marrow inside, which confirmed his idea from the look of the others.

Dropping the bone with a dull clatter, he repressed a shiver.

He started forward again, realizing he needed to keep moving. After retrieving the bat from where he'd leaned it against the tunnel wall, he continued onward, his shoes cracking the brittle fossils with each step he took. Every step sounded like a gun blast, but the bones were everywhere on the ground, there was no way for him to avoid them.

He walked for another quarter mile with nothing but pale bones for company.

Then the tunnel light began to grow brighter and he placed the lighter back into his pocket, the hot metal burning his thigh.

He barely noticed, his concentration only on the path in front of him.

Soon, he saw yet more light and hoped he'd finally made it to the end of his small journey. The bones were gone from underfoot, and the ground became hard packed red dirt again.

For ten more minutes he walked, and when he finally reached the end of the tunnel, he paused at the entrance just to make sure nothing was waiting for him to step out into the open.

With the aluminum bat in his hands, he took a deep breath and slowly slid out of the side of the tunnel, hugging the far wall. The opening was clear.

No signs of life or his son could be seen anywhere in the immediate area. He gazed up to the sky, expecting to see the typical blue he had always seen, but instead his eyes were greeted with a sky the color of blood. A few yellow clouds floated by on the vermillion horizon and Jason gulped as he stared openmouthed.

After a few minutes of staring like a child at the circus, he regained a small amount of his composure and realized he needed to keep moving if he was going to save his son.

To his right was what looked like a path leading away from the mouth of the tunnel and he decided the trail would be his best course of action. In front of him, it appeared he was on a mountain or cliff face. With a quick glance around him again, he walked straight to the end of the wide platform in front of the tunnel opening.

He stopped at the edge, now able to look down on the austere landscape below. His jaw dropped and he felt his heart beating faster from terror. His legs felt uneasy and he had to lean against a nearby boulder for support.

Below him sprawled the creature's world.

Jason's eyes tried to take it all in, but it was an overload of sights he'd only seen in his worst nightmares.

Slowly he regained his composure and closed his mouth; though he still continued to gape at the territory below him, not able to tear his eyes away.

An old movie his mother used to watch floated into his head, one of the more popular sayings from the film seeming to fit perfectly with his present predicament.

"Toto, I don't think we're in Kansas anymore," he muttered under his breath.

# Chapter Sixteen

J ASON GAZED OUT at the new world he found himself in.

Directly below him he saw the trail that snaked along the side of the mountain, the thin line cutting through the rocks and boulders like a tear in the earth.

As he looked out across the landscape to the horizon, he saw nothing but devastation. It reminded him of what the bombs had done to Hiroshima at the end of World War Two.

No buildings or structures could be seen from his present point of reference and no living trees or foliage for as far as he could see. He saw what appeared to be pools of stagnant water interlaced amongst the dead trees scattered across the land below him. The trees were a purplish color, with skeletal-like branches which pointed every which way.

The landscape itself was a darkish red, maroon color, reminding him of dried blood. He looked everywhere, hoping to catch some movement of his son and his captor, but nothing showed itself.

Deciding he better get moving, he started down the trail. So far he'd seen no animal life, not even a few insects to break the silence of his surroundings.

Walking down the trail, his feet crunching in the dry dirt, he continually kept looking behind him, watching the empty trail for signs he was being followed. The dead silence let his imagination go wild and he half-expected something to jump out from behind a boulder and attack him at any moment.

But nothing happened, and after a little more than an hour, he had made it to the bottom of the mountain.

There was still a clear trail leading away from the foot of the mountain, and after a quick glance around, he moved on, following the beaten down path.

After another hour had come and gone, his mouth became dry from his exertions, so he stopped at one of the many stagnant pools that dotted the landscape.

Falling to his knees in exhaustion, he knelt down and brushed away the reddish algae-like coating that covered the pool's surface and cupped some water in his hands.

He was about to take a drink when something swam by him, just under the surface of the water. He immediately jumped back surprised, not knowing what exactly it was he'd seen.

If his eyes hadn't deceived him, then he'd seen some form of fish that resembled a melding of a snake and a slug. Deciding he wasn't that thirsty after all, he wiped his hands clean on his pants and started down the trail again.

He walked for hours until he was barely able to see the mountain he'd descended behind him and he was beginning to lose hope. He was tired and his feet were killing him. Plus, he still had no idea if his son was alive or even if he was going in the right direction to find him.

He climbed over to a two-foot high rock on the side of the trail and sat down. He leaned over, placing his head between his hands. He was so weary and worried for RJ, he felt like crying. While he sat there contemplating his fate, his nose picked up the scent of something burning. If he had to take a guess to what it could be, he would have figured it was some kind of wood.

Standing up, he started walking off the trail, not really knowing where he was going, but figuring there was nothing to lose. He walked for another twenty minutes, being careful to avoid the many pools of stagnant water, until he came to the side of a small cliff. The cliff face went straight up for more than a thousand feet. Jason looked over its vertical surface, but could see no way of scaling the edifice even if he had felt the need, but luckily that wasn't where he needed to go. When he moved closer to the cliff side, he saw a number of dried foliage and a few old trees which had been cut down. Now the large logs lay on their side, and as Jason stood and stared, his nose still smelling the smoke, a man appeared from around the tree logs and stopped cold. His jaw dropped when he spotted Jason, and he stared at him for almost a full thirty seconds, then he turned around and bolted out of sight back behind the logs and stray brush.

"Wait, I don't mean you any harm!" Jason called, running after the man. Jason had thrown caution to the wind, too excited about finding another human being alive. If the man had wished Jason harm, Jason would never have seen it coming since the man had been hidden from view before he'd stepped out from behind the logs. Lucky for Jason, the man seemed more scared of him than Jason might have been of him.

Jason ran around the logs to discover a small cave opening a little more than four feet high. Ducking his head, he ran into the cave, heedless of his safety. There was a small campfire in the middle of the octagon like space and the man was at the back wall, standing still. He had a large club in his hand and he held it in a defensive posture. Jason stopped on the other side of the fire and lowered the bat in his hand.

"Hey, there, my God you don't know how good it is to see another person. I was beginning to think I was the only thing alive around here," Jason smiled at the man.

The club lowered slightly, the man's eyes staring into Jason like a cornered animal.

"Who the hell are you and how'd you get here?" The man asked. His voice was rough, like he had a bad cold.

Jason took another step forward. "My name's Jason. Jason Lawson. I'm looking for my son. Can you help me?"

"Your son? What the hell are you talking about?"

Jason sighed, realizing if he was going to get anywhere with this man, he was going to have to gain his trust. Jason sat down on one of the logs near the fire. They had been dragged inside the cave for just this purpose and Jason laid the bat at his feet. He looked up at the man and smiled again, hoping it looked genuine. He then told the man the story of how he'd found this strange place and how he was searching for his son. He told the man about the black-shaped creature that shrugged off bullets, the pool with the strange marine life, and how he had found his way to the man's cave by following the scent of the campfire.

The entire time Jason wove his tale, the man stood quietly and listened. With the exception of the club being lowered to the ground, the man's cautious stance never changed. When Jason finished his story, the man stood taller, and then walked over to the campfire and dropped down across from Jason with a groan of tired bones.

The flames reflected off his eyes, giving the man a feral look. His hair was shoulder length, but the top was thinning. He had a good three week's worth of a beard on his face and his clothes were nothing but tattered rags. With the man closer, Jason could see the remnants of his clothes seemed to be a pair of chinos and a button down, long sleeve shirt.

The man leaned forward so close to the fire Jason thought his beard might burn from the heat of the flames.

"It's a good thing you didn't drink that water from any of the pools. You need to boil that stuff at least twice before it's safe to drink. There's small parasites that live in that water. If you drink it straight from the pond, the little bastards feed on your insides until they get so big they…" He stopped and leaned back on his log. "Well, let me put it this way, did you ever see that movie Alien?"

Jason gulped and nodded assent.

"So, you really don't know where you are, huh?" The man asked.

Jason shook his head. "No idea, I'd be grateful for any information you could give me."

The man leaned over and picked up what looked like a hollowed out gourd. He handed it to Jason. Jason took it, and upon hearing the sloshing liquid inside, suddenly felt his thirst returning stronger than before. But he didn't drink, thinking about the warning he'd just received.

The man chuckled. "Go 'head, it's safe. Boiled it myself just this morning."

Jason grinned slightly and took a sip. The liquid tasted coppery with a hint of peppermint. He drank greedily, not realizing how thirsty he'd been. After a few minutes, his thirst was slaked and he handed the gourd back to the man.

"Damn, boy, you sure were thirsty," he exclaimed upon feeling the weight of the gourd.

"Sorry," Jason said, wiping his mouth on his sleeve.

The man waved the remark away. "I'm just jokin'. It's good to have someone to talk to again. So you want the lowdown on this place or what?"

Jason nodded yes.

"All right then. My names Clyde Bowen and if I had to guess, I'd say I've been in this place for almost three months or so. There's others like us. Humans, I mean. Mostly children. They're in a camp on the other side of the ridge. But it's not really a camp; it's more like a prison. A breeding prison. I reckon you've seen those things that live here?"

"Oh, yeah, that's why I'm here. One of those bastards took my son and I'm going to find him and get him back if it kills me." Then in a softer voice he added. "That is, if he isn't already dead."

Clyde's eyebrows went up in surprise. "Dead? I doubt it. You see, a lot of years ago the creatures that call this place home pretty much ate everything worth eating. They started hunting on earth and other planets. At first they just ate what they caught, but then one of 'em got the idea to catch us and raise us like cattle; keep us reproducin'. Once we're big and fat, well, that's when they eat us. Shit, on this world, we're nothing but heifers to be raised and slaughtered."

"So, you think my son's still alive?" Jason asked hopefully.

Clyde nodded. "Yup, if he's just a boy, then the bastard that caught him probably took him back to his camp. Your son will end up staying there for the rest of his life, breeding and working, until the bastards decide it's his time. Then the bastard'll take him away for dinner."

Clyde tossed a dried, purplish branch into the fire, the flames consuming it with a surge of multicolored light .

"If you haven't realized it, time passes quicker here than on earth. That's why your son was long gone when you came through that portal, even though you were only a second or so behind him. If I had to guess, I'd say a full day has passed since you came here."

"And where is here exactly, and how the hell do you know so much?" Jason inquired.

Clyde chuckled again, clearly enjoying being a tutor to Jason. "Well, a lot of what I know came down from others who'd been here longer than me. You see, I was a prisoner of one of the camps, too, but one night I managed to escape. See, being an adult, the creature would eat me first, keeps the young ones for breeding. So I took a chance one night with a few others and made a break for it. I made it, the others didn't." His eyes looked into the fire as he remembered.

"Been on my own now for almost a month. It's not the Ritz, but at least I don't have to worry about being the main course every night. As for where we are, well, no one really knows. Some think it's another dimension and others think we're all dead and this is Hell. That's why we named this place Hellioth."

"Hellioth? What does that mean?" Jason asked.

Clyde spit into the fire, the saliva sizzling as it evaporated.

"That's easy, it's short for Hell on Earth. And after you spend some time here, you'll realize it's the goddamn truth."

# CHAPTER SEVENTEEN

RJ HAD NEVER been so scared in his life.

Even when he knew Ronnie had him cornered and he was expecting to be beaten up, he'd never felt the terror which was swelling within him, threatening to rip his heart from his chest.

When the creature scooped him up in its arms, he'd felt the air on his face just before they had plunged into his closet and the waiting portal. He had seen his father's terrified face and then he was gone, lost in a sea of bright lights. The next moment he opened his eyes to find himself in some kind of cave.

He saw the creature press its clawed hand into an imprint in the wall near the opening and then it turned and started down a long, dark tunnel. Even in his terror, RJ filed away the cave impressions to the back of his mind for future consideration.

He bounced on its back, like a sack of potatoes, helpless. He did his best to squirm his way free, but the creature's talons squeezed tighter on his arms whenever he tried to escape, causing him to cry out in pain. After multiple times with the same result, he gave up and just lay submissively, knowing if he fought to be free, he'd receive more of the same.

He only saw where he had been, his position on the creature's shoulder set up so his butt faced forward and his head faced their back trail. He strained his head to look up at the sky, but it was so dark he could see nothing but shadows. The creature's footsteps echoed on the trail as its body moved at what would be considered a dead run for a human. But though it was hard to believe, RJ realized he was in no way being carried by a human being. The thing below him was all black and had a tough hide all over its body that seemed to absorb all ambient light surrounding it.

But it was the smell that really gave it away. RJ had to constantly breathe through his nose or he was liable to end up puking all over the creature's back. The odor of the thing reminded him of the smell of ammonia and something dead. He knew the redolence well because one time his mom found a dead rat in their basement. The small rodent had seemed to pulse and the fur rippled as the maggots inside its body fed and moved around. His mom had scraped the carcass into a garbage bag and had used ammonia to wash the area down. But the small corpse had been there for a while and some of the bodily fluids had seeped into the concrete floor of the cellar. Although the ammonia covered the stench of death, it didn't totally eradicate it, and the two odors mixed to create an entirely new fragrance which had his mom opening all the windows in the cellar for more than a week.

That same smell was always with him now as the creature moved swiftly down the mountain side. It had a light coat of ink black hair draping down from its shoulders. The hair caught the wind from its passing and floated behind them like some kind of thin, stringy cape.

RJ winced as the creature jumped over a large rock in the road, its shoulder pressing into his kidneys. With all the bouncing around, he suddenly realized he had to go pee, though he wasn't about to ask the monster if it would pullover to the side of the road for a moment so he could go.

His heart continued pounding in his temple, the only sounds to be heard were the creature's heavy footfalls as it moved down the trail. Boulders and tall skeletal trees flashed by in the darkness, and despite the fact he was a prisoner, he also was glad he wasn't all alone on the trail.

He started to cry again, even though he didn't want to. He knew he needed to be brave, like his dad. But he couldn't help it. He had no idea where he was or what had happened to his father. He didn't know what the thing carrying him wanted with him, although he'd watched way too many horror movies to think it just wanted a friend because it was lonely.

Time jumbled together and for what must have been at least two hours, the creature jogged across the terrain. It seemed to be indefatigable, its long legs eating up the miles, as large tufts of dirt shot out behind it as it loped down across the terrain.

Then it slowed and stopped in the road. It turned around in a circle, as if it was making sure the area surrounding it was clear, then it took off again. When it had turned around, RJ managed to catch a glimpse of light a little ways off the trail on what seemed to be a rise in the terrain.

The creature veered off the main path, and in the wan light, RJ could see yet another path below him, this one even more flattened by the many footsteps that had worn it down over the years.

Within a few minutes the creature slowed and finally stopped. RJ felt himself being lifted off the thing's shoulder and unceremoniously dropped to the dirt ground. He landed in a puff of dust, his butt hurting from the rough landing.

He looked around him to see a fenced in enclave.

A man was walking toward the gate with a small torch in his hand. Upon reaching the gate, he unlocked it. RJ could see it was some kind of locking mechanism, but not like anything he'd ever seen before.

The gate opened just wide enough to allow RJ to be passed through the opening. The creature picked him up by the collar of his shirt and tossed him into the compound like a sack of potatoes.

Without another look at RJ, the creature hissed at the man, swaying back and forth on its legs like a man-sized snake. The man nodded back, as if he'd heard some unspoken orders and was agreeing to them. Then the creature moved off across the hill, covering the distance in seconds now that its burden was released. RJ watched it departing until he saw it stop in a small structure on the top of the hill. The structure looked like it was made out of clay or mud, like in those documentaries he used to watch about indigenous tribes living in other countries. The creature stopped at the doorway for a moment, looking back on the compound, and with a shake of its head, disappeared into the building.

RJ was yanked to his feet by the man, the pull so strong RJ let out a yelp of pain. When he was standing, he yanked his arm free and stood there, trying to look as defiant as he could under his dire circumstances.

"Where am I? Where's my dad? Who are you and why am I here?" RJ said with as must conviction as he could muster.

The man chuckled like RJ had just told him a joke.

"Look, kid, it's late and I'm tired. You'll find out everything you need to know in the morning." He grabbed RJ by the scruff of his shirt and started to drag him towards a one-story building in the center of the camp.

"No, I'm not going anywhere with you, I want to go home!" RJ yelled, managing to pull free from his grip when his shirt collar ripped. He was about to turn and run when he saw that the entire camp was surrounded by some kind of wooden fencing.

There was nowhere to run.

When he turned back to the man in defeat, he saw a fist coming straight for his face. Before RJ could do anything, the man's fist struck him in the left cheek, the soft flesh in his mouth tearing against his teeth. RJ was thrown to the ground, his head reeling from the blow.

Even Ronnie had never hit him like that. In his eleven and a half years on earth, no one had ever struck him with the power behind the blow he'd just received. With his vision blurring and his head throbbing from the blow, the man picked him off the ground and pushed him towards the one-story building.

RJ fell forward onto his hands, but kept himself moving. After a few seconds of deep breathing, he stood up and kept walking. He was done protesting. If he could help it, he didn't want to do anything more to make the man hit him again.

With tears rolling down his cheeks from pain and terror, he picked himself up and walked to the building. Once he was on the ramshackle porch, the man opened the only door RJ could see.

Without any preamble, or a word of warning, the man raised his boot and placed it firmly on RJ's back. Then he kicked out, sending RJ flying into the building.

"Welcome to your new home, kid. You'll be spending the rest of your life here. But don't worry about that, 'cause it just might not be that long." With a chuckle to himself, the man closed the door.

RJ lay on the floor, spread flat. It hurt too much to move and he figured he'd just rest for a moment before he had to get up.

His ears caught the sound of rustling, like many feet moving at the same time.

The room was almost pitch black, a dull gloom illuminating the area around him. Only the outlines of shapes were visible and he had to blink his eyes to hopefully get a better view of his surroundings.

He decided to sit up, and when he began searching the room, he could barely make out the forms of black, shadowy shapes coming towards him. He tried to back up on the floor, crawling like a crab, but his back came up against the  locked door.

His breath came in gasps and he waited for the shapes to grow close enough to grab him and finish what the creature had started hours before.

He put his arms in front of his face and screamed; "No, leave me alone! I don't want to die!"

Then it was too late.

The figures swarmed over him and he became smothered by the weight of many bodies, the shadowy figures converging on him en masse.

# CHAPTER EIGHTEEN

"LET ME GET this straight," Jason said while he stood up and walked around the campfire. "You think this is some kind of parallel dimension or something and we're all trapped here?"

Clyde nodded. "You bethcha. Far as I know, the only ones that can open the portals are the Snatchers."

"Snatchers? Is that what they're called?" Jason asked.

Clyde turned around on his log to see Jason better. He knew what his new friend was going through. He was trying to accept the unacceptable and he needed to keep moving. Clyde knew in time, Jason would calm down and accept what was right in front of him.

"To tell you the truth, I don't think anyone really knows what they're called, but the name just kind of stuck. I mean, that's how they grab us from our dimension. They open a portal and then pop in, grab their prey, then pop back here with no one the wiser back home."

Jason turned and sat back down by the fire. He stared into the glowing embers and his eyes seemed to become lost in the dancing flames while he spoke.

"My father was taken by one of those Snatchers when I was a kid. It bit his head off and then took the rest of him back through the portal it had made. No one believed me; they all said I was crazy. Until now, I had pretty much convinced myself that I must have been hallucinating the entire thing." He turned and looked at Clyde. "Guess now I know I wasn't imagining things."

"Seems to be," Clyde said with a subtle smirk.

Jason stood up again, facing Clyde. "And now one of those bastards has my son and I'll be damned if it's going to take him, too."

He grabbed Clyde by the arm. "You have to take me to the camp. My son has to be there," Jason told him, the desperation in his face apparent.

Clyde held up his hands in a slow down gesture. "Now wait a minute there, pal. I was lucky enough to get out of there in one piece and I sure as hell don't want to go back."

"But you have to. Jesus man, he's my son. He's only eleven for Christ sake."

Clyde saw the pain in Jason's eyes and sat back down, thinking.

"Well, I suppose we could do a recon of the area in the daylight. The Snatchers sleep during the day and hunt at night."

"How many of those things are there?" Jason asked.

"Shit, that's a tough one. I know from what I've heard there's not that many left. Years ago, they had even taken to attacking and eating each other. If only they could have wiped themselves out, then none of us would be here now."

He walked over to the tunnel opening, and let out a loud fart. He grinned at Jason.

"Sorry about that, figured I'd come over here so it would float outside," he said while waving his hand behind his ass.

"Yeah, thanks," Jason said, wanting to hear more about his new enemies. "So what happened next?"

After a moment, feeling ventilated, Clyde walked back to the fire and sat down.

"Well, it seems as the years went by the stronger ones wiped out the weaker ones, so now only the most determined, the most powerful and ruthless, are still around. They made these camps and started to breed us, so they would have a replenishing food supply. So far it's worked well for them." He spoke the next sentence more softly. "Hasn't worked so well for us, though."

"So how many of them are at the camp?" Jason asked, eager to hear the rest.

Clyde took a sip of water from the gourd. Rinsed his mouth good, and then spit it into the fire. "Well, there's good news for you, I guess. The Snatchers don't play well with others so they've set their camps up far apart from the others as possible. Far as I know, the next closest camp is more than five miles away. Guess they're territorial."

Jason's face lit up with hope. "Does that mean my son should be at the camp that's nearby?"

Clyde nodded his head slowly. "It's possible, but it's just as likely that another Snatcher took him and then ran the miles back to its lair. There's really no way to know for sure without getting in there and seeing with our own eyes. And once you got in there, believe me, you're not gonna get out again. Hell, when I escaped there were four of us. By the time we had made it out of there and the Snatcher had hunted us down, I was the only one left. The only reason I survived was I thought quick and hid in one of those pools. The damn thing walked right by me and never knew I was at its feet. They don't like water much. Let me tell ya, after it left it was a good thing I was in the water already because my pants needed a good washing."

Jason nodded, not relishing the picture. Then he walked over to Clyde, his face set in stone.

"All right then, when do we leave?" Jason asked, eager to go find his son.

Clyde walked to the tunnel opening again and looked out onto the wide open landscape. The red sun was just starting to set, the horizon turning dark violet. There was no moon anywhere in the sky. When night fell, the darkness was complete. Clyde turned back to Jason, his mouth set into a tight line.

"Look, Jason, no matter how bad you want to go, night's falling. We'll go first thing in the morning."

"How long is that, is it the same as back home?" Jason asked.

Clyde shook his head.

"No, actually it's a little shorter. The day and night cycle on this planet is about eighteen hours, so it'll be daylight again in about nine hours or so. Until then, why don't you relax and have something to eat."

Jason watched Clyde rummage around in the corner of the cave. The man kept digging and after a few minutes came back with something that resembled a mushroom.

"What the hell is that?" Jason asked, staring at the brown fungus.

"That's supper. Hope you like it, 'cause that's all there is to eat in this place. Even if I wanted to eat meat, the Snatchers wiped out every other animal. They don't eat plants or greens so there's plenty of this stuff growing around here. It grows on one side of those ugly lookin' trees that are all over the place."

"What about fish? I thought I saw some swimming in the pool I almost drank from." Jason said, studying the mushroom like fungus in

Clyde's hand.

Clyde shook his head. "Poisonous. Shit, if they weren't, the damn Snatchers would have eaten them years ago."

Jason just sat there, listening. Clyde pushed the mushroom closer to his face and Jason took it. He hesitated for a moment while Clyde stood there, watching him.

"Go on, try it, hell, you might even like it," Clyde said.

Feeling like a guest in someone's house who had cooked all day and you just feel obliged to be polite and try some, Jason took a small bite.

Preparing to spit out the fungus the second it touched his tongue, he was surprised to find it didn't taste that bad. While it didn't taste like mushrooms from back home, it reminded him of what it was like to eat a potato raw. It had a soft texture, like tripe, but once in his mouth it softened, his saliva breaking it down quickly.

"So, what do you think?" Clyde asked, smiling.

Jason took another bite. "It's edible, I guess. Reminds me of a raw potato."

Clyde slapped his knee and laughed. "Son of a bitch, that's what I thought the first time I had one." He came and sat back down next to Jason, a mushroom in his dirty hand.

"You're all right, pal. I think you and me are gonna get along just fine," he said, taking a bite from his mushroom.

Jason smiled back politely. As help went, Clyde could be much worse than he was. But then again, he could be much better. Not that it mattered, where Jason was and what he needed to do, beggars couldn't be choosers, and he was definitely a beggar.

Jason sat quietly and chewed his food, while next to him Clyde rambled on. The man was happy to have another soul to talk to and was taking full advantage of it.

Jason just continued eating, nodding when he thought it was appropriate, knowing whether it was a shorter night than from back home or not, he had a feeling it was going to be one of the longest nights of his life.

He sent a silent prayer to his son to just hold on for one more night and tomorrow he would save him. He knew his son couldn't hear him, but then, maybe there was enough craziness in this new world that if he really tried hard enough, RJ would hear him and not give up hope.

# Chapter Nineteen

R J WAS PULLED roughly to his feet and he realized almost immediately it wasn't more of those creatures surrounding him, but other people, other kids, like him. Hands pulled him to the left and right, and raised voices argued over who would get to talk with him first. Finally, one voice rose over the others, seeming to squash the others cries in one loud clap.

"Enough! I'll say where he goes and who he talks to," said a loud male, disembodied voice as the owner slowly moved closer through the crowd, pushing without a care for who was struck. More kids crowded closer and were promptly pushed aside as the mysterious someone pushed and shoved like he were at a rock concert trying to get the autograph of the lead singer.

Children were thrust aside, making room for the owner of the disembodied voice, and after a moment the kid stood in front of him, staring at him with hard eyes.

RJ could only stand in place, too shocked to move.

Someone lit a torch and the room was flooded with a dim glow. Shadows covered everything, giving the faces staring at him an evil countenance.

But that was his first impression.

As things began to quiet down in the large building, RJ realized the faces staring back at him looked as scared and frightened as his own face must look.

The only difference was the faces looking at him were dirtier, the hair was disheveled, and the clothes they wore were ripped and torn in far too many places to count.

The owner of the voice was a tall boy in his early teens. His face was covered in dirt, and his long, dark brown hair gave him the look of a rock star. The pair of Levis he wore were ripped and dirty, and the muscle shirt he wore was so thin his skin peeked through in multiple places.

"What are you going to do with him, Patrick?" One of the kids asked, from behind him, the face hidden from view.

The teen ignored the question and grabbed RJ by the arm, dragging him across the room, the others following along, all curious about what would happen next. RJ was still too shocked to do anything other than let himself be led where Patrick wanted him.

While RJ was moving through the room, he was able to catch glances of the bedrolls on the floor. All were lined up in neat rows, one row on each side of the room. Miscellaneous items were scattered at the top and bottom of the bedrolls, reminding RJ of what an orphanage looked like.

He saw a boy in the corner, sitting over a hole in the floor with his pants down. He watched the boy stand up and pull his pants back on. Finished, the boy walked away, never giving RJ the slightest idea he cared if he was being watched.

When they reached the back of the room, the teen pushed RJ onto one of the bedrolls, hard. RJ's elbows and backside hit the blanket with a thud as Patrick had planned and the hard ground underneath RJ caused him to wince in pain, his teeth snapping shut with a click.

In a brief flash, he imagined what might have happened if his tongue had been between his teeth. A visceral image of his severed tongue lying on the blanket in front of him, while he drowned in blood flooded his mind, until he shook it away. That hadn't happened, so there was no reason to dwell on it.

The teen smiled cruelly and kneeled down to stare into RJ's eyes, enjoying the pain he'd inflicted on the new arrival. His breath smelled horrible and RJ wanted to turn away, but had a feeling it wouldn't be a very good move right about now.

"Listen up, newbie. I'm Patrick and I run this place. Stay out of my way and I won't pound you into the dirt and feed what's left of you to the Snatcher." Then he stood up and pushed his way through the crowd of other boys and girls. When they wouldn't move fast enough, he'd punch or elbow someone in the stomach or ribs while he made his way through the mass of people.

RJ sat perfectly still, trying to grasp what was happening to him. Then a small boy, no more than ten, sat down next to him on the closest bedroll.

"Hi, I'm Teddy. Don't listen to Patrick; he's just a big bully. If you leave him alone, he probably won't bother you."

RJ nodded, thinking of Ronnie back home. "I'm RJ, and I already have some experience with bullies and that's not always true."

RJ was now able to look around a little better. He turned to Teddy, now seeing the boy for the first time. Teddy had long blonde hair that kept falling in front of his face. He had small skinny arms and his coveralls seemed to be about two sizes too big. He reminded RJ of a freshly made scarecrow which was now ready to be put out in the farmer's field.

"I don't see any adults anywhere, where are they?" RJ asked.

Another boy sat down across from them and smiled wanly. "There aren't any here. Whenever the Snatcher brings a grown-up back they usually don't stay long, sometimes only hours, or if we're lucky, maybe days," the small boy said.

"That's Matt," Teddy told RJ. "He's eleven. Patrick doesn't like him, so he's always beating him up."

RJ looked a little closer at Matt's face, studying the lines under the dirt and grime. He could clearly make out the dark bruises and scrapes from his most recent beating. RJ felt anger building inside him that had never been there before. No matter where he went, there was always a bully to make things worse.

RJ noticed Patrick across the floor sitting with the few girls in the room. He gestured to them with his chin and asked Teddy.

"What's with all the girls over there with Patrick?" He asked.

Teddy followed his gaze and grinned slightly. "Patrick keeps all the girls with him. He's older and he likes kissing them and stuff." Teddy made a face as if he'd tasted something distasteful. "That's fine with me, girls are gross."

Matt nodded an assent and winced when he pulled a muscle from his last beating. He carefully stretched out on his bedroll, making twisted faces while he became more comfortable.

RJ looked back at Teddy. "How long have you been here?" He asked the boy.

Teddy shrugged. "Don't know really. If I had to guess, I'd say a few months or so. No one keeps track, so it's hard to tell." He pointed to

Patrick. "He's been here the longest, though. The Snatcher doesn't take him 'cause he keeps things in order around here."

"Take him where? What do you mean?" RJ asked, not understanding.

Teddy's voice grew cold as he shared with RJ what he knew.

"The Snatcher keeps us for food. We're like chickens or pigs on a farm. When he gets hungry, he comes and takes one of us. After that, they never return. He takes all the adults and eats them first. He wants some of us to get older and make babies so he has more food. Its like we're farm animals waiting for the butcher's knife." He smiled at the analogy, thinking he was clever. "That's what my dad used to say sometimes. Seems to fit here, I suppose."

RJ shook his head, barely believing what he'd just heard, but everything in front of his eyes was saying it was the truth.

"I saw one adult out front when that thing brought me in, what about him?"

RJ asked.

"Oh, that's old Harry," Matt answered. "He's a mean bastard. No one knows why the Snatcher keeps him alive. Guess someone has to be out there to keep track of us and keep us breathing, and old Harry got the job." Matt leaned in closer so only RJ and Teddy could hear him.

"Sometimes during the day, when the Snatcher's sleeping, Harry comes and takes one of the girls away for a while. When he brings them back they're always crying. Sometimes, he even takes one of the boys. Don't know what he does with them, nobody will talk about it, but I know I don't want to go with him," Matt said with a touch of fear in his voice.

RJ sat perfectly still, like a living statue, still not believing what had happened to him. It was like some crazy nightmare he should be waking up from any minute. Probably a result of eating that second hamburger his mom had made him for supper. Then he'd wake up and it would be morning and he would run downstairs in his new house and eat a big stack of pancakes while his mom smothered him with kisses he would keep trying to fend off with his extra hand, while the other one kept shoveling pancakes into his mouth.

Then he thought of his father.

Was he trying to find him? Or had that creature, that thing, killed him before he'd gone through the portal or whatever it was? Despite the fact he wasn't alone, he felt a fresh wave of tears coming on. Teddy saw this and leaned over, rubbing RJ's shoulder with his hand.

"It's okay, RJ, we've all been there. You'll feel better in time, or at least accept where you are. I mean, we're all still scared, but you get used to it. You have to or you'll go crazy," Teddy said.

"Yeah, RJ, don't worry if you want to cry, we all did, believe me, and still do almost every night," Matt told him.

RJ let the tears flow, knowing his new friends seemed to understand what he was feeling. The rest of the kids ignored him, not interested in his tears. They had already been through what RJ had to accept and they wanted no reminders of how it felt to be scared and alone without their parents and a giant creature outside that wanted to eat you for dinner.

With the sound of the other kids talking amongst themselves, RJ cried long into the night, his two new friends staying by his side, trying their best to console him.

# Chapter Twenty

THE LONG NIGHT had finally ended, Jason awake the entire time with the exception of an hour or so when exhaustion finally settled in. Now he was standing by the opening to the small cave, watching the red sun rise on the horizon. It was so strange, so unfamiliar, he thought, as he gazed out on an alien world.

Wherever he was, it sure as hell wasn't earth. But as for another planet or dimension? Well, he tried not to dwell on any of that. All it would do was depress him more than he already was. In the late hours of the night, he'd tried to figure out what to do when he found his son.

Sure they would be together again, but what good would that do if they could never find their way back home? He thought of Emma and wondered how she was, what she must be thinking. What had she done after all the noise from the room had filtered down to her? What had she done when she'd entered RJ's room and found it empty?

Had she called the police, had she screamed? Perhaps she'd fainted, understanding on some small level that things were most definitely out of whack.

Then thoughts of his son flooded through his mind. What was his son doing right now, at this very moment? Was he all right or was he suffering. He tried to tell himself RJ had to be alive, the alternative far too unbearable to contemplate.

Clyde stirred behind him and Jason turned to see the man rolling over in his bed of straw and twigs. The straw was a dull purplish color, like most of the plant life on this world.

Jason turned from the opening and walked over to the prone man, kneeling down once he'd reached him.

"So when do we leave? It's light out and I want to get moving as soon as possible," Jason said to the still groggy man.

Clyde sat up with a few moans and groans, then rubbed his eyes clear of sleep. "Whoa there, partner, now just slow down. We'll get going, just give me a chance to take a piss and maybe eat something. It s a good two miles or so of a walk over rough terrain. You better just sit down and relax. Trust me; if your son made it through the night alive, then he's fine. The Snatcher's sleep in the day so even if your son was next on the menu, it wouldn't be until tonight."

Jason said nothing, merely watching Clyde, his right hand tapping impatiently on  his leg while he waited for the man to get up.

Clyde let out a sigh, knowing it was hopeless to try and talk Jason out of waiting.

Rolling to his feet with another louder groan, he moved about the cave with purpose. A hole was dug in the ground at the back of the cave, and Clyde relieved himself there, then he picked up another mushroom, and while chewing thoughtfully and slowly, sat down on a log and looked across the cave at Jason.

"So what exactly do you plan on doing once we get there?" Clyde inquired.

"What do you mean? We'll slip in, grab my son and then get the hell out of there."

Clyde chuckled at that. "I'm afraid it's not that easy. For one thing, there's a guard posted all day while the Snatcher sleeps. His name's Harry and he's a mean old pervert. The Snatcher needs someone to watch his flock, so that mean old bastard volunteered. If he sees us, he's got this kind of whistle carved from human bone. If he blows it, that damn Snatcher will be down on us so fast we'd be dead before we know it's happened."

Jason sat down on the nearest log and lowered his head in thought.

"Shit, you're right, I never really gave it too much thought. I've just been making it up as I go." He looked up at Clyde. "Do you have any suggestions?"

Clyde smiled. "Maybe, but you need to remember there are other kids in that camp, too. If we grab your son, then we need to take them with us," Clyde told him.

Jason nodded. "Agreed, but what about the…Snatcher?" He said, pausing at the name of the creature. It seemed unreal calling it by a title, any title other than creature or thing.

Clyde pointed to Jason's back. "Well, you got that gun there, maybe that'll help. Until now, no one around here ever had a firearm before."

Jason frowned. "Maybe, but when I shot it in my son's bedroom, the bullet seemed to go right through it."

Clyde nodded and wiped his mouth with his already filthy sleeve. "Maybe, but the Snatcher's form is different when it's in our dimension. This is its home. Its shape is permanent here, although the goddamn thing is still so damn fast it'll rip your head off before you can blink at it. Just be glad we only have to deal with one of them. If there was more than one, this rescue of yours would be nothing more than a suicide mission."

"And what are our odds now?" Jason asked.

Clyde spit the little bit of mushroom still in his mouth into the cold ashes of the campfire. "Shit, I'd say between one and zero. But what the hell, I got nothin' better to do." With that said, he stood up and gathered a few things. A walking stick and a rag he used as a hat for his head and a few other miscellaneous items.

He pointed to Jason's aluminum bat. "Don't forget to take that. Should make a good club. Hell, its better than nothing."

Jason did as he was asked, and a few minutes later the two men were ready to depart the cave. Besides his weapons, Jason was now carrying a gourd on a string so they would have water with them. With a last look around the cave to make sure he had everything he needed, Clyde looked over to Jason.

"All right then, let's go get your boy, and don't forget to remind me to lock up after we leave."

Jason did a double take, wondering what Clyde was talking about until he saw Clyde smiling, and returned it with one of his own.

"Very funny, Clyde, I'm laughing on the inside," Jason said.

Clyde walked by him and into the harsh daylight. "That's fine with me, just as long as you're laughing somewhere."

With the red sun spreading its crimson rays on a new day, the two men headed back to the trail that would lead them to the Snatcher's camp, and hopefully, to Jason's son.

*     *     *

The bright red sun was hot on their heads as they made their way across the unforgiving landscape. Jason stopped and wiped his forehead with his sleeve, the sheen of perspiration soaking his shirt with each swipe. They were on a small slope, the land curving downward. From Jason's perspective, the surrounding territory reminded him of Nevada or maybe Arizona, the only difference being the red color ground and the pools of stagnant water.

Clyde was a few yards ahead of him and he stopped to wait for Jason to catch up.

Jason let out a tired sigh and started off again.

For most of the trek the two men had been silent, using all their energy to watch where they were walking and try to conserve whatever was left for breathing. The air was hot and dry and if Jason had to guess, he would have figured it was in the high nineties. Luckily, there was little to no humidity and the two men made steady progress. The water gourd was more than half empty by the time they made it to the bottom of a low ridge. Clyde pointed up to a ridge a few hundred feet away and leaned back against the husk of a long dead tree.

"The camps just over that ridge. I suggest you go all the way around and come at it from the backside, that way Harry probably won't see you. But be careful, some of the young ones have been here for a long time and the Snatcher lets them live to keep the others in line. If one of them sees you, you better believe they'll sound the alarm," Clyde said while sipping from the water gourd.

Jason listened quietly to every bit of information Clyde gave him. Who knew what piece might be the clue to freeing his son and escaping?

Clyde stopped talking and looked at his scuffed work boots. "Listen, Jason, I've taken you this far, but this is it. I'll wait here for you, but I'm not going any closer. If you'd seen what I'd seen, you'd understand. I'm sorry if you're not happy about it, but it's just the way it is."

Jason nodded, understanding. "No, Clyde, that's okay. I'm grateful for what you've already done for me. Who knows what might have happened if I hadn't found you. Whatever happens from this moment on, I still thank you." He held out his hand for Clyde to take.

The man looked at the outstretched hand and took it, pumping twice.

"Thanks for understanding; and good luck." Then he handed Jason the water gourd back.

"Here, take this, I can get more." He stopped for a moment and his eyes looked out onto the distant horizon. "I hope you find your son," he said softly.

Jason turned to begin moving away. "Me, too, Clyde; me, too," he said under his breath.

He skirted the edge of the ridge and in no time was in the proper position. Just before Jason disappeared over the top, he glanced back to Clyde, and with one last wave to Clyde, disappeared from view.

Clyde stood there for a few minutes, feeling the coward for not helping Jason further, but he knew what dangers the man was willingly walking into, and while he wished him well, he'd be damned if he was going to walk back into the lion's den if he didn't have to. With Jason gone, he could now face the truth. Chances are the boy was long dead, nothing left but a few chewed bones.

Not knowing why, Clyde climbed the ridge and hunkered down under an old, purplish tree, its wide, but dead, branches lending him some much needed shade. He could see the small figure of Jason making his way across the difficult terrain. If he had listened to Clyde's advice, then the figure should be moving off to the east to circle around the compound.

Then as if Clyde had willed it, Jason did just that. Clyde nodded and smiled. At least the man was able to take advice from others.

Now all Clyde could do was wait. He figured if Jason didn't returned by the time the sun had reached its zenith, then the man was dead.

Picking up a stray twig, Clyde drew himself a game of Tic-Tac-Toe in the red earth. It wasn't fun playing by himself, but after the past few months he'd grown accustomed to it.

While overhead in the sky, a crimson sun beat down on a dark red world.

<h1 style="text-align:center">CHAPTER TWENTY-ONE</h1>

THE NEXT MORNING RJ woke up to a restless stirring of commotion by the other kids inside the room. It seemed old Harry had brought them breakfast. RJ stood up, wiping sleep from his eyes and wandered over to the table where all the kids seemed to be crowding around.

Once each kid grabbed a piece of the food, they would then back off and go to their beds to eat. There was a lot of fighting between some of them, the older kids trying to bully the younger ones to give them their share of the food.

When RJ was close enough, he saw what they were fighting over. There seemed to be some kind of big mushrooms piled on the table, the red dirt still sticking to them. Next to the mushrooms was a large bucket of what RJ hoped contained water. There was an assortment of battered cups and plates on the table the kids used to hold the liquid. The mushrooms they just carried around in their hands. RJ was almost near the table, and as he moved closer, he saw both Matt and Teddy get in front of him. Both had food in their hands until Patrick came up to them and snarled at them both. They looked down at the floor and gave their food to him, too frightened to argue or put up a fight.

With a hearty laugh, Patrick broke off a few inches of one of the mushrooms and tossed it back to the boys. The boys gave him a broken smile and shrunk away to eat their meager breakfast in peace. Patrick and a few other kids who appeared to be his goons just laughed while they ate more of their stolen food.

When RJ reached the table, he quickly grabbed the last piece of mushroom. It was a decent sized piece and he'd already decided to share it with his two new friends. But before he was able to get away, Patrick got in his way, stopping his progress while his two goons silently slipped behind him.

He was now trapped among the three larger boys with nowhere to go. He quickly tried to make eye contact with some of the other kids, hoping someone would help him, but no one would look at him.

He quickly realized he was alone.

Patrick looked down at him, the four inches of height he had on RJ feeling more like a foot than only a few inches.

"What ya got there, newbie, my breakfast maybe?" Patrick asked with the other two goons snickering merrily.

RJ held the food close to his chest. "No, it's mine, besides, you already took Matt and Teddy's food, haven't you got enough?" RJ demanded. Despite the fact that he was trying to be brave, the familiar butterflies had come back to his stomach, like they always did when Ronnie had him cornered back home.

"Shit, newbie, there's never enough, now give me your 'shroom or I'm gonna have to pound you and then take it anyway," Patrick told him. "It's your choice."

Despite being terrified, he realized what was happening to him right now was no different than back home when Ronnie would get him cornered in an alley and take his lunch money. But unlike at home, if he didn't eat, he would never be able to keep up his strength. And that would mean he would always be prey to Patrick and his bullies.

RJ stood perfectly still and looked up at Patrick. He remembered something his father had told him more than a week ago. He still remembered sitting in their car while his father drove them home, his bicycle sticking out of the trunk.

"Now, son," his father had said, "I know I tell you not to be violent, but one of these days you just might have to take the initiative."

Remembering those words, RJ stood looking up at Patrick, his goons surrounding him, and realized this was one of those times. He needed to summon the courage to fight back or he would be picked on by Patrick for as long as he was here.

With his heart beating so fast he thought he was going to pass out, he tossed the mushroom into the air in front of Patrick. The teen's eyes followed the food and his hands went up to catch it. With his attention distracted, RJ kicked him in the groin with everything he had in him.

But he didn't stop there, before the two goons could so much as cry out in shock, he rammed both his elbows, one at a time, into the goon's stomachs, like he'd seen his favorite wrestlers do on TV.

One second RJ was being threatened to give his food to Patrick, the next second Patrick was doubled over on the floor, cupping his balls with his hands, a small stream of bile seeping from his mouth, while his two goons were bending at the waist trying to catch their breath.

That was enough courage for RJ, he was spent. He bent over and retrieved his breakfast from the floor, stepped over Patrick, and dashed to the back of the room where he found a spot in a corner.

The room was wreathed in silence, no one spoke or breathed. Every kid was in shock. No one had ever stood up to Patrick before and no one knew what to do about it. RJ stood by his bedroll, Matt and Teddy next to him. Both of the smaller boy's mouths were hanging open as they watched Patrick writhe on the ground.

Minutes ticked by and Patrick finally sat up, wiping the corner of his mouth clean with the edge of his ratty shirt. Then he slowly stood up on unsteady legs with the help of his two goons.

Patrick's face was red with rage and RJ knew he was dead meat. Whatever had given him the courage to punch the older kids had blown away like smoke in the wind.

Patrick walked through the bedrolls, directly to RJ.

RJ swallowed hard, not looking forward to what was coming next. He took a few hesitant steps forward, hoping if he got it over with quick, maybe it wouldn't be so bad.

Patrick stopped in front of RJ, his two goons directly behind him, and RJ was expecting the first punch in the stomach or face any second, but nothing happened.

Patrick just stood there, looking down at RJ, and then his gaze drifted behind him. RJ was to afraid to look, to see what was so interesting behind him, fearing it was some sort of trick, so Patrick could hit him when he focused his attention elsewhere.

Patrick's mouth curled up into a snarl and he leaned closer to RJ.

"This isn't over, newbie, not by a long shot." Then he turned and walked away. One of the goons tried to comfort Patrick and he thrust off the hand like it was on fire. Patrick retreated back to his bedroll, and once he was away from RJ, all the kids started talking. First in low murmurs, then in excited utterances.

RJ turned around to see more than seven kids standing behind him, including Matt and Teddy. One of the kids he didn't know, a heavy set boy with chubby cheeks, walked up and slapped RJ on the shoulder.

"Oh, man, that was friggin' awesome," Chubby said. "Where'd you learn how to fight like that?"

RJ just shrugged, still so scared inside he could barely speak. He realized these kids had stood behind him and were prepared to defend him if Patrick had wanted to take it to the next level.

Matt came up to RJ and patted his arm. "That was so great, all of us have wanted to do that, but we're too scared. But when you punched Patrick, Liam here said we needed to get your back. And oh my God, it worked, he backed down!" Matt said excitedly, almost jumping up and down with his fervor..

RJ just nodded and handed Matt the mushroom still in his hands. "Here, Matt, give this to Teddy and save some for me, okay?" RJ asked.

Matt nodded so hard RJ thought his head was going to fall off, and then he moved away, disappearing amongst the other kids. Numerous kids slapped him on the back and congratulated him on his victory over Patrick. For his part, RJ just nodded and mumbled thanks. He didn't understand what the big deal was; he just did what he had to do. He'd had no choice, unless he wanted to be picked on for as long as he was going to be in the camp.

While everyone tried to introduce themselves and patted him on the back again and again, RJ snuck a glance over to the corner where Patrick was. The older teen didn't look happy, and by the way he was looking at RJ, their feud was far from over. But before he could start to worry about it, he was pulled to his corner of the room, the other kids talking and cheering, like their evil king had been overthrown by the brave night.

RJ decided to just relax and go with it, because after seeing Patrick's face, he knew his troubles were far from over.

# CHAPTER TWENTY-TWO

JASON CIRCLED WIDE around the perimeter of the camp, praying he wouldn't be seen by the guard. As he moved quickly through the dips in the land, his eyes tried to take in as much of the scenery as possible, but at the same time trying to remain hidden.

The camp seemed to be composed of a few buildings that were made of clay or dirt. And one structure was made up of mostly wood, with a wooden door; the blood-red tint to the wood identifying it as coming from local trees. When he circled around to the back of the camp, he saw a lone building sitting on the top of the nearby hill overlooking the entire site.

That must be where the Snatcher lived, he thought, slowing his movements.

The sun was beating down on his head, making him sweat uncontrollably. He paused to take another drink of the tepid water in the gourd and then began moving again. The gun's muzzle dug into his back, and the aluminum bat weighed heavy in his hand, and for the second time since heading out, he wished he could just leave it in the dirt. After all, how much could it help him, after he'd seen the power of the creature?

Ignoring those thoughts, and deciding he should keep every weapon he had in his possession, he scurried closer to the fence surrounding the camp. From a distance the fence looked almost like chain-link metal mesh, but when he was close enough to touch it, he quickly realized it was just wood and vines. He tried to pull on a section, but the fence held strong. Evidently, they made trees very strong around here.

He circled the perimeter a little more; following the contours of the wooden fence, trying to find a weakness. So far he didn't see any way in, with the exception of scaling the eight foot high fence. Unfortunately that was out of the question. The moment he did, the possibility of being spotted would triple.

He was about to try another route when he heard a piercing whistle-blow coming from the front of the camp. He ducked down low and watched for signs of life, wondering if he'd been spotted, or if the alarm was sounding for some other reason. Then he got his first view of the guard when an old man in a pair of patched coveralls ran out and stood in the middle of the camp.

Jason stayed where he was, realizing if he moved, he'd be spotted, but he soon realized it was way too late for that. He heard the sound of heavy footfalls and he poked his head over the small dirt impression he was hiding behind, to see the Snatcher come charging through the front gate.

It stood about eight feet tall and its black skin seemed to absorb the light around it like a sponge. The old man pointed in his direction and Jason realized he'd definitely been discovered.

The Snatcher seemed to stand even taller as it studied Jason's position. Then it started running toward him, a blur of speed and muscle.

Deciding running away was the better part of valor; Jason stood up and started sprinting away from the camp, toward where Clyde should be waiting for him. He didn't mean to bring the creature back to Clyde, but in his panic it was the only place he could think to go.

His arms were pumping in front of him, the bat now a hindrance, and his legs were pushing him forward like a marathon runner. At first he didn't look over his shoulder, too scared he'd trip on a loose rock or tree root, but he soon realized he needed to know where the creature was.

When he'd made it to an open clearing of level ground, he took a quick glance over his shoulder.

It wasn't good.

The Snatcher was moving at a steady pace, the obsidian form's long, muscular legs eating up the distance separating hunter from prey.

Cursing under his breath, he redoubled his efforts, forcing his legs to move faster, pushing the boundaries of what his body would allow, but he soon realized it was hopeless. He wasn't in that good of shape before all this had happened, and despite the adrenalin coursing through his veins, he still felt he was at the end of his rope. To make matters worse, he started to feel a sharp stabbing pain in his side that told him he'd pushed his body too hard.

Slowing down, he turned to see the creature quickly gaining on him, so he decided he might as well make his stand where he was. He noticed he'd run almost all the way back to the ridge from where the recce had started from when he had set out for the camp, the ridge now at his back.

He was on a slight incline to the land and the Snatcher would have the disadvantage of taking the low ground to reach him.

It wasn't much, but it was better than nothing. Jason pulled the .38 from his waistband, thanking God or anyone who would listen that it was still there and hadn't fallen out somewhere on his mad dash to escape the camp.

Flicking off the safety, he lined up the creature in his sights. It wasn't hard, the black shape stood out on the barren clearing like a black spot on a white sheet.

Jason let out a breath, the hand holding the gun in his outstretched arm already growing sweaty, and sent his first bullet toward the creature.

The bullet went wide, kicking up a puff of dirt more than two feet from the Snatcher.

It never slowed, but just kept coming, like an unstoppable behemoth.

At that moment, Jason wondered if he should keep running. He was only a few feet away from the ridge where Clyde should be waiting for him. But even if he did make it to his friend, what then? The man was unarmed; all Jason would succeed in doing is getting Clyde killed with him.

Deciding he was stuck with either shooting the Snatcher dead or becoming its lunch, he lined up another shot and fired the revolver. With the creature closer now, Jason's marksmanship became better. The second bullet struck the Snatcher in the shoulder, but instead of the round passing through the body like it was a ghost, like it had done in RJ's bedroom, this time the bullet struck some form of resistance.

The Snatcher seemed to stumble for a moment, but then shrugged it off and doubled its speed.

"Oh, shit," Jason mumbled, realizing all he may have accomplished was to anger it more than it already was. Not that it mattered very much. The creature already wanted to kill him and devour him. How much worse could it get?

He aimed again, this time squeezing the trigger two more times, sending the third round lower and then letting the muzzle climb bring the barrel up so when the fourth bullet was released from its prison, it was heading directly for the neck of the creature. The third round missed, shooting between the creature legs, but the fourth round struck it in the side of the neck, grazing its black flesh. The creature screamed and actually hesitated in its charge.

Jason felt relief. Whatever may happen, at least he knew it didn't like bullets, although at the moment, all they seemed to do is piss it off.

The Snatcher paused for a moment, shaking its head, and then started toward him again, the long legs loping across the terrain like some macabre deer. Jason sent his fifth and six rounds at the black beast, but he never knew if they struck it. Before he realized what was happening, the Snatcher was only yards away, and he realized he was out of bullets with no time to reload. Dropping the gun, he bent over and picked up the aluminum bat which had fallen to the red earth so he could fire the gun.

He stood on the clearing, legs spread wide in a battle stance, the silver bat held in front of him and reflecting the red sunlight, looking for all purposes like a knight preparing to slay the dragon. But he had a feeling the outcome wouldn't be as valorous as in one of those mythical tales.

The Snatcher came charging up the hill, its mouth or something similar, Jason wasn't sure, opened wide, baring its blackened teeth.

Talons were ready to slash at Jason, disemboweling him with the first swipe.

Jason stood his ground, knowing if he was going to die, then at least he'd see it coming. Although inside himself he was so scared he strongly hoped he could prevent himself from pissing all over his pants and feet.

The Snatcher hissed and charged up the hill and Jason readied the bat. When it was right on top of him, he ducked low and sent a swing at the Snatcher's legs.

Talon-like hands swiped over his head, so close he could feel the passage of the air as they clipped some of the stray hairs on his head. Instead of taking his head off, however, they just found empty air.

But Jason's swing was true. The bat reverberated in his hand as the metal club struck the Snatcher where a shin would be on a human being. The creature let out a howl composed more of rage and annoyance than of actual pain. It turned around sharply and prepared to jump on Jason, but Jason was already rolling away. The Snatcher landed where Jason was just a moment before, the dust rising from its landing. Jason rolled to his feet, his adrenalin pumping. He was so intent on fighting; there was no time to be scared. All he knew was that this thing stood between him and his son.

He swiped the air back and forth with the bat threateningly, the Snatcher slowing its attack for a moment. Usually it took its prey down with one swipe, but for some reason this prey was more resilient, craftier.

It was about to strike again, when a large rock fell from the ridge above, striking the Snatcher on the shoulder. It cried out in pain and Jason saw something black, much blacker than its skin, leaking from where the rock had struck it.

It was only a pinprick, but it was still damage.

Jason took the distraction as an opportunity he couldn't ignore and he stepped in like a swordsman and hacked at the creature's arm. The bat caught on one of the Snatcher's talon-like-hands, making jagged scrapes and burrs on the bat's surface. Because of the damage to the aluminum, there were sharp points of metal along the shaft. If he was to rub them on his own skin, they would easily tear his flesh to ribbons; they were so jagged.

The creature reared back, not understanding what was happening. Then another head-sized boulder fell from the ridge. The Snatcher jumped aside, but it soon realized it was being attacked on two fronts.

It hissed at Jason and then up at the ridge. Deciding Jason was the easier target, it attacked him again. Jason backpedaled away from slashing talons, but the Snatcher's reach was longer and he screamed when one of the talons scraped the flesh on his chest. He swung the bat, more for defense than offense, and the jagged scrapes on the bat rubbed across the Snatcher's right arm. The creature pulled away, the bat dragging across its obsidian hide. The beast screamed, a high-pitched scream that made Jason want to fall to his knees and place his hands on his ears.

But he didn't.

Fighting the piercing headache pounding in his head, he backed away from his opponent. Another head sized rock flew from the ridge, this time striking the Snatcher on the left leg.

Jason saw where the bat had struck the Snatcher's arm. It was bleeding heavily, the black ichor falling to the red earth. The creature took its free hand and cradled the arm against its breast like a child with a bad cut, then it lowered its back and began moving away from him.

It looked like the Snatcher had endured enough. With a hiss that told Jason how pissed off the beast truly was, and the arm leaking blood from where the bat had struck it, the Snatcher turned around and loped off back to the camp.

Jason stood immobile for a few seconds, not believing he was still alive. When he saw the black shape disappear over the farthest hill, he fell to the ground and lay there. His breath came in heavy gasps, his body shaking from the exertion and the comedown of all the adrenalin pumping through his system.

He heard shifting rocks and then footsteps coming towards him. He reached out for the bat, but realized he was too tired to pick it up.

A shadow stood over him and he looked up at the smiling face of Clyde.

His friend sat down in the dirt next to him, picking up a stray rock and tossing it away in the direction the creature had taken.

"Good God, Jason, if that wasn't the damdest thing I've ever seen. If I had to guess, I'd say that you're probably the first person to ever walk away from a fight with that black bastard."

Jason lay silently with his eyes closed, his chest moving up and down. The shallow cuts on his chest were minor, already clotting. He'd live to fight another day. At the moment he ignored them, concentrating on breathing and slowing his heartbeat.

Clyde grabbed Jason's arm. "Hey, pal, did you see what that bat of yours did to it. If I had to take a guess, I'd say the Snatcher doesn't like aluminum like a werewolf doesn't like silver, though I don't think the aluminum will kill it, just mess it up some."

Jason opened his eyes and sat up with a grunt of pain. It felt like every muscle in his body was on fire, but that was okay. In fact, he relished it. Pain meant he was still alive and that he still had a chance to save his son.

"What the hell are you talking about, Clyde?" Jason asked in a dry whisper.

Clyde turned to him, spitting into the dirt. "What am I talking about? Shit, Jason, how many rounds for that gun do you have left?"

Jason felt in his pocket for the extra bullets. Before leaving the cave, he'd taken them out of the box so they wouldn't make so much noise. After reaching into his pocket, he pulled out a handful.

Clyde took them, holding one up to the vermilion sunlight.

"Excellent. I have an idea that just might work." Then he shrugged. "Or it just might get us both killed, your choice," he said excitedly.

Jason answered him by rolling onto his side and vomiting up what was left of his dinner from the night before, bits of digested mushroom splashing onto the red earth thanks to the water he'd consumed. Clyde rubbed his back for moral support and grinned at the sky.

"I'll take that as a yes," Clyde said with a large smirk.

When Jason was done throwing up, he wiped his mouth with his sleeve and let Clyde help him to stand. At first Jason was wobbly, but Clyde was patient and waited for him to regain his balance.

While the two men hobbled up the ridge, with Clyde in the lead and Jason holding the bat and gun.

Upon reaching the peak of the ridge, Clyde held out his hand to help Jason over the lip and asked politely: "So where the hell is my water gourd?"

Jason just laughed, his laughter floating out over the blood-red prairie to be lost on the horizon.

# Chapter Twenty-three

THE TROUBLE STARTED just as RJ expected less than two hours later. He'd been sitting and talking with his new friends on the floor of the large room. Next to him were Matt and Teddy, the chubby kid, Liam, and two other boys named Mark and Clay.

They appeared to have become his crew similar, to the kids Patrick had managed to gather around himself, with the exception that his crew was young, fat and skinny while Patrick's crew were older, stronger and tougher.

It didn't bode well for RJ or his new gang.

RJ had been ready for Patrick, though, and had always kept one eye in his direction. When he saw the older teen finally get up and begin to move his way, he was ready.

Within seconds, all of RJ's friends were standing by his side and prepared to face Patrick and his goons. It seemed RJ had instilled in them the fighting spirit and they had decided if they were going to get beat up, then they would go down fighting.

Every kid with RJ was holding something in their hands to use as a weapon. Mostly pieces of hard clay or rock taken from the building's foundation, but Matt had managed to find a heavy tree root to use as a makeshift club.

Like warriors of old, the two groups moved into the middle of the room, prepared to do battle. The other kids pressed up against the structure's sides, not wanting any part of the battle, but yet each child cheered privately for the group they wished would be victorious.

With his heart in his throat and butterflies attacking his stomach like they were going to chew out of his body at any second, he forced down his fear and faced his sworn enemy. Because he now realized that's what Patrick was. He was an evil just as bad as the Snatcher. He fed on the suffering of his fellow kids and beat them up for the shear pleasure of it.

He was a monster even worse than the Snatcher. At least the Snatcher had to eat, it was only following its nature, but Patrick had chosen to be like he was.

And RJ had decided to end it here and now.

The two groups stopped in the middle of the room, and before Patrick could throw the first punch, the door to their prison was thrown open and old Harry stood there. He had a large club in his hand and knew how to wield it, as most of the kids had experienced first hand.

He stepped only a few feet into the room, wary of the kids nonetheless.

Everyone in the room stopped what they were doing, and turned to stare at the filthy, old man. In reality, Harry was only in his late forties, but hard living under the Snatcher's heavy-taloned hands had made him appear older than he was.

Beneath his dirty, torn coveralls, was the strength and muscle of a healthy, middle-aged male.

Some of the older kids had found that out when they'd thought they could take him. Harry had beaten the kids close to death that day and had ended any more mutinies.

Harry's eyes roamed the room, looking at each child in turn. RJ stood perfectly still, not understanding what was happening. Were they going out on some kind of work detail? Or maybe they all had to line up in the yard for exercises like he'd seen on countless movies at home.

Harry's eyes continued roving until his gaze fell on Liam. The man grinned and pointed his club directly at the chubby boy.

"Him, I want him," he said in a level tone.

Liam shrank away from Harry and tried to melt into the corner of the room. Every kid in the room started talking at once as the fate of one of their own was decided. To them this was just another part of their new life, like eating mushrooms for every meal and shitting in a hole in the floor.

"Silence!" Harry said to the room, his voice rising in pitch. He looked at Patrick and pointed at Liam.

"Bring him here, Patrick. And be quick about it. The Snatcher's hungry and doesn't want to wait…unless you'd like to take his place," Henry smirked.

That put Patrick into action. He gestured to his two goons and they moved forward to grab Liam. The heavy boy let out a shriek and tried to borrow into the wall to escape Patrick, but there was nowhere to go. RJ blocked Patrick's path, not knowing if his friends were behind him or not, but he wasn't going to let Patrick just take Liam like he was nothing but a piece of meat.

RJ stood defiantly, looking up into Patrick's face and was surprised to see a single tear sliding down the older teen's face. Patrick sniffed and wiped it away with a casual rubbing of his nose to hide the gesture.

"Look, newbie, don't make this harder than it has to be. This is how it is around here, I have no choice. None of us do. Just let me do my job; this has nothing to do with us."

RJ didn't know how to respond to what the teen had just said. Patrick became something else in that moment. Not a monster, but just another kid forced to do what he had to in order to survive.

Though it broke his heart, RJ stepped aside.

Patrick moved past him, the tear gone now, and no one the wiser it had ever been there in the first place. He reached the back of the room and grabbed Liam's arm. Liam screamed and tried to fight him, shrieking like stuck pig, but the other two goons grabbed his arms and yanked him to his feet.

Liam fought for a few more seconds and then realized the futility of it. He was firmly in the hands of three older kids who had him good and tight and no one around him was doing a thing to stop it.

As one group, the three teens began dragging Liam to the only door…and Harry.

"No wait; you can't do this to me! It's not fair! I just got here!" He pleaded, his voice raising an octave with each word spoken. His face was filled with terror as to his approaching fate. His eyes flashed to Matt and he turned to Patrick. "Take him, he's smaller. He's been here longer than me, take him instead!" He screamed.

But no one was listening. The boy started crying, long wide tears rolling down his cheeks to splatter on the dirt floor, his two chins shaking like pudding.

When Patrick had the boy in front of Harry, he dropped him and stepped back. Patrick's face was impassive while he stood watching the older man.

Harry looked down at Liam and poked him with the club. "Come on, Fatty, man up. Go out with at least a shred of decency for Christ sakes." Then he grabbed his arm and pulled the boy to his feet.

The entire time the drama was unfolding; RJ had stared and watched, not really understanding exactly what was happening. He watched Harry pick Liam up by one of his arms, then turn and drag the boy behind him. When Liam's formidable weight slowed Harry down, the older man began pushing the boy through the doorway and into the scarlet sunlight.

RJ only was able to glimpse Liam hit the ground in a puff of dry dust, and then Harry slammed the door closed. Muffled cries could be heard from the other side of the door and most of the kids turned away, as if the matter was over, the problem settled.

Matt tapped RJ on the back and pulled him to the far wall of the room.

"Come over here, RJ, I think you need to see this, if only to know what you're in for." Matt said this in a serious tone that RJ hadn't heard from the small boy before.

Matt led him to the wall and after his fingers worried at the dirt and clay near the foundation; he managed to pull some of it away. When he was finished, there were small pinpricks of daylight shining through. RJ looked to his left and right to see other kids doing the same thing as him and Matt. He turned to look over his shoulder to see others who appeared to have no interest whatsoever in what was happening outside. RJ pressed his eyes to the tiny hole and looked out onto the open area between the gate and the barracks. His view was limited, but he could see a large portion of the camp by twisting his head back and forth.

He could see Harry dragging Liam with him, the boy falling to his knees in screams and pleadings and Harry kicking him in the butt to continue moving the boy forward.

Then RJ looked past the two people and his breath locked in his throat. Standing a few yards away was the creature; the one that had taken him from his bedroom and carried him to this place.

It was the monster the kids called the Snatcher.

The black beast stood tall in the daylight, seeming to absorb the crimson sun's rays, its black hair falling from its shoulders to dance in the wind. He couldn't tell for sure, but it seemed to look hurt. Black stuff dripped down its arm to fall into the dirt at its feet.

RJ watched Harry push Liam in front of the creature, then the old man stepped away. Harry moved more than ten feet away, and for the life of him, RJ had no idea what was going on.

Liam was on his knees crying, his belly jiggling and his face contorted in terror as he screamed for his mom to come and save him. Next to RJ, hushed voices were talking as if the climax to something was coming.

RJ changed eyes as he peeked through the hole, his left eye getting bleary from lack of blinking, and the orb widened when he saw the Snatcher pick Liam up in its claws. The boy's legs dangled in the air like he was a cloth doll held in a five-year-old child's hands. His screams became softer as his terror locked his voice inside him. RJ watched the Snatcher hold Liam up to eye level, as if it was studying him.

Before RJ realized what happened, like a snake attacking its victim, the Snatcher's head came down over Liam's skull, swallowing it whole.

Inside the building, all voices in the room stopped and silence reigned. RJ stared in disbelief as the creature chomped down on his friend, swallowing the head whole. Blood squirted from between the creature's mouth where it met Liam's shoulders, but the Snatcher kept on sucking, the noise drifting over to the building the kids were trapped in.

When what seemed like minutes, but was only seconds went by, the creature stopped feeding and removed its bloody mouth. Liam's head was gone, only a jagged stump of ripped and torn flesh remaining from where sharp teeth had severed the head from the boy's body. The Snatcher howled to the sky, then took the corpse, shifted position with it, and tossed it over its back like a bag of cement, then it loped off, first going to the gate and then up the hill that led to the small round structure of rocks and clay.

Even in his shock, RJ assumed that must be where it lived, like a farmer's house near his stable.

RJ fell back from the hole, his legs giving out on him, and sat down on the floor, too shocked to do anything but sit there. He'd just watched his new friend be eaten alive. Shivers went up and down his body while he attempted to process what he had just seen, his mind wanting to reject it, but the rational part of him knowing it was true.

Matt sat down next to him and placed his hand on RJ's arm.

"I'm really sorry I had to show you that, RJ, but you needed to see it. That's why we're here, and that's where we're all gonna end up sooner or later. It's our fate," the small boy said quietly, sounding older than his few years.

Teddy dropped down on the other side of RJ and the three boys sat for more than ten minutes until RJ couldn't hold it back and he started to cry again. Deep inside his mind, he wished his mom or dad would come and save him, but he knew it was a hopeless wish. Placing his head in his hands, he cried softly, his two friends sitting on either side of him.

Their faces were dry, their tears long used up, but they could comfort their friend, at least.

Outside, in the open area in front of the clay and wood building, the blood from Liam slowly disappeared, evaporating into the air as well as being absorbed back into the violet soil. In less than five minutes there would be no trace to mark what had happened to the boy, the ground swallowing up the plasma like a living sponge. No flies covered the area, this world devoid of insects.

Harry was still standing perfectly still near the guard shack by the gate. He spit into the red earth and then walked away, swinging the club by his side like he was about to go play baseball with a few friends. He stepped into his small shack and the area became empty once again, nothing but the wind blowing small dust devils across the courtyard.

As for the black ichor left by the Snatcher's wounded arm; that too, slowly disappeared, until there was nothing remaining but a slightly darker spot of red staining the denuded earth.

# Chapter Twenty-four

J ASON AND CLYDE made their way over the rough terrain, moving fast as physically possible. Many times during their return journey to Clyde's cave, the man had to hold Jason back from stepping too close to one of the numerous stagnant pools dotting the red land. The ground near the pools had softened over years of water leakage and had turned into deadly spots of quicksand.

In one particularly bad moment, Jason had sunk into the quicksand up to his right knee before Clyde managed to pull him out with a loud sucking sound. Jason had landed on top of the man, crushing the wind from Clyde's chest.

When Jason had rolled off him, he'd found he was missing his shoe.

Luckily, he was able to stick his hand back into the slurry and find the stray piece of footwear. Since then, as they walked across the barren landscape, Jason's shoe would squish like a wet fart from all the excess moisture it had absorbed.

Every time Jason took a step, Clyde would chuckle from the sound. Jason pretended he didn't hear him.

This went on for almost a half hour until the heat of the day finally sucked all the moisture from his soggy shoe.

When they were almost back to the cave, the two men took shelter near a large boulder. The massive rock was tall enough it protected them from the worst of the red sun's rays, allowing the two weary men to take a much needed rest. With nothing to drink, they just sat in silence, trying to save what little energy they had left for the final leg of their journey.

Finally, standing up to work a cramp out of his right leg, Jason spoke up, cutting the silence.

"So, Clyde, you never told me how you wound up here," Jason stated

Clyde leaned back against the boulder and wiped his brow with his hand. "Now that is an interesting story, if you want to hear it."

Jason nodded. "Well, I don't have much else to do at the moment, so go for it," Jason grinned back.

"All right," he said, sitting taller, getting ready to tell his tale. Jason slid down to the ground and stretched out his aching feet. His chest wounds had stopped bleeding a while ago and now they'd started to itch.

"Well, for starter's, I lived in California; San Diego actually. I was a janitor at a middle school. Now it wasn't the most glamorous job, but it paid the bills nicely. I was never much of a spender, always saved my pennies. So, one night I was working late. The floor in the teacher's lounge needed to be stripped and rewaxed. As far as I knew, I was the only one left in the school that night. It was Friday night, you see, and all the kids would usually be gone by five at the latest.

Well, I worked for a few hours and then, after the floor had been stripped, I decided to take a break while it dried.

I walked out into the hallway, figuring I'd go down to the cafeteria and grab myself a snack from one of the vending machines. Let me tell you, Jason, the choice of food those kids get to eat compared to when we were kids, although I think I'm a touch older than you are. Oh wait; I'm getting off course aren't I?"

Jason smiled and nodded. It felt good to take his mind off of where he was, even if it was for just a few minutes.

"Okay, sorry 'bout that, where was I? Oh yeah, the cafeteria. So I went down to the cafeteria to get a snack and about ten minutes later I wandered back, figuring the floor should be dry enough to wax. When I walked by one of the supply closets, I stopped. My eye had caught some light shining from under the door and when I looked at the wall switch it was clear the light was in the off position. I just figured it must have been a couple of kids hiding, maybe waiting for me to leave so they could tear up the place or something. So, I walked over to the door and opened it quick, thinking I was about to scare the hell out of a couple of delinquents, but instead I looked the Snatcher straight in the face.

Now I wouldn't be lying if I told you I pissed my pants right there and then. I tried to slam the door shut, but it stuck one of those talons in the doorframe and blocked it; so I turned and ran for my life." He rubbed his nose, uncomfortable with reliving the experience.

"The big bastard caught me before I'd gone more than four feet. It slammed me against a locker and I went crashing to the floor. Then it picked me up by my foot and started to drag me back to the supply closet. I tell you, Jason, I was so scared it was a miracle I didn't shit myself right there, but I was too preoccupied trying to get away to do it. My fingers scraped on the smooth tile in the hallway, and with the squeaking sound of my hands trying to find purchase, it pulled me into the closet with it. Then it got even weirder as I know you're aware. It stepped through some kind of portal at the back of the closet, and the next thing I knew I was in a cave, with lots of writing on the walls. Well, I figured my best bet for staying alive, seems that it hadn't killed me already, was to play possum, so that's what I did. It picked me up and carried me to the camp you were at today. That's where I saw all the kids and figured your son must be there, if he's still alive, that is. I worked with Harry for a while. I guess the Snatcher needs some people to control the younger ones. I never saw where any other adults were. Harry said something about them being eaten almost as soon as he brings them back, but that's all he ever said.

Well, after working with Harry and watching the sadistic bastard feed those kids to the Snatcher like a steak dinner, I just couldn't do it anymore. I decided to try and escape, and if it caught me, then so be it. Anything was better than having a hand in killing those poor kids.

A few days later a few more adults arrived, two men and a woman. I convinced them we needed to escape as soon as possible and they all agreed. We didn't get more than a quarter of a mile before that damn thing hunted us down. It killed the two men and dragged me and the woman back to the camp.

The next day it ate the woman, so the day after that I took another chance and was able to sneak out of the camp when Harry was sleeping. I ran as far and as fast as I could. That's when I found my cave and it's been my home ever since."

"Jesus, that's some story," Jason said, shaking his head as he took it all in. "I'm sorry you're here with me, Clyde, but at the same time I'm glad you are. Do you know what I mean?" Jason asked him.

Clyde stood up, dusting the back of his pants free of dirt with his hands.

"Yeah, Jason, I'm afraid I do, and if it's the last thing we do, we're gonna get your son and free the rest of them, too. Come on, it's getting late, we only have a few more hours of sunlight and we need to make it back to the cave before its gets dark. The Snatchers hunt at night and now that it knows we're out here, you better believe it's gonna come looking for us. Not to mention there are others that roam around. Hell, some go for miles out of their way trying to find food. Guess it gets worse every year, too."

With a proffered hand, Clyde helped Jason to his feet and the two men headed off again. Jason thought about Clyde's story, wondering how many people on earth had been taken over the years and were now presumed dead or missing by the local authorities and family members.

He set his jaw while he walked.

Whatever happened, he would get his son back and hopefully, somehow, he would kill that thing so it never took another child again.

*   *   *

When they finally arrived at the cave hours later, both men practically tumbled face down onto the dirt by the cold campfire. They were exhausted, Jason especially. He'd fought with a creature from the pits of Hell and was still able to talk about it, and worst of all, if he wanted to rescue his son, he would have to return and dare to battle the creature again, and this time he needed to win.

Clyde lay on his back, his chest moving up and down while he tried to control his breathing.

"Jesus, I'm getting to old for this shit," he whispered.

Jason chuckled. "Next time, let's just call a cab," he joked.

That started Clyde laughing and the two men started chuckling while they lay on the ground. It was a stress reliever and both men opened themselves to it happily. After a few minutes of giggling like school girls, Jason managed to regain control. Sitting up, he cleared his throat.

"All right, Clyde, we've already wasted enough time. I need to get back there and get my son, but first you said something about an idea."

Clyde sat up, also, his breathing more under control. His face was streaked with dirt and he rubbed his eyes with the back of his hands.

"And we'll deal with it, but first we need more water." He leaned over the closest log and pulled another gourd from under some loose rags. Handing the gourd to Jason, he pointed to the cave entrance.

"You go fill that with water while I get a fire going. Once we boil it, we can drink our fill, then I'll tell you what I've got planned," Clyde told him.

Jason rolled to his feet with a grunt of pain. He stood over Clyde, and after a moment, walked out of the cave for the nearest pool. From his comings and goings, Jason knew the closest one was only a dozen yards away off to the right of the entrance.

Stepping back out into the waning violet sunlight, blinking from the glare of the dipping red orb, he heard Clyde behind him already preparing the fire, singing a song to himself.

Jason stumbled down the small ridge the cave was on and walked the short distance to the pool, his legs and feet protesting the entire time. Upon reaching the pool, he leaned over and began using his hand to clear away the red algae on the surface, then he plunged the gourd into the water. He saw things swimming just out of range of his vision and he quickly pulled the gourd out of the water and returned to the cave. When he stepped inside, a roaring fire was burning. Jason handed Clyde the gourd and sat back down on one of the logs while the older man got to work transferring the water to a large basin that looked like it had been carved from rock. The rock formation was purely natural and was just a coincidence it could be used as a kettle, but it had served Clyde well since he'd first found it on one of his walks around his new home.

Once the water had been boiled to Clyde's specifications, the men let it cool. They talked about trivial things while they were waiting and Jason was really becoming aggravated with Clyde for not telling him his great idea. Just when Jason was at the end of his frayed temper, Clyde set the gourd down after taking a swig and smiled at Jason.

"Okay then, that's good. Now it's time to make plans. Do you remember when you shot at the Snatcher?" Clyde asked him.

Jason nodded. "Yeah, though the bullets didn't seem to do much but piss it off."

Clyde nodded. "Exactly, but what happened when you hit it with the scratched bat?"

Jason thought about it. "It cut it up pretty bad."

"That's right; it didn't like the taste of aluminum very much. Tell you the truth, I doubt if that kind of metal even exists on this world," Clyde said.

"So what you're saying is…"

Clyde cut him off. "What I'm saying is…is that you've got your silver for your werewolf."

Jason frowned. "Damn, Clyde. I can't fight that thing with a bat. If you hadn't started throwing rocks at it, it would have ripped me to pieces."

"True, but what if we melt some of the bat and coat the rest of your bullet tips with aluminum?"

Comprehension flooded Jason's face. "Yeah, the bullets would mess it up pretty good." Then his face became more downcast. "Oh, wait a minute, how the hell are we going to do it? I mean, it's not like you have a machine shop in your pocket."

Clyde waved his hand at him in a no big deal gesture. "Nah, Jason, it's no problem. All we need is a few rocks and a big fire. Aluminum should melt pretty easy, it's a soft metal compared to iron or brass. Then all we have to do is dip the tips of the rounds in the liquid metal and, wallah, instant silver bullets."

Jason sat perfectly still, the fire casting his face in shadows while he thought about Clyde's suggestion. When a solid full minute had come and gone he sat taller, his back rigid. With a disgusted look on his face, Jason turned to look Clyde straight in the eyes.

"Christ, Clyde, that's the craziest goddamn idea I have ever heard."

Clyde seemed hurt from Jason's criticism and he stayed silent.

But then Jason's face blossomed into a large smile and he grabbed Clyde's arm, pulling the man up while Jason jumped up with him. "So when do we start?"

Clyde was taken aback, until he realized Jason had approved of his idea.

"Well, shit, we can get started right now. If things go well, we should be finished by late tonight. First thing in the morning, we'll head out and save your son."

Jason slapped Clyde on the back; his spirits higher than they'd been since he'd first arrived in this crazy world.

With the two men getting to work, Jason stopped and looked at Clyde.

"If all goes well, there's going to be one less Snatcher on Hellioth in the morning." Clyde nodded, agreeing with Jason, and the two men doubled their efforts. There was a lot to get done and little time to do it in.

With the sun finishing its descent across the red sky, the fire in the cave burned hotter, the shadows of the two men moving about quickly, as if their lives depended on it. And if not theirs, Jason was damn sure for the life of his lost son.

# Chapter Twenty-Five

I T HAD ALREADY been two hours since the death of Liam. The children all sat quietly, with the exception of a few small groups who seemed to be more resilient than the others. As for RJ, he was just starting to get over his shock of seeing one of his new friends slaughtered like a prize bull.

Old Harry had brought them their midday meal, nothing more than a stack of more mushrooms. Matt had told him the fungus was all they ever ate. The Snatchers had hunted the land dry and there were no other animals alive. In the harsh terrain, only the mushrooms continued to grow.

The table near the door was still covered with almost half the supply of mushrooms Harry had brought in. Most of the kids were still too traumatized to want food.

RJ stood up, realizing immediately if any of them wanted to survive, they needed to escape their prison. Walking over to Patrick, he stopped at the edge of the teen's section of the room.

He was quickly blocked by two of Patrick's goons, who raised hands in front of their chests in a threatening gesture. RJ ignored them, looking past their upraised arms to Patrick.

"We need to talk," RJ said seriously.

Patrick made a face of disgust. "About what? There's nothing we have to talk about."

RJ shook his head. "I disagree. But I want to talk to you alone, where no one else can hear us. It has to be private," RJ said. He hoped if he was able to separate the teen from his gang, he might be able to have a true conversation with him. Maybe without all the posturing Patrick would normally have to do in front of his friends for appearances, the boy might listen to reason.

Patrick looked back at his friends, almost as if he was waiting for them to tell him what to do. All he got in return was impassive faces.

Shrugging, he turned back to RJ. "Fine, newbie, let's go, and it better be good."

The two goons lowered their arms, letting Patrick pass.

RJ moved over to the only door in the room, where the area was devoid of bedrolls and other kids. He took a deep breath, preparing his words in his mind. He had one chance to make this sound convincing, or Patrick was going to tell him to go to hell.

"Look, Patrick, I know you're top dog around here, but sooner or later even you're gonna end up dead. We need to get out of here, like now."

Patrick looked down at RJ like the younger boy had just said the craziest thing he'd ever heard.

"Oh really, and even if I agreed with you, where exactly do you think we're gonna go? In case you haven't noticed, we're pretty far from home."

RJ's brow furrowed in concentration and he stared at Patrick's face, the hard chin, the slightly pointed nose, the freckles, small but there nonetheless. Then he looked up into Patrick's eyes.

"Look, it doesn't matter where we go, just as long as it's away from here."

Patrick shook his head. "You're crazy, newbie. I've got a good thing going here and I'm not leaving."

RJ let out a sigh of frustration. "Okay, fine, but will you try to stop some of us if we want to make a break for it?"

Patrick looked over RJ's shoulder at his own friends waiting for him in the corner of the room. He stood there contemplating RJ's request, and RJ was already thinking his jailbreak was over before it had even begun when Patrick lowered his head, shaking it back and forth, his hair brushing over his shoulder.

"No, newbie, I won't stop you, but you're making a big mistake. You're gonna get a lot of kids killed."

"Maybe, but if we don't try, we're all dead anyway," RJ told him.

"Fine, whatever, just leave me out of it," he said and with a wave of his hand in dismissal, walked away, leaving RJ to stand alone. RJ watched the older teen as he went back to join his friends. Some of the other kids started asking him what their talk was about, but Patrick just waved their questions away. Evidently, he was a man of his word and would keep RJ's confidence.

RJ moved across the room until he was with Matt, Teddy and a few others. All together, Matt and Teddy had recruited nearly half the room to go with them. All these kids were frightened out of their wits and would readily follow anyone who acted like they had a plan.

And at the present moment it appeared to be RJ.

RJ gathered a few of the bigger kids around him and told them to go to the rear of the room and start digging away the clay and mud that held the structure's foundation together. Some of the weaker kids were to stand in front of them, blocking the view of the workers. RJ then interrogated every kid on what the camp was like outside the walls of their prison. Most could only shrug. With the exception of what could be seen through the cracks in the foundation overlooking the clearing in the middle of the camp, none of the other children had been outside the walls of the barracks.

An hour later, one of the boys, a beefy looking kid named Leon, moved close to RJ and told him they'd made a hole big enough for all of them to crawl through. RJ nodded and told him to gather everyone who was going with them and to be ready.

RJ then walked to the middle of the room, where Patrick could see him. When the older teen saw RJ waiting for him, he rolled to his feet from his bedroll, and after a quick stretch, walked into the middle of the room to join him.

RJ looked up at the cold face.

"We're ready to go. You can still come with us. We could use your help," RJ said.

Patrick chuckled. "Help? Shit, newbie, you are in for one hard lesson. Don't say I didn't warn you." Without another word, he turned away and walked back to his bedroll.

RJ had already forgotten the teen, having more important things to deal with. In the few seconds his dialogue with Patrick had taken, all eighteen kids who had decided to try and run for it were ready and waiting.

RJ moved to the back of the room, pushing past the kids waiting for him. He made eye contact with each one, nodding and slapping a few on the shoulder like a general about to send his men to war. The open hole let the light in from outside, chasing away some of the shadows.

"Okay then, once we're all through the hole, we run for the back fence. Once we're there, we climb it or burrow under it or whatever it takes to get away. Is everyone with me?"

Eighteen frightened faces nodded yes.

"Okay then." He smiled back at the scared, dirty faces. "See you on the other side." And then he slipped through the hole, the first one into the breach.

The first thing that happened upon crawling through the hole was he became blinded by the bright light of the day. After being in the darkened room for almost two days, his eyes needed to adjust to the brighter light of the courtyard. He closed his eyes tight, seeing tiny white spots dance before his mind's eye. After almost ten seconds had come and gone, he slowly opened them. At first he had to squint, but then his eyes adjusted and he was able to see much better.

Behind him, the other kids crawled through the hole one by one, each suffering like RJ had, all blinking again and again until they could see. It took almost five agonizing minutes to get everyone through and adjusted to the bright sunlight, but once everyone had made it, RJ gathered them in a close circle.

"All right now, keep the talking down, we don't want to be heard. If someone sees us, then run. It's only the old man and the Snatcher. They can't catch us all if we split up." Then he took off at a quick jog, his destination the rear fence.

The entire group was no more than halfway to the fence when RJ heard a piercing whistle split the silence of the day. He turned to see Harry standing in the middle of the courtyard. The man's pant's zipper was still undone --the man having just finished taking a quick whiz--as he blew on the bone instrument.

RJ cursed something his mom would have yelled at him for. Of all the bad luck. They had chosen to make a run for it while Harry had decided to take a piss break.

"Run, he can't catch us all!" RJ said to the large group behind him. Like a rock thrown into a flock of pigeons gathering in a New York park, the kids disbursed, each running in whatever way he or she thought was best.

RJ ran too, but took another glance over his shoulder to see Harry still standing still. The man wasn't chasing them. RJ thought that was odd.

But then he realized why.

He looked up the slight slope to the small, round building where he'd seen the Snatcher enter earlier after Liam had been killed. Now the black figure stood at the entrance, its talons opening and closing as it looked down on the camp.

Its head looked up at the sky and let out a piercing scream. The shriek so loud it sent a shiver down RJ's back. So that was why old Harry wasn't chasing them. He'd called the Snatcher to clean up the mess.

The black beast charged down the small hill, its long legs covering the distance in seconds, and slowed only when it approached the gate. Harry had started moving, too, and was there to open the gate wide, the Snatcher running inside. It slowed for a moment, as its head turned left and right, like it was sniffing the air.

Kids were running everywhere and the creature couldn't decide who to try to recapture first.

One of the kids who RJ didn't know by name was running without purpose and he strayed to close to the Snatcher. Just before the boy ran into the dark form, he realized his mistake, and with his shoes spraying dust, tried to turn and run the opposite way.

The black beast swiveled on its claw-like feet and grabbed the child by the left arm. RJ had made it to the side of what reminded him of an old Western trough for watering horses, and he hunkered down and hid for a second, trying to decide what to do next. Should he try to get by the Snatcher and run through the now opened gate? Or should he try for the rear fence and attempt to scale it while the Snatcher was occupied?

Before he could decide what to do, however, his eyes became riveted to the Snatcher and the boy in its grasp. RJ watched, assuming the beast would give the boy to Harry so the man could return the child to the barracks. But what he expected to happen and what actually did was the stuff of nightmares.

The boy was dangling in the air by one arm, his legs kicking as he screamed to be let go. The Snatcher grabbed his other flailing arm and while RJ watched in horror, the beast pulled the child apart like he was a chicken bone and the beast was trying to make a wish.

A sickening, ripping sound filled the yard, overriding the screams of the frightened children. Blood splattered all around the creature, its black coat turning red from all the gore. The child's intestines and miscellaneous organs fell into the dirt with a splat. It dropped the small corpse to the ground with another wet smack, leaned over and with two talons plucked out of the visceral what appeared to RJ to be the dead boy's heart.

Like he was just pausing for a snack, the Snatcher plopped it into his mouth like an appetizer, then its head swiveled around, looking for more prey. RJ stared in horror, not believing the unbelievable scene he'd just witnessed. He thought things could never degrade more than they already had and his mind raced for what to do next.

But then things became much, much worse.

From his hiding place behind the trough, he saw the Snatcher's head swivel back and forth like an owl would do before flying off a tree branch to attack its prey, then it shot after its next victim, a small girl who couldn't be older than seven or eight.

It pounced on her like a tiger, its head diving down and tearing out her throat in one bite. Only a gargling sound could be heard as the girl's dirty pink dress turned red. The Snatcher barely noticed. Before the girl was fully prone in the red dirt, twitching in her death spasms, the creature was on the move again.

A boy about RJ's age tried to climb the rear fence. He was more than halfway there when he was grabbed from behind by the Snatcher. It yanked the boy off the fence, the mid-sized body striking the ground with a puff of dust. Before the gasping boy could do more than shriek in terror, he was disemboweled, intestines spilling out to splatter in the dirt. The boy's hands tried to push the slimy red tendrils back into his abdomen, but it was no use. His tears flowed as he cried and screamed for his mommy. The Snatcher may not have realized it, but at that moment in time he gave the boy mercy. Leaning down, the beast swiped a razor-sharp talon across the boy's throat, severing his carotid artery. A fountain of scarlet rose into the air for a heartbeat, the red liquid reflecting the crimson sunlight. Then the boy's heart stopped pumping and his body stopped moving, the boy's arms flopping down to his sides like a toy with the batteries yanked from it in mid-play.

RJ held back the screams he wanted to let loose, the tears of terror and sadness inside him too much to bear. He watched child after child be eviscerated and realized Patrick had been right. This had been the biggest mistake of his life.

That was when he realized he needed to get back to the hole in the rear wall and get back inside. Only then was there hope he wouldn't be slaughtered with the other children.

The Snatcher was across the yard, tearing into a skinny boy whose name had been Ricky. RJ had listened to the boy tell him about his cat Smoky and how he missed him and his parents. Now the boy was in multiple bloody pieces, his head lying at an unnatural angle in the red earth.

With his heart in his throat, RJ forced his paralyzed legs to move. At first he could barely walk, the terror inside him so strong, but with one footstep at a time, he began moving faster until he was running. Every kid near him he yelled to, telling them to get back inside the building before it was too late. Some heard him, but some were too far gone, the terror and chaos surrounding them overwhelming their senses to really hear what RJ was trying to tell them.

Reaching the rear of the building, RJ waited for another kid he didn't know to crawl in. Just before he was ready to go in himself, Matt charged into him, his breathing heavy like he'd just run a race.

"Oh my God, RJ, the Snatcher's killing everyone, why's it doing that?" Matt asked frantically.

RJ had no answer for him, other then to push his friend back through the hole.

Two more kids had made it as well and RJ pushed them inside the building.

Then he dived through the hole with hands pulling him through from the inside.

Once he was through, he spun around on his knees and looked back out into the courtyard to see if he could help anyone else.

That's when he saw Teddy running as fast as his legs would let him towards the hole.

"Come on, Teddy, hurry, its right behind you!" RJ screamed. It was true; the Snatcher had finished with its latest victim and had caught the movement of Teddy in the corner of its eye. With the utmost grace, the creature had turned and leaped for the child. Teddy was running full out, his arms pumping back and forth, spittle flying as he put everything into one last dash to safety.

"That's it Teddy, you're almost there, just a little closer," RJ coached him. He was so close, only a few more feet.

Then the Snatcher made a superhuman leap and landed directly behind Teddy's running body. With one scythe-like swipe of its arm, it severed Teddy's head from his body. Teddy's body kept running, though, the body not yet realizing it was dead.

An object in motion will stay in motion, he'd learned that in science class and it was exactly what happened.

Teddy's legs kept running, the last order from the brain still being followed. When the decapitated corpse was no more than three feet from the hole, its coordination finally collapsed and the body toppled to the earth like a fallen tree.

The jagged stump where his head used to be landed directly in front of the hole in the wall. RJ wasn't able to move in time and bright red blood from the jagged stump shot out of the neck and into his face.

Shrieking in terror, RJ jumped back, striking the kids behind him. Blood pooled at the foot of the hole in the wall and then slowed when Teddy's body went dry.

RJ was on his back, wiping his face frantically. His eyes were closed, but the image of his friend's head when it was sent flying, and the jagged stump landing in front of him, was burned into his retinas.

Some of the other kids helped wipe his face clean with a spare cloth and RJ was helped to a sitting position on the floor. He looked up at half the faces he'd started with, the rest, dead or dying outside in the courtyard. Another high pitched scream from another child filtered through the open hole, making him wince even more.

All the kids with him were in shock, still not comprehending the massacre they had just witnessed.

No one moved and no one talked. Patrick and the other kids sat in their corner, trying to be as inconspicuous as possible, some shaking with fear.

Outside, the cries for help and the calls for moms and dads stopped, only silence coming from the open courtyard. Inside the building, the only sound to be heard was the heavy breathing of frightened children, and sometimes the sniff of a runny nose.

More than ten minutes went by with everyone in the room waiting for the Snatcher to kick in the door and finish the rest of them off, but it never happened.

Night started to fall and some of the kids began to realize despite what had happened, they appeared to be safe inside their room.

Adrenaline stopped flowing and the kids began taking inventory of who had lived and who hadn't made it back. Slowly but surely, the tears started flowing as grief flooded each child, one at a time.

As for RJ, he still couldn't believe what had happened. Like most twelve-year-old boys, he believed he was immortal. That no matter what happened around him or who else might die; the spirit of death would never touch him. For the first time in his young life, he realized he could die, and more than nine young cooling corpses could attend to the fact outside in the drawing dusk.

He crawled over to the hole and started putting the rocks and clay back, trying to pack it the way it was before. As each piece of stone was placed in the hole, the headless corpse of his friend slowly began to disappear.

When he was placing the last rock that would finally make his friend's body disappear for good, there was a scratching in the dirt outside the hole and the small headless body was yanked away, only the thin trail of plasma remaining. RJ jumped back, thinking the Snatcher would grab him, but nothing came for him. After a full ten minutes, his heart finally slowed and he finished filling the hole. The entire time the tears spilled off his cheeks to land on the dirt floor.

RJ patted the repaired hole, making sure it looked sturdy enough to at least pass a cursory inspection and then crawled over to his bedroll. Matt was next to him, crying into his makeshift pillow and RJ dropped down next to him.

The shadows in the room continued to grow until a dim gloom suffused all. RJ held out his hand for Matt to take. The boy lifted his head up, sniffed for a moment, then took the proffered hand. The two lay there all through the night, too frightened to let go, taking whatever comfort they could from each other, while the sounds of crying and misery filled the shadow-enshrouded room for the rest of the night.

# Chapter Twenty-Six

T HE MIDDLE OF the night had come and gone, both Jason and Clyde finally finishing their duties. Jason was sitting outside the cave entrance, staring up at the night sky, the area around him almost pitch black. Clyde was still in the cave finishing up. Jason could hear the man banging away on something. Clyde had said he had an idea for a use for the rest of the bat not melted down and Jason had told him to go for it.

It was useless to him now, more than half of it all melted and deformed

As he looked up at the inky blackness of the sky, he had to admit it certainly was different here, wherever here was.

He felt like Robinson Caruso, trapped on another planet instead of a deserted island. The night sky was so unfamiliar to him, his eyes continually scanning its vastness searching for something, anything to hold onto. There had to be something in that alien sky that would remind him of home.

It was strange with no moon shining down, and all the stars were in the wrong places. He wished he was more knowledgeable with astronomy. Perhaps if he was able to chart the different stars, he might be able to figure out just where he was in the universe.

He looked up at the sound of footsteps behind him. Clyde was there, perspiration covering his face.

"Well, that's it, we're done," he said, wiping his brow with a piece of cloth.

Jason just nodded, enjoying the quiet.

Clyde sat down next to him. The man smelled of wood smoke and sweat, but Jason didn't mind. He figured he probably smelled the same way to Clyde.

With a soft moan when he stretched his legs out, Clyde looked up at the night sky, as well.

"Pretty isn't it? I usually come out here every night and just stare up at the stars. Not much else to do. You know, Jason, since you showed up; I really had no idea how lonely I was. I'm sorry you and your boy wound up here, but at the same time I'm a little glad it happened." He turned to look at Jason in the dark, but all he saw was a shadowy outline from the ambient light coming from the cave. "I bet you think I'm a real asshole for saying that."

Jason shrugged, then realizing Clyde wouldn't be able to see the gesture, he spoke up.

"No, Clyde I don't think you're an asshole. I know exactly what you mean. When I was a kid my father was taken by one of those creatures, those Snatchers. For years I had to deny what I saw or risk spending my life in a nuthouse. Although it's terrible that I'm here and I fear for my son's life, I also know I have never felt as whole as I do since arriving here. I finally know that I'm not crazy."

"Really, your father? Jesus, Jason that sucks."

"Maybe, but you see, when we go after that bastard tomorrow, I'm getting payback for two people I love; my son and my father."

Clyde sat quiet, not really knowing how to respond. After a handful of seconds, he spoke up, changing the subject.

"You know, I lived alone in California, didn't have any family. Parents died a few years back. One had cancer and the other died of a broken heart. They say that happens sometimes. Can't imagine loving someone so much that after they die you give up living yourself." Clyde hesitated for a few heartbeats. "Must be nice, though."

Jason moved in his seat on the ground, sending a few pebbles to roll away down the incline. Then he stood up, dusting off the back of his pants.

"We should probably turn in. It's going to be a busy morning." He looked up at the night sky one last time. "How much longer before its light out again?"

Clyde sniffed in the dark, then spit. "Oh, I'd say a couple of hours. Bet you miss a working clock, huh?"

Jason chuckled. "Yeah, I guess. But you know what I really miss?"

"No, what."

"A bath."

Clyde chuckled at that. "If you stay here long enough, you'll get used to being dirty, trust me."

Jason turned and moved inside the cave, Clyde following him. "I doubt that'll happen, Clyde, 'cause by tomorrow, I'll either have my son back with me or I'll be dead."

"Yeah, but even if everything goes as planned, how the hell are you going to get back home?"

Jason frowned at that question. "You know, I haven't really thought that far ahead. I figure until my son's back with me, all the rest is just irrelevant." Then he disappeared into the cave.

Clyde stood at the entrance for another minute, letting a loud fart leave his backside. He waited a minute for the wind to carry the odor away, then he too, stepped inside the cave.

He grinned as he entered, proud of himself. That was the polite thing to do, he thought, letting the odor blow away instead of being trapped inside the cave.

His momma had raised him right.

*     *     *

Jason awoke to a gentle shoving on his shoulder by Clyde. Despite being anxious to get his son, he'd fallen asleep just before dawn, the previous day's activities finally catching up to him in a wave of exhaustion.

He had slept hard for the next two hours and despite his eyes being open and looking at Clyde, for the briefest of time he had no idea where he was.

Then it came rushing back like a flash flood, filling his mind with images of black creatures of death and portals to other worlds. Rubbing his eyes and knowing he wasn't ready to stand yet, he looked up at the blurry figure of Clyde.

"What time is it?" He mumbled.

Clyde chuckled at the question. "Well, I'd say that's kind of redundant around here, but if you want me to generalize, I'd have to say it's about a half hour after sunrise."

Jason's eyes snapped open and he became fully alert. Jumping to his feet and wobbling for a moment, he looked around the cave, trying to do everything at once.

Clyde moved next to him and held his arm tight. "Whoa there, sport, slow down, there's plenty of time to rush to your death."

Jason turned to look at the man, a flash of anger in his eyes.

"Dammit, Clyde we should have already left. For all we know, my son could've died in the half hour we lost while I was sleeping."

Clyde held his hands up in surrender. "That may be, but if you didn't get at least a few hours rest, then in what condition would you be in to rescue him?"

Jason was ready for a rebuttal, but stopped himself. Deep down he knew Clyde had a point, though in his ill temper he'd be damned if he would admit it to him.

"Whatever, let's just get going, we're already running late," Jason told him while moving off to find his shoes that he'd kicked off the night before.

Clyde grinned, watching Jason digging around the cave. He knew he was right and so did Jason. He didn't feel the need to have it said out loud.

The minutes ticked by on the clock in Jason's head and less than fifteen minutes later by his calculations, he was ready to go. The revolver was in the back of his pants, now with aluminum tipped rounds. He had a dozen extra in his pocket, though he would bet he'd have no time to reload. If there was one thing he'd taken with him from his last encounter with the creature was it was fast and strong. Touching the bandaged cuts and feeling some of the bruises from the day before, he wasn't relishing their next meeting.

Clyde was standing next to him, waiting.

Jason turned to his friend and nodded. "All right, let's go kick some Snatcher ass."

The two men walked out into the light of a new day. The crimson sky was clear, the desolate landscape calling to them. Waves of heat could be seen coming off the ground in front of them, like massive microwaves, slowly baking the earth.

Jason still found it odd there were no other animals or insect life around them. Nothing fluttered in the trees or attempted to bite his flesh to suck at his blood.

No bees hovered by the strange purple foliage or squirrels running up and down the skeletal like trees.

It was all so surreal, like he was in a three dimensional movie.

Clyde walked behind him, his footsteps the only other sound besides Jason's own dirt-crunching steps.

They walked in silence, neither having much to say. The time for small talk was far from over, the two men now moving and acting like two medieval warriors off to battle the mythical beast.

Sweat poured down their faces and lodged in the curve of their backs, causing them mild discomfort. Still, neither man slowed. Clyde handed Jason a gourd full of tepid water and Jason drank eagerly, downing more than half in a few gulps.

Clyde said nothing. It was doubtful they would need water for the return trip as they would probably both be dead. It was only luck which had chased the Snatcher away last time. Next time the ebony beast would be ready for them, now knowing Jason's strengths and weaknesses.

The path rolled by under their feet as they trudged on, making good time, but still not as fast as Jason would have preferred. But he knew he needed to save his energy for what would come next, so despite his heart wanting him to dash down the trail like a marathon runner, he held back and walked a steady walking pace.

The sun was sitting high in the sky when they finally made it to the last hill before the camp. Jason slowed his pace, with Clyde matching his speed. Reaching the top of the ridge, Jason stopped and rested on his haunches for a moment. Clyde copied him, his knees cracking from the change in position.

Jason repositioned his gear, making sure everything was in reach of his hands.

Clyde gestured with his chin to the camp spread out before them in the distance.

"You reckon they'll be expecting us?"

Jason shrugged. "Don't know and frankly, I don't care. I'm getting my son one way or the other."

"Fair enough," he said, standing back up and stretching his back muscles. Okay then, I'll head off to the other side. When I distract it; you get in there and grab your son and the other kids."

Jason nodded. The two men had already decided long ago when they were making plans that if it at all possible, Jason would try to save as many children as he could. The question was; how to pull it off. But like so much of their plan it was wait and see.

They started moving again, walking more slowly when the last leg of their journey came into view. The scarlet sky cast an ominous background to the camp of lost souls.

Jason looked at Clyde and the man nodded, then moved off on a course that would take him around the front gate and have him on the other side of the camp, ending up exactly opposite Jason's position.

Jason edged a little closer, halting when he was no more than a dozen yards away. A grouping of sparse foliage was growing through the rocky soil and Jason hunkered down to wait for Clyde to get into position. Then he had to wait for Clyde's signal.

He'd asked the man how he would know the signal when Clyde gave it and the older man had just chuckled.

"Believe me," Clyde had said, "you'll know it when I send it."

So Jason tried to be as small as possible in the shrubs, while he waited for the mysterious signal. The sun beat down on his head and back and for the hundredth time he wished he'd brought a hat.

He chuckled softly to himself while thinking about it, telling himself the next time he was planning to travel to another dimension, he would have to make sure to pack better.

He flexed his right leg, trying to get a kink out of it, then settled down for the long wait. It would take Clyde a little more than ten minutes to circle around--going out far enough to prevent from being spotted-- before he was in position to make his move.

With his pulse beating a steady rhythm in his head, Jason tried to control his fear and prepare himself for what would come next. He ground his teeth in with nervousness and continually swallowed the accumulated saliva in his throat. He knew he wasn't ready; after all, he was a businessman for God's sakes, not some kind of gladiatorial warrior. But if that was what he had to become to save his son, then so be it.

He sent out a mental prayer to whoever might be listening to let his son still be alive and well. Then he stretched out and tried to get more comfortable. Despite the amount of time he had to wait could be measured in mere minutes, he felt every tick of the clock in his head like it was an eternity.

Letting out a deep breath, he closed his eyes and tried to think of the good times with his son and wife. He wondered if he would ever get the chance to make new memories with either of them. Thinking of Emma filled him with pangs of loss. God how he missed her, but he knew if he was ever going to see her again, he would have his son by his side, the alternative too damn hard to contemplate.

His ears perked up at the sound of gunfire and then a piercing scream filled the day, shattering his reverie.

That had to be the signal!

He stood up and prepared himself to run for the camp, all other thoughts and remembrances pushed down where they wouldn't be a distraction.

He watched the Snatcher take off across the open plain, away from the camp. He sent Clyde his prayers, hoping the man would be fine, and stood up and started running.

With his legs pumping, he darted toward the gate, and the man called Harry, who was blocking the opening with an evil grin on his face as he watched the Snatcher disappear over the next ridge.

# CHAPTER TWENTY-SEVEN

WITHIN MINUTES OF the same morning and time Jason was darting across the austere land towards Harry, with, the vermilion rays of the red sun cascading across the landscape and the camp, RJ stood up and walked over to the wall of the room with the small holes in the foundation. Peeking out into the courtyard, he could see nothing but dirt. From his position, he was able to see a few patches of darker earth where the kids had been slaughtered the day before, but otherwise the yard was clear. Sometime in the night, the Snatcher or Harry had taken away the bifurcated and disemboweled corpses.

He turned away from the hole and stopped when Patrick blocked his path. The older boy looked tired; the circles under his eyes making him look older than his years.

"I told you, newbie. I hope you're satisfied. You got a lot of kids killed last night. That means there's less for the Snatcher to eat. That means your life expectancy was just cut down by half."

RJ pushed by Patrick, planning to go back to Matt. "Go to hell, Patrick; don't you think I feel bad enough? I don't need to hear your shit."

Patrick placed a hand on RJ's arm, turning him around. RJ let the teen do it and when he was facing him again, RJ's face was set in a tight grimace, his eyes hard.

"You really don't want to mess with me right now, Patrick. I'm not afraid of you," RJ growled in a low voice, his hands curled into fists by his side.

Patrick paused for a heartbeat, looking into RJ's eyes. There must have been something in there the older teen hadn't seen before, because he took his hand away from RJ's arm and took a step back.

"Fine, newbie, but this shit isn't over." Turning, he walked away. No one else had heard the exchange, both of their voices kept low.

RJ turned and moved through the downtrodden kids. Once he was standing over Matt, he sat down wearily.

Matt sat up, his eyes red from crying. "Why did Teddy have to die, RJ? It's not fair, he was my friend," Matt cried.

RJ had no answer for the distraught boy. What could he possibly say? So, instead he leaned closer to the boy and hugged him, the younger child falling into his arms. Matt's shoulders shook as he began to cry again.

RJ held him silently. He was done crying for a while; now all that was left inside him was anger. Anger for the monster outside for taking him from his home. Anger for slaughtering his friends like they were nothing but cattle.

Memories of him watching his friends being ripped to pieces by the Snatcher flooded his mind and he pushed them back down, using the pain as fuel for his anger. His hands curled into fists around Matt's shoulders and he swore somehow the beast would pay.

*   *   *

Clyde had circled around to the opposite side of the fence and was now prepared to make a suitable distraction to allow Jason to slip in unnoticed. He reached into his pocket and pulled out a few wrinkled pieces of notebook paper. They had originally been his list of nightly chores at the school he'd worked at and he had kept them the entire time he'd been on this hellish new world.

He knew he wasn't likely to find any more paper, so he'd held them close, knowing there would be a time when they would be needed. Whether it was to start an emergency fire or to write some desperate note to God knows who, he knew sooner or later he'd be glad he kept them.

And that time was now.

After he and Jason had coated the bullets with aluminum, Clyde had taken a few rounds and opened them to get the gunpowder inside.

He had poured the powder into each of the strips of paper, curling the ends tight.

Using strips of bark taken from one of the old trees, he'd wrapped them around a fist-sized rock, one paper for each rock. Now all he had to do was light them and toss them towards the fence. When the paper burned through, the gunpowder inside would ignite, making a very decent distraction, given his limited resources.

When he was in position, he pulled out the lighter Jason had given him. Luckily, the man had come through the portal with it. Jason had no idea what a find it was for Clyde, who had to continuously rub sticks together like an over-the-hill boy scout to light a fire every night.

The paper caught on the first light, the slight breeze not a hindrance. When the paper was burning nicely, he tossed it towards the gate. While that projectile was in the air, he quickly lit the other three, sending them after the first.

One at a time the mini grenades landed by the gate, small bits of rock and dirt exploding outward. Harry came running at the firecracker-sized blasts, his club in his hand. Upon seeing the mini explosions, he started blowing his bone whistle, summoning the Snatcher.

Clyde looked up to the gentle slope to see the Snatcher step out of its home. It looked left and right, then charged down the hill like a deformed gazelle.

Clyde decided it was now or never.

He stood up and yelled across the distance separating him from the gate.

"Hey you piece of shit, why don't you take a bite out of this!" He hollered, waving his ass at the black beast. The Snatcher slowed as it approached the gate, its head swiveling in Clyde's direction. It raised its head and hissed, then charged at the man.

"Oh shit," Clyde gasped and started running away. His plan was to draw the Snatcher as far away from the camp as he could, giving Jason the time he needed to find his son, then he planned to dive into one of the pools and hide.

But as he took a quick glance over his shoulder at the black shimmering thing behind him, he quickly re-evaluated his plan. Knowing it was too late to change it now, he ran faster, hoping he could make it to the closest pool before he was caught and torn to pieces by the slavering beast slowly closing the gap behind him.

∗   ∗   ∗

RJ's head perked up at the sound of large bangs coming from outside the building. The noise reminded him of an old car backfiring or…no, it couldn't be, gunfire?

But how? As far as any of the kids knew, there were no guns or firearms of any kind in the camp. Not even the basic metals could be found, only dirt, rocks and water.

RJ sat up and looked around the dim room. The other kids had heard it and were now talking animatedly to each other.

RJ ran to the foundation, Patrick next to him.

"Did you hear that?" RJ asked him.

"Sure did, but what was it?" Patrick asked with his face pressed against on of the tiny holes.

"Ever heard it before?" RJ asked him, trying to see what was happening outside. Every kid was trying to see through the small holes in the foundation, wondering what was happening. From their vantage point, the gate was just out of sight, so all they could do was sit and wait.

Frustrated, RJ pushed himself from the hole, another boy filling his spot in seconds.

Despite the carnage from the previous day, he found himself getting hungry. Looking over to the table where the mushrooms would be, he frowned. If Harry was going to bring food he had yet to do the job. Maybe they wouldn't be fed as punishment for yesterday's botched breakout.

With nothing else to do, he went and sat down on his bedroll. Matt was at the hole, too, trying to see anything in the courtyard. At least he was up and moving around now, RJ thought.

RJ lay back on the floor, cupping his hands behind his head, trying to keep his fate from intruding on his thoughts. Whatever was happening outside probably didn't matter to him anyway.

# CHAPTER TWENTY-EIGHT

J ASON WATCHED THE Snatcher disappear over the next hill and he forced his legs to move faster. The man in front of the gate still hadn't noticed him yet, his eyes only for the beast as it ran after Clyde.

Jason had made it to within twenty feet of the gate when his running footsteps carried to the older man's ears. Harry swiveled at the waist, his eyes opening wide when he saw Jason charging towards him. Jason had his hands free, the revolver wedged into the back of his waistband. As he ran, he could feel it rubbing his back, a reassuring feeling that it was still there. Not wanting to waste a bullet that would be needed for the Snatcher, nor the sound of the weapon alerting the creature what was happening back at the camp, Jason hoped he could deal with Harry with just his hands.

Harry turned his body and raised the wooden club, waiting for Jason to come closer. Jason never slowed. His mind was only for his son, the man in front of him merely an obstacle to be overcome.

Jason plowed into Harry at full speed, tucking his head into his chest so as not to snap his own neck. At the exact same time Jason was ramming him, Harry brought the club down onto Jason's back, the soft thump of wood on flesh carrying to his ears.

Jason's vision became a white light as the pain from the blow flared in his head. But his momentum was so great, he continued forward, knocking Harry to the ground, and then landing on top of him before his own force of motion had Jason rolling over his head to land sprawled on his back on the red earth.

Jason lay still for a moment, trying to catch his breath. His back was screaming with pain and he feared something might have been shattered from the heavy club.

Opening his eyes, he looked up just as Harry brought the club down in an overhand blow that was intended to split Jason's skull in two. Just before the blow connected, Jason rolled away, the club coming so close to his head his ear was scraped by the rough wood. Jason rolled some more, Harry following him. Every time the man brought the club down, Jason would avoid it, but then Harry scored and struck a glancing blow off Jason's shoulder. He screamed with pain, feeling like his shoulder had popped out of the joint. Harry grinned, yellow teeth flaring in the sun. He raised his club again; knowing this time Jason wouldn't be able to avoid it.

With an intake of breath, Jason kicked out with his foot, the bottom of his shoe connecting with Harry's right knee. With his leg knocked askew, the blow went wide, missing Jason by more than six inches. Harry stumbled forward, not prepared for the miss. Jason rolled to his knees and punched the man straight in his balls. Harry let out a high pitched scream that was cut short when the pain from his groin filled his body. He stood perfectly still, his breath coming in ragged gasps, his body bent over from the agony of having his testicles crushed, like he was bowing to Jason's superior fighting prowess.

Jason stood up, never stopping. He brought his knee straight into Harry's face, sending the man's head flying backwards, his body falling to the dirt. The older man lay flat on his back, staring up at the sky. His nose was shattered, blood pouring out in rivulets. The man realized he could drown on his own blood and rolled over, the bright red fluid dripping off his face into the earth below him.

Harry's hand was searching for his club and Jason kicked it away, far out of reach. Jason was about to hit the man again, but it looked like the fight was out of old Harry.

Only a handful of seconds had gone by and Jason knew the time it would take to tie the man up would be time he didn't have, so he left the prone man where he lay and ran for the building he believed his son to be in. Pain flared from his back and shoulder, but he ignored it. Reaching the wood and stone structure seconds later, he undid the heavy, horizontal piece of wood holding the door closed.

Throwing the door open, he charged inside, his son's name already on his lips. That's when he was swarmed by more than a dozen bodies and forced to the floor. His mouth was covered by someone's arm and he felt more claustrophobic than he could ever have remembered in his life.

Someone punched him in the face and he felt another kick to the thigh of his left leg. He cried out in pain and realized he was trapped.

It had all been for nothing, he thought as he became smothered by the torso of yet another body.

*   *   *

RJ was lying on his bedroll, cursing his fate when one of the other kids, who was looking out onto the courtyard through one of the holes shouted out.

"Hey, guys, there's someone fighting Harry!"

RJ stood up and ran to the wall. He could only see a hint of the battle, the area just out of sight. The shadows of the fighters danced on the dusty ground, tempting him with a leg or an arm, but nothing more.

"Damn it, I can't see a thing. Does anyone have a better view?" RJ cried out.

All answers were to the negative and RJ cursed under his breath. Then a voice near the door hollered above the rest. "Wait, someone's coming to the door."

"Who is it, is it Harry?" Another voice asked.

"Can't tell, the head's blocked."

RJ ran to Patrick. "It's got to be Harry, maybe he's gonna make us leave or who knows what. We've got to jump him when he comes in. There's a lot more of us than him and he'll never expect it," RJ reasoned. "Patrick, this could be our chance, our only chance!"

Patrick bit his lip, thinking. He knew he had only seconds to decide. RJ stood in front of him, his face eager for an answer.

"Oh, screw it," Patrick finally said. "Let's get the old bastard. I owe him for more beatings than I can count."

"All right, that's great!" RJ yelled. "All right, everybody listen up; when Harry gets here, we're gonna jump him. Kick his ass the way the jerk deserves it."

"But what about the Snatcher, he'll be mad?" Matt said near his side.

RJ turned and looked at the small boy.

"So what. What's he gonna do, kill us? Shit, he's going to do that anyway, why not get a little payback."

"Yeah, let's do it!" Someone yelled.

"Let's get the prick, kick his ass once and for all," another voice said.

RJ gathered everyone near the front, Patrick getting them ready, as well. Some picked up blankets made of some course material not found on earth, ready to cover Harry's head with them. Fists were raised and faces were determined. They'd had enough, and if they were gong to die, they were going to go down fighting.

The door rattled in its frame as the wood on the front was lifted. The door swung open, blinding the kids with the bright light shining in. A figure stepped inside, and before the man could do or say anything, the kids jumped him, forcing him to the floor. Patrick punched the man right in the face and RJ saw Matt kick him in the thigh. As he watched the small boy, RJ thought this was the first time the boy didn't looked scared and frightened.

Muffled screams of pain floated from the pile of kids and RJ heard muffled words. Then the man was able to push off a kid who was on his face and a voice rang out in the room.

"Jesus Christ, stop, I'm here to help you!"

RJ's breath caught in his throat and he wondered if he was hearing things. He knew that voice. But how? It was impossible, wasn't it?

He dived into the mass of kids, pulling as many away as he could. Angry yells greeted him, as the kids wondered what he was doing. Patrick had straddled the man and was repeatedly punching him in the face. RJ pushed Patrick off as hard as he could, the older teen falling away with a loud curse of his own. RJ looked down at the bruised face of his father. His cheek was cut and he had a fat lip, but otherwise seemed to be okay.

"Dad! Oh my God, is it really you?" RJ yelled at the prone man.

Jason opened his bruised eyes and stared up at the face of his son.

"RJ? Oh, thank God you're alive!" Jason screamed. RJ fell on top of Jason, the supine man groaning from the weight. They hugged for a full minute, each ecstatic to have found each other. Then Jason pushed his son off into the midst of the other kids who were standing very still, watching; not quite understanding what was going on.

"All right, that's enough of that. We need to go, now, before the Snatcher returns."

"Returns?" RJ asked.

Jason nodded. "I've got a friend running decoy for us, but it won't be long before it returns, we need to be gone before that."

RJ nodded, looking at the other faces around him. "Well then, let's get the hell out of here?"

Cries of delight filled the room as kids jumped up and down, happy to be rescued. But Jason wasn't so happy. He knew they were far from free.

"Come on, we have to leave now. Everyone get outside to the yard, and stay close together," Jason ordered them. His eyes took in some of the small faces as they moved by him and his heart broke. All were filthy, wearing nothing more than rags, but now their eyes had a spark for freedom.

With barely controlled chaos, the kids moved through the door, pushing and shoving. RJ stood by his father, hugging him. He looked up at Jason and smiled.

"Are we going home, Dad? Are we leaving this place for good?"

Jason didn't quite know how to answer that just yet, so he decided on a half truth.

"What do you say we worry about getting away from here first and then we'll deal with the rest, okay?"

RJ nodded, just happy to be safe in his father's arms again. They were the last two out and Jason wasted no time in herding them to the open gates. Just before the first kid was sliding through the egress, Harry jumped out from behind the small security shack he lived in. His club was in the air and he was ready to hit any kid who tried to leave the camp.

Patrick was near the front of the line of kids, and the second he saw Harry blocking their way, he jumped the man. Harry swung the club, hitting Patrick on the left shoulder, but with the club down after the blow, the other kids quickly swarmed over him. Harry went down under a wave of small arms and legs. His muffled cries drifted from under the bodies and more than a minute of pain for the old man had ticked by before the kids stepped away.

When the last child had climbed off Harry, Jason moved forward, the kids moving out of his way.

Jason looked down at the barely conscious form of old Harry. His face was barely recognizable, all the bones in his cheeks shattered by dozens of blows and kicks by determined feet and hands. His clothes were ripped and bite marks could be seen on his arms and chest.

He'd treated the children like animals and they had responded in kind. Jason nudged him with his shoe, but the man only moaned. He was barely conscious and a threat to no one.

Jason moved to the front of the line, waving the kids to move up the path.

"Come on, guys, he's harmless now, lets get moving."

The kids obeyed, Patrick now taking on the roll as point man. As the older teen moved down the trail, the others following, Jason looked over to where Clyde had been, wondering if his friend was okay.

With the last kid moving by him, he and RJ brought up the rear. They had a long walk back to the cave on the mountain, and sooner or later, he knew the Snatcher was coming for them.

He could only hope they would all make it to the cave first and then he would somehow figure out a way to get the portal open back to Earth.

# Chapter Twenty-nine

CLYDE WAS RUNNING for his life, his legs eating up the terrain. His arms were pumping in front of him like a sprinter as he ran across the rocky landscape. His breath came in gasps and he seriously wondered if he might just fall over dead from a heart attack. That would be the king of all ironies, he thought.

The Snatcher was closing the gap far too quickly for his liking. He had about two minutes if he was lucky, and with each yard covered, his legs grew heavier. He had never been that much of an exercise nut and the only reason he was still moving at all was sheer fear and adrenaline.

He jumped over a knee high boulder, losing his balance for a moment. Just before he went head first into the ground, though, he managed to keep moving forward, his own momentum helping him.

There was a taller boulder, at least ten feet in height, coming up in his path. He knew what was behind it. He took the corner around the rock so tight he scraped his arm on the side of the rough surface.

For just a heartbeat, he was out of sight of the Snatcher. The pool in front of him, shaded by the sun's rays by the boulder and covered with red algae, looked as uninviting as jumping into a pile of shit, but he knew it was either that or face the Snatcher's talons.

He never slowed.

Reaching into his pocket while he ran, he tossed the Bic lighter away from him, not wanting to get it wet, then dived into the pool, doing his best to slice into the water. His outstretched arms were in front of his head, pointed like a spear, when he slid into the murky shallows of the pool. But he was off balance and instead of a graceful dive, it was more like a belly flop. His stomach smacked the surface of the water, sending the red slime covering flying in every direction.

He was under before he realized it, the cool liquid still feeling good on his sweating body. He stopped when he hit the muddy floor and turned to look up at the surface, out onto the edge of the water.

At first he could see nothing, his body stirring up the sediment on the floor of the pool, but after a minute or so the water began to clear, allowing him a view of the water's edge.

The Snatcher was there.

It knew he was in the water, but Clyde had learned early on when arriving in the camp that Snatchers disliked water to the point they would rather die than touch it. The creature received the necessary moisture needed to survive by consuming its prey's blood. So Clyde knew he was safe, but the million dollar question was would the beast wait him out, or return to the camp.

Clyde's lungs were screaming for air, and though he knew he could probably surface to gather more oxygen, that would just enrage the Snatcher more. Better to stay hidden and hope it gave up. Something swam by his face, the tail touching his cheek. He almost cried out before stopping himself.

He had only seconds left before he would have to surface. His vision was starting to dim and he knew his lungs were going to try to suck in fresh air whether it was oxygen or water.

Then Clyde saw the Snatcher's head swivel around to its back trail. It seemed to hesitate for another second and then it turned and loped away.

Clyde counted five more seconds, hopefully letting the creature get far enough away so it wouldn't hear him surface, and then he kicked his legs off the floor of the pool and shot upward. His lungs gave out before he was out of the water and he started to breath in the disgusting liquid.

His head broke the surface and he gagged. With gasps of coughing and vomiting, he swam back to the edge of the pool. With a small heave, using his last strength, he pulled himself out of the water. He fell onto his back and stared up at the vermilion sky, happy to be alive.

When he turned his head to the side, he saw the Bic lighter lying in the dirt where he'd tossed it. Reaching out, he wrapped wet fingers around it and held it tight. He would hold the lighter for now, not wanting to put it in his waterlogged pants. But they would dry soon enough in the arid weather.

While he sucked in great big lungfuls of air, he sent a silent prayer to Jason, hoping his distraction had worked and given the man enough time to save his son and the other children.

*     *     *

One minute ago.

The Snatcher stood by the pool's edge, staring down at the water. His skin shriveled from being so close to the hated liquid. He knew the prey was in the water, but it might as well be on another planet for all it mattered. He stood there frustrated, deciding what to do, when he caught the sound of yells and voices being raised in excitement. His head swiveled so his ear canals could pick up more of the ambient noise. Then he heard it again, coming from the camp. His prey was moving. All the hunts would be ruined unless he stopped them. His lair was piled to the wall with the slaughtered children from the day before. He would feast for a week on their small corpses, but if the others escaped, then he would starve as the years ticked by, trapped on the dead world he called home.

Turning away from the pool, he took off at a run. The man he'd chased was irrelevant; he needed to catch the small ones first. The Snatcher had already decided the one called Harry would be next on his list of prey. In the past few days the old man had caused nothing but problems and his use to him was at an end.

With muscular legs pumping, the Snatcher crossed the distance he'd traveled while chasing the man, backtracking in half the time, and slowed when he reached the gate to the camp. The gate was wide open, the one called Harry lying prone in the dirt. The Snatcher moved closer, his olfactory senses picking up every nuance of the escaped prey.

And one other.

The human he had battled recently, the man's scent was mixed in with the others. The Snatcher was intelligent enough to figure out what had happened. The human had come and attacked Harry and had then set his property free.

Harry stirred on the ground, moaning in pain. The Snatcher walked over to him and stood over his battered body. The tall form blotted out the sun, casting Harry's face in shadows. The old man looked up into the Snatcher's face, or what would be a face on a human being. He saw sharpened teeth and slits where eyes would be.

Harry spit out some broken teeth and tried to say he was sorry, that he would make it right, but he never got the chance.

Like the sound of a steam engine letting off extra steam, the Snatcher raised both arms into the air and swiped razor-sharp talons across Harry's throat.

Harry lay twitching on the ground, gargling in spilled blood. He was drowning, and he looked up into the face of death, he realized it was long overdue. The Snatcher looked away from the dying man, senses picking up the trail of the children, then with Harry choking his last breaths, the Snatcher loped away to find and kill the escaped prey.

This time there would be no mercy; he would kill them all and feed on their corpses until the next planetary alignment. It wouldn't be as pleasant as live food, but it would do.

The Snatcher knew what revenge was and it wanted to exact it on the human who had set all the recent events in motion. With a digging of sharp claws into the red earth, the Snatcher doubled its speed up the path. He knew the children were close and he would find them soon.

*    *    *

Patrick and RJ walked side by side up the winding dirt path. Jason was in the lead, keeping everyone moving. The two boys had become fast friends in the past half hour, the things they had experienced drawing them closer.

"I'm really sorry I was such a jerk to you and the others," Patrick said ruefully. "I guess I let my own fear cloud my judgment. You know, back home I was never a bully, hell, I used to stand up for the little guy." He walked in silence for a moment, and RJ was wondering if he was finished, but then he started talking again.

"This place changed me, and though I know I did it to survive, I wish I'd done things differently," Patrick finished.

"Jesus, Patrick, you were an ass, but after everything you'd seen who can blame you. I'm just glad you realized it," RJ said with a smile.

"Gee, you're all heart," Patrick joked.

The two walked silently for a few more minutes, concentrating on the winding path until RJ stopped suddenly. Patrick noticed immediately and slowed down as well, the other kids moving on up the trail, ignoring them.

"What's wrong?" Patrick asked, curious.

"Thought I heard something." He waited for the sound to occur again, but when it remained quiet, he shrugged. "Must be my imagination, getting jumpy I guess."

"Who could blame you, with all you've seen," Patrick jibed.

RJ was about to give him a witty rejoinder when Patrick's eyes lit up with surprise and fear. RJ never got the chance to ask what was wrong before Patrick slammed into RJ, pushing the smaller boy to the ground.

RJ rolled over, ready to give Patrick some serious shit, especially after the talk they'd just had, when his breath caught in his throat.

The Snatcher had come out of the dry, sparse foliage on the side of the trail and its claws had been aiming directly for RJ's neck. Patrick had seen this and had known there was no time for a warning. The older teen had just reacted, pushing him to the ground and taking the talons on his own collarbone.

Razor-sharp talons sliced into skin, sliding into the teen's throat. Patrick had just enough time for a soft squeak before his mouth was filled with blood and his vocal cords were severed. The Snatcher took its other arm and swiped it across Patrick's neck again, decapitating the boy and putting him out of his suffering.

The head jumped off the torso, bouncing on the dirt path to roll to a stop next to RJ.

RJ looked down at Patrick's severed head, the mouth was still trying to talk, the jaw moving up and down, his brain not realizing he was dead.

RJ had read back home that the brain stays alive for almost thirty seconds after the head is separated from the body. Until this moment, he never believed a word of it…until now

Patrick's body stood perfectly still, the legs still locked in a standing position; the teen's hands twitching by his sides. Time seemed to stand still, RJ imagining he could see every drop of blood spraying from the severed stump of Patrick's neck. Then the body toppled over, the muscles giving in to death.

RJ lay on his back, his elbows propping him up. He was speechless, looking up at the black terror called the Snatcher. The creature raised its talons to the sky, blood dripping from the razor-sharp points. Its head looked down and stared at RJ, preparing to repeat the same slaughter on his body, mimicking what it had just done to Patrick.

RJ was frozen with fear.

Sounding like it was from a distance, he heard the muffled sound of children screaming as they tried to run away from the obsidian nightmare which had kept them all in a state of perpetual terror for months; some even longer.

RJ saw the Snatcher's talons curving forward, preparing to cut him open from waist to neck, but he was too paralyzed to move. All he could do in that brief instance before the claws struck was pray it would be quick and send his father a silent, I love you.

# Chapter Thirty

JASON SPUN AROUND from the front of the line after the first frightened scream floated over the children's heads and his blood ran cold when he spotted the reason for their terror.

The Snatcher had found them.

He turned to the next kid in line, an older teen who had been friends with Patrick.

"Take the kids and get them as far up the path as you can. Don't stop for anything," he told him.

"Yes, sir," the frightened teen said, doing what he was told, pushing and pulling the children further down the path, away from the commotion at the rear of the line.

Jason muttered a few choice imprecations under his breath.

He knew the black beast would have found them eventually, but deep down in his heart, there was still a shred of hope they might have made it far enough away to perhaps throw off their scent from the following creature, but he had no way of knowing if the Snatcher hunted by sight or smell.

He pushed one of the kids aside who accidentally got in his way and he bolted to the back of the line. More than twenty faces looked up at him, as he hustled past them, and all had tears in their eyes, some not yet comprehending what was happening, but sensing the terror of their fellow travelers.

Jason could only watch helplessly as Patrick was beheaded, his body falling to the red earth. Then he saw his son laying prone on the ground, the Snatcher towering over him.

He knew he would never reach RJ in time and he remembered the revolver in his waistband.

He had his gun!

In the time it would take to let out a breath, he cursed himself for being a fool. He was so wrapped up in the moment, he'd forgotten about the firearm tucked into his pants.

His right arm flew to his back, and for just a brief second, he felt fear in his heart when he couldn't feel the grip.

Then his hand wrapped around the butt of the .38, and he pulled it free. The gun had shifted while he was walking and he hadn't realized it.

There was no time to try to line up a shot; even now the Snatcher was preparing to rip RJ open from head to toe. Jason screamed at the top of his lungs, hoping to catch the Snatcher's attention. Then squeezed the trigger.

The bullet had less than twenty-five feet to travel and that was Jason's saving grace. Before the round went wide, it clipped the Snatcher's upraised arm. The aluminum tipped bullet slicing into its black flesh, causing the arm to pull back as if the creature had been stung by a metal bee, the black body spinning around.

But it wasn't enough to stop it from killing his son. Before Jason realized it, the Snatcher had recovered and was preparing to finish what it had started. Jason never hesitated; continuing to move closer. From ten feet away he squeezed the trigger again. The second round hit the Snatcher straight in the upper chest, where the heart would be in a human being. The creature fell back as if it had been punched by a giant hand, talons raking empty air. The steam whistle scream rent the air with fury, the Snatcher not pleased at being halted and its prey slipping from its grasp.

Jason had made it to RJ's side, and he nearly wrenched his son's arm from its socket, while pulling him roughly to his feet.

"Get out of here, son, follow the other kids up the path!" Jason told him.

"But what about you?" RJ asked, his voice hoarse and frantic.

Jason shoved his son away from him towards the retreating backs of the running children. "I need to deal with this bastard. If we don't stop it, it'll just keep coming after us…now go!" He had just enough time to order his son to move and then he turned to face the Snatcher, the muzzle of the revolver already searching for a target.

The Snatcher had regained its balance and was now trying to decide what to do. Should it go after the fleeing prey? Or deal with the human who had hurt it before and was doing so once again.

Jason answered that question for it, sending another round at the black body.

The bullet hit the Snatcher in the thigh, causing the creature to bellow in pain. Jason could see black ichor leaking from the bullet holes in its flesh, but the creature still seemed to just be annoyed by the wounds, although the silver bullets definitely seemed to enrage it more. If Jason didn't hit a vital area soon, the fight would be over before it had begun.

Jason didn't hesitate, knowing time was against him, and squeezed the trigger again. The bullet went wide, the creature dropping to the ground at the sound of the gun shot. Jason cursed; it was getting smarter and had realized what the revolver could do.

Like a sprinter taking off at the sound of the starting pistol, the Snatcher dug its claws into the dirt and powered at Jason. Its talons were held out in front of it, preparing to rip the man apart.

He tried to line up another shot, but the creature kept zigzagging back and forth, making for a difficult target. He fired again, but the bullet flew harmlessly over its shoulder to strike a nearby boulder.

Then it was on him, talons raking him and its mouth-like orifice blowing its fetid breath on his face. He still had the revolver in his hand and he realized it was jammed against the Snatcher's body. Sending a silent prayer that the weapon was facing the right direction, he squeezed the trigger. There was a muffled pop, the gun blast barely heard from in between the pressed bodies, and for a fearful minute Jason wondered if he'd just managed to shoot himself in the chest or stomach. But then the Snatcher fell away from their embrace as if Jason had pushed it.

A hole had appeared where its stomach would be and the steam whistle scream filled the area, causing Jason to wince. When it was over, Jason raised the .38 and prepared to fire yet again, knowing he was almost out of rounds. Actually he had no idea how many he'd fired, losing count in the heat of battle. And he knew once again there would be no time to reload.

The Snatcher's bulbous head was in his sights and he knew this would finish the battle once and for all. With a cry of victory, he lined up the face and squeezed the trigger, expecting to feel the weapon jerk in his hand, and a moment later the Snatcher's face would explode in a viscous spray of black ichor.

Nothing but a dry click came from the gun.

He was out of bullets!

And just as he thought, there was no time to attempt to reload the weapon.

Then the Snatcher was on him. It swiped the gun from his hand, one of the talons catching the flesh of his palm and slicing it like a razor blade. Jason let out a yell and pulled his hand away as the Snatcher came at him. Jason jumped away, only his adrenalin keeping him sane as he stared at the horror trying to disembowel him.

The talons came at him again, ready to decapitate him in one swipe. Jason tried to back up and his feet tripped over Patrick's headless corpse. He felt himself falling backward, the talons missing him by mere inches, thanks to his fall.

He landed hard on the ground, his head striking a rock embedded in the path. He saw stars for a moment and shook his head to clear them. When his vision cleared, less than half a second had passed, but it was enough to seal his doom. The Snatcher was standing over him, its chest heaving up and down as it prepared to fillet him like a flounder on a fisherman's table. The wounds on its body still leaked black ichor, and the creature looked weaker for it, but unfortunately none of the bullet wounds appeared to look fatal.

In that half of a heartbeat that was the rest of his life, Jason looked up at the Snatcher and the red sky behind it. It had been a good fight. He'd been crazy to think he would have triumphed to begin with. He could only hope with the time it took for him to be killed, it would be enough for his son and the other children to make it to safety.

Then the talons came down and blocked out the sunlight.

# Chapter Thirty-One

JASON SCREAMED LONG and loudly, his eyes wide with terror, as he watched the ebony talons approaching his head. But instead of feeling the cold razor-sharp points of the Snatcher's talons, at the last moment the Snatcher was knocked off balance and its claws sliced into the dirt, digging deep into the hard soil only an inch from Jason's horrified face.

Jason looked up at the slavering orifice, teeth flashing in the sun. Then he looked at its chest to see the tip of something silver jutting out of the beast's sternum, like a seedling trying to fight its way through the earth to reach the surface of the soil.

Jason was terrified, but something told him if he wanted to live, he needed to move now. So he tucked his head under the Snatcher's arm and rolled away, his face becoming covered in dust and dirt. He rolled to his feet, wiping his eyes clear of grit to see the Snatcher pulling itself to its full height. Behind it stood Clyde. The man was still holding the large knife he'd fashioned from the rest of the aluminum baseball bat. Jason remembered hearing the pounding from outside the cave the night before and realized what it had meant.

They had only used a fraction of the bat and Clyde had softened the hollow tip and formed it into a crude broadsword. Only the first four inches were sharp, the rest just pounded flat, but it seemed to have worked remarkably well.

The shaft slid through the Snatcher like butter and the wounded creature screamed in pain.

Clyde was still behind the howling beast, too surprised with what he'd just done to realize he needed to run away. Jason's voice caught in his throat and he watched helplessly as the Snatcher spun around with talons out, slicing at Clyde. When the beast spun, the sword was ripped from Clyde's fingers, the blade still embedded in the beast's torso.

Clyde tried to escape, falling backward, but not before receiving a severe cut across his abdomen. He dropped to the ground and the Snatcher moved to finish him off, forgetting about Jason in its rage and pain.

Jason was too focused in the moment to be frightened. His friend was hurt, and if he didn't do something quick, the Snatcher was surely going to kill him.

Jason threw caution to the wind and charged the back of the Snatcher. Reaching out to the handle, he pulled the makeshift sword free and stepped back. The creature reeled in pain, its cries filling the path yet again.

Jason never slowed.

When the creature turned to face the reason for his pain, Jason stepped inside the dagger-like talons, his nose almost touching the Snatcher's chest. Looking up at the slavering head, he leaned back and thrust up with the sword, putting everything he had into the blow. The sharp point of the aluminum blade sliced upward at a slight angle into the Snatcher's chin, continuing until the black ichor stained tip broke free of the flesh on the back of the beast's neck.

Blood poured out of the wound like a waterfall and Jason was smothered in the beast's blood. He closed his eyes and spit out the disgusting, vicious fluid.

His grip was firm, the black electrical tape on the handle keeping his hands from slipping. Without realizing it, he twisted the bat in his grip and the Snatcher squealed in pain. The sides of the tip, honed to sharpness by Clyde, cut tendon and muscles, almost severing the head from the beast's broad shoulders.

Jason couldn't see anything, the black ichor pouring over his head and covering his face, burning his eyes with its viscosity.

The Snatcher's body convulsed and its long arms flailed wildly, one of them striking Jason and sending him reeling away to land hard in the dirt.

At the moment he was blind. He had no idea what was happening and he expected to be ripped to pieces at any moment. The cries of the

Snatcher slowed in intensity and Jason heard the sound of something heavy falling to the earth.

With his ears ringing, he rolled to his feet. Ripping the buttons on his shirt, he pulled it off, hoping to find a dry spot, and then wiped his eyes and face clear of the disgusting ink-colored blood. He blinked a few times until his vision began to return and he gasped when he saw what was in front of him. The Snatcher lay on the ground, its head partially severed from its shoulders. Black ichor was shooting out into the dirt, but with each passing second, Jason could see the flow was slowing.

He heard a groan on the other side of the prone Snatcher and realized it was Clyde. Running over to his friend, still wary of slashing talons, despite the beast's current condition, he knelt down on the red dirt and helped Clyde to a sitting position.

Clyde coughed, spitting blood, a thin ribbon of scarlet dripping down his chin.

"Easy there, buddy, you're going to be fine," Jason told him without conviction.

Clyde tried to laugh, but quickly stopped when pain racked his body.

"Don't bullshit a bullshitter, Jason. We both know I'm fucked," he said in a soft whisper.

Jason looked down at Clyde's chest and stomach and knew the man was right. The Snatcher had managed to open his lower torso with one of its talons. Jason had to look away, the sight of Clyde's ribs and intestines poking out of the wound enough to make him want to gag. As Jason studied the mortal wound, he couldn't imagine how his friend was still breathing at all.

Clyde coughed again, his face creasing from the intolerable pain he was feeling. It was like someone had poured acid in his veins and had sent the entire corrosive fluid through his body, the acid now eating him from the inside out.

"How the hell did you find us so fast?" Jason asked.

Clyde sucked in air, his face showing the pain it took. "Once the Snatcher left me, I crawled out of the pool. I figured you'd need my help, so I headed up the path to find you as fast as I could run." He coughed some more. "Looks like it's a good thing I did." He looked up into Jason's face. "It's all right Jason, I'm ready to die. I've been ready ever since I got to this damn place." His hand went into his pocket and he managed to pull something out. It was the Bic lighter. "Here, I saved this from a dunking, figured you might need it again."

Jason nodded and took the lighter, sliding it into his back pocket. He barely noticed he was doing it, his attention on Clyde.

"I'm so sorry, Clyde. If you hadn't tried to save me then you'd be fine now."

"That's bullshit, Jason. You saved me. Until you arrived here, I had no idea how lonely I was. I wasn't living Jason, I was simply existing." More coughs racked his body and Clyde lost consciousness for a few moments.

Jason looked up at the sound of footsteps coming down the path to see RJ and one of the older teens moving towards him. Jason held up his hand for them to stop where they were and then looked down at Clyde again.

The man's eyes were open and he was staring up at the sky, a single tear slipping out of the corner of his left eye. "You know, it really is a beautiful sky, all red and dark." He looked to Jason, his gaze locking with his. "Do you think they have a Heaven around here?"

Jason fought back the tears struggling to break free as he cradled his friend's head in his arms.

He nodded slowly. "Sure they do, buddy and you know you're going there."

Jason squeezed his eyes shut to try and get control of himself and when he opened them again and looked down at Clyde, he saw the man's gaze was nothing but a dead stare. Jason looked down at Clyde's ravaged torso to see his chest was still.

Reaching out with a bloody hand, he closed Clyde's eyelids.

With a sob in his throat, he gently set the man's head down and stood up. His son was waiting quietly near the edge of the path, not moving, barely breathing.

Then Jason stepped around Clyde and the Snatcher and opened his arms for his son. RJ ran into them and crushed his head against his father's chest. Father and son hugged until RJ thought he couldn't breathe.

He said nothing, relishing the feeling.

After a few minutes had passed, Jason separated RJ from him. His son looked down at the Snatcher's still form.

No words needed to be said.

Then Jason realized the danger was finally over and his son was safe and he fell to his knees and cried. All the fear, worry and hopelessness he'd felt for the past couple of days hitting him like a freight train; his friends death the capper to it all.

RJ moved next to him, and this time it was Jason who crushed his face to his son's chest. His shoulders heaved for a few moments as he let it out, then he regained control of himself.

Pushing away from his son, he looked embarrassed.

"Sorry about that, son, I guess that wasn't very manly of me huh?"

RJ shrugged. "That's okay, Dad. I won't tell anybody if you won't."

Jason grinned at his son's quip, and with RJ to lean on, stood up. He looked over to the body of Clyde and then looked down at his son.

"We have to bury him, son, I'm not going to just leave him like that."

RJ nodded and the two got to work digging a shallow grave on the side of the path. When asked, the other teen also helped. RJ and Jason found out his name was Chad and he was from New Jersey. The three of them talked the entire time they worked, the sound of their voices soothing one another.

The work went quick, the dry soil on the edge of the path easy to work with even with nothing more than the aluminum sword and a few flat rocks for shovels.

When they were finished, and Clyde was in the shallow red earth with rocks over the grave, Jason stood over the mound.

He said nothing; he felt there was nothing to say.

Both RJ and Chad knew what had happened and Clyde wouldn't hear him, so he just turned away from the grave and started up the path.

"Come on, boys, let's get to the others. Hell, they probably figure we're all dead."

Just as they began to head up the trail, RJ stopped and looked down on the corpse of the Snatcher. His eyes roamed over the strong legs and the sharp talons. Then something clicked in his mind, something he remembered when the creature had first brought him through the portal. He turned to Jason and raised his hand for him to wait.

"Hold up, Dad, I need to do something before we go. Can I have the sword?"

With a shrug, Jason handed it to him, for the life of him not understanding why his son would want it.

Bending over the Snatcher's corpse, RJ raised the blade high over his head, the aluminum catching the light and reflecting it like a mirror.

"RJ, what the hell are you doing? Get away from that thing. Hell, we don't even know if it's dead!" Jason yelled at him.

RJ ignored him, concentrating on hitting his mark. Holding the sword tightly, he moved to a position where he was standing above the taloned right hand of the Snatcher, and like a lumberjack chopping firewood, he brought the sword down, the side of the blade biting deep. But the flesh was strong and RJ raised the sword again and this time when aluminum met black flesh, the blow was true, and he severed the taloned hand from the arm.

Jason ran over to him, but the deed was done. RJ handed his father the sword and bent over and picked up the severed hand.

"What the hell did you do that for?" Jason asked, shocked.

RJ smiled, looking down at the clawed hand. "If I'm right, this is our ticket out of here."

Jason wanted to ask what his son was talking about, but RJ took off up the path, not giving him a chance. Jason looked to Chad who just shrugged, not understanding anything that was happening. With a weary sigh, Jason glanced one last time to Clyde's grave, and then he and the teen followed RJ up the trail, leaving the corpse of the Snatcher to rot in the sun.

# CHAPTER THIRTY-TWO

ABOUT A QUARTER mile up the path, Jason caught up with the rest of the children. They were all sitting on the edges of the winding trail, not really having a place to go. Without Jason, they had no leadership and had waited patiently, hoping he would return. When he did, coming around one of the dog-legged corners of the trail, children jumped to their feet and ran to him, almost knocking him over in their enthusiasm.

"Whoa, all right, take it easy," Jason said, trying to disengage some of the kids who had locked on to him. RJ was at his side and he squeezed Jason's arm to get his attention.

"We need to get back to the cave where the Snatcher brought me through," RJ told him.

Jason nodded, and over the laughing, clapping children, he replied. "You mean the one with all the bones on the ground?"

RJ nodded. "Yeah, that's the one. Can you get us back there?"

Jason's jaw went taut as he tried to remember how he had come to the path. It had been pretty straight-forward, the Snatcher having crushed all the sparse, dry foliage in the area from its frequent trips from the cave every time it had acquired new prey.

Finally, he nodded curtly. "Yeah, son, I think I can get us back there, why?"

RJ held up the severed hand he'd taken from the Snatcher's dead body. "Because I think I can get us home with this," RJ said with a grin.

Jason looked down at the severed limb, but didn't say anything. He was constantly being bombarded with questions from the other children which made it hard to talk to his son.

Finally, he held up his hands and screamed. "Enough already, shut up, everyone!"

Silence descended over the path and Jason breathed a sigh of relief. Then he walked to a nearby boulder about four feet high and climbed on top of it.

"All right guys, here's what's going to happen." He pointed to the mountain about a half mile or so away with his hand, "We're going to march over there."

"How come, what's there?" Chad asked.

"Are we going home now?" Matt asked in a subdued voice.

Jason nodded, his face set in a grimace. "I honestly don't know, but it's our best chance, so everyone line up and let's move out in a single file." Then he jumped down off the boulder and moved to the front of the line with RJ by his side.

They started their march, one foot in front of the other, trudging along the winding path. The sun was hot on their heads and after only an hour, everyone began to complain of thirst and exhaustion, the dry heat sapping their strength. The children talked in low voices, some thinking they were leaving, others not as trusting. All followed Jason and RJ, and as the crimson sun reached its zenith, the rag tag group of survivors reached the foot of the mountain.

Jason started moving upwards, making sure everyone was following him. The path was treacherous. Many times the trail would shrink to only a foot or so, the other side overlooking the perilous edge. If one of the children should slip, they would plummet down to the ground below.

Jason was exhausted by the time he reached the opening to the long tunnel which would lead to the actual cave filled with wall carvings inside the mountain. The darkness seemed a little less threatening, knowing the Snatcher was dead. He pulled the Bic lighter from his pocket and an image of Clyde came to the front of his mind. Smiling at the thought of the man, he flicked the lighter to light it. It took four times before it lit, thanks to some dust damage from the fall into the red soil, back when Clyde had dropped it to dive into the pool to escape the Snatcher. With a steady flame to light the way, he sucked in a lungful of oxygen and headed inside like he was diving into the ocean and would need to hold his breath.

Though one Snatcher was dead, he remembered Clyde telling him how more than one of the beasts hunted the area near the mountain, and he was prepared if that eventuality occurred, the .38 fully loaded with aluminum tipped rounds once again, though he prayed with every fiber of his being that wouldn't happen. He'd barely managed to survive the first battle with one of the ebony beasts; he had no desire to try for two.

One by one the children followed, the younger ones becoming scared, the older ones comforting them. They had become a family in the short time since escaping from the camp. All were equal and they showed it to each other in different ways, whether it was helping a fallen comrade when he slipped on a smooth patch of terrain or catching a body when they slipped on a loose stone. Boy, girl, teen or child, they all worked together.

RJ saw all this and smiled, wishing Patrick could have seen it. On their trek away from the camp, RJ had seen a different side of the teen and had realized Patrick had been just as scared as the rest of them, only he showed it in a very different way.

Jason slowed when he stepped on the first bleached bones that littered the tunnel floor, and sounds of terror could be heard coming from the back of the line.

"We're almost there, son, just a few more minutes," Jason told him, ducking below a low overhang of stone.

After following the dark tunnel for what seemed like forever, Jason was the first to enter the cave itself, RJ right behind him. The football was still on the ground where he'd kicked it, the bleached, cracked bones scattered everywhere.

More than half of the children shuffled into the cave behind him, the rest having to wait in the tunnel. Heads would poke up as eager faces tried to jump up and see what was happening.

Jason turned to his son, his hands out at his sides. "Well, son, we're here, what now?"

Jason walked around the cave for a moment, getting his bearings, then in the dim light he saw the markings on the wall. He walked over to them, examining them closely like an archeologist with a new find. They reminded him of hieroglyphics, pictures or instructions of what the Snatcher did to open the gateway back to earth.

RJ brought up the severed limb in his right hand and stood in front of the markings. He swallowed hard, his mouth becoming dry, and then he turned his head and looked to Jason.

Jason nodded, encouraging his son in whatever he was going to do.

RJ placed the severed hand into an indentation on the right side of the markings. He'd remembered when the Snatcher had carried him through the portal, and how the creature had pressed its taloned hand into the indentation. He now did the same thing.

Holding the hand tight, making sure each talon was in the correct position, RJ waited. Behind him, voices grew louder as everyone wondered what was happening.

He stayed there, not moving for more than a minute, but nothing happened. When he was ready to give up, realizing it had been a false hope, the cave wall started to glow. RJ stepped back, not knowing what was happening and saw an oval light appear. It spiraled out from the middle, the lights changing color constantly from reds to oranges to blues.

He turned to look at his dad. "If I'm right, that's the way home," he said over the calamity of the upraised voices filling the cave.

Jason's face was a giant smile. "Well, I don't think we have a choice. All right, everybody through the gate or portal or whatever!" He yelled.

One at a time the children did as they were told, their faces filled with excitement and nervousness of the unknown. One after another they disappeared until it was only Jason and RJ standing side by side in the barren cave.

Jason grabbed his son's arm tightly in his hand.

"Ready, son?" He asked.

RJ nodded and together they jumped into the portal. There was a moment of pure white light and then both Jason and RJ fell to the floor of wherever they were. Behind them, the portal disappeared, like a light switch had been turned off. Hands were all around Jason, helping him to his feet and holding him up.

Glancing behind him, Jason saw he'd fallen out of a utility closet, the mops and cleaning supplies knocked askew from the chaotic reentry back to his home world.

He looked around some more, RJ next to him and recognized immediately where he was.

It was a school, the metal lockers, flyers and posters on the tiled walls as recognizable to him as the giant M in McDonald's was to a ten-year-old.

All the kids were jumping up and down, hugging each other and laughing.

They had made it home!

Jason looked up when an old man in his late sixties wearing a janitorial uniform appeared from around the hallway corner. He wore a baseball cap and had a red rag dangling from his left back pocket.

"What the…? Who the hell are you kids, and how did you get into the school?" He demanded, in a crotchety tone, clearly upset.

Jason walked over to him, smiling from ear to ear.

"Well, now that's a long story." Then he took another look around, giving the school some more thought, and turned back to the janitor, taking a stab at a hunch he was having. "Hey, mister, let me ask you something. You wouldn't know a guy named Clyde would you?"

The janitor seemed taken aback by the question. "You mean Clyde Williams? Yeah, I know him. Or better yet, I knew him. About six months ago he upped and quit right in the middle of his shift, didn't even come back for his last paycheck. No one's seen him since. Why?"

Jason shrugged and his smile grew so big his jaw hurt. Then he asked one more question, already knowing the answer.

"Say, how's the weather in California today, is it nice outside?"

The janitor fixed his ball cap, his eyes growing to slits in suspicion of this strange man surrounded by a bus load of kids, and looked at Jason like he was crazy.

"Yeah, the weather's fine, why the hell did you ask me that? Look, buddy, you need to get these kids out of here or I'm gonna call the police."

For some reason Jason found that hilarious and he began laughing, a rich, hearty laugh he couldn't control, nor did he want to. He hugged his son, happy to be alive, while the other kids clapped and cheered merrily around them.

"Yeah, you do that, in fact, mister, I insist. I bet there's a lot of parents all over America that'll want to know that their children are safe and sound."

The janitor scratched his head and pulled out a cell phone, dialing 911. As for Jason, he settled to the floor exhausted, RJ sitting next to him, their backs against a couple of lockers.

Of all the places to wind up, what were the odds?

And then he decided, on second thought, it didn't matter one bit.

# Epilogue

## Two Weeks Later

R J WAS PEDALING his bike home from school, feeling good about just being alive. The sun was shining and it was a beautiful day, even though it was the middle of January.

New England was going through a bout of warm weather, the temperature hovering in the low fifties and high forties. Cold to some, but for most New Englanders, it was like a spring day, a small sign of the warmer weather coming only a few months away.

There was only a small amount of snow still left on the ground from the last snowfall from the week before. Now all that was left was a few piles of blackened slush, the dirt from the street mixing with the once white crystals.

RJ paid the mounds of snow and ice no mind. His attention was on the street in front of him, as he swerved around the spreading puddles of melting snow.

He'd seen Nancy a few times since he had returned home from the Snatcher's world and he was hoping to see her later today.

He smiled when he thought back to the day he and his dad had found themselves in the school in California.

Jason and RJ had slipped through a fire door and had then called his mom. To say Emma was glad to hear from them was an understatement. She had quickly wired them money so they could fly home. His dad had looked a little out of place at first on the streets of

California, however. He was missing his shirt and his face was bruised and bloody. He'd managed to clean himself up at a nearby gas station and then had 'borrowed' a sweatshirt from a nearby clothes line from one of the many one-story homes lining the street. Then they had gone to the airport to wait for the wired money. After that, it had been simple to purchase new clothes and fly home.

Emma had been ecstatic, hugging and kissing them both upon their arrival to Logan Airport. When she'd asked where they had been, Jason had concocted a lie to appease her. His dad knew she didn't believe a word of it, but she was so happy to have her family back she didn't care.

But RJ knew that once things got back to normal again, both he and his dad were going to have to tell her something.

He wasn't looking forward to it.

As for his dad, they were closer than ever before. Now that Jason had someone to share what had happened to his father all those years ago, he was at peace with himself.

There had been a few changes in the house, as well. For one thing, Jason had removed all of the closet doors from the bedrooms and had tossed them into the basement; then he'd built cinderblock walls inside the backs of the closets. Emma had thought he was crazy, but had let him do it if it made him feel better.

It was just one more thing to explain to her one day.

RJ didn't know if the stone blocks would stop another Snatcher from coming through to their world, but if it made his dad feel better than what was the harm.

RJ pedaled a little harder, enjoying the exertion of his body. He thought it funny how he now enjoyed the little things he'd once taken for granted.

He thought about all the children who had been on the news in the past few weeks. Stories of kids who were thought to have disappeared forever and had then mysteriously appeared in a public school in San Diego, California.

He chuckled at that, like anyone would ever believe the true story of where they'd been.

RJ turned the street corner, now only a few streets from his house when he felt his back tire get hit by something from behind. He managed to regain control and slowed to a stop to see Ronnie and Chris behind him.

RJ stepped off his bike, making sure to use the kickstand. He turned to face the bully and his sidekick. Since his return home two months ago, he hadn't seen Ronnie or his friend. They had always just missed each other. As for Kyle's disappearance, well, no one knew where the boy had gone. Some thought he had run away, but RJ knew better. While he didn't believe the boy had deserved death by the Snatcher, he also knew that you sow what you reap. If Kyle hadn't been chasing him that day in his grandmother's house, he never would have been taken.

Just one more thing RJ had to keep to silent about.

Ronnie walked up to him, cracking his knuckles as he walked.

"Hey, Lawson, I was wondering when I might see you again, my fists have missed your face." Chris chuckled behind the bully, acting like Ronnie was the king of standup.

RJ just stood with arms at his sides, waiting. There was nothing he wanted to say to Ronnie except go to hell, but he knew that would just be taking the bully's bait.

Ronnie stopped when he was face to face with RJ, his breath blowing in his face.

RJ turned his nose a little to the right, the odor unsettling. Ronnie's breath smelled like Slim Jims and Ruffles and it didn't smell very appetizing.

RJ took a half-step back, Ronnie smiling when he did. He knew Lawson would back away, acting like the coward as always. RJ waved his hand in front of his face, wincing at the stink of Ronnie's breath.

"Gees, Ronnie, brush much?" RJ said; the sarcasm clear in his voice.

Chris actually chuckled slightly at the jibe to his leader, but a stern look from Ronnie silenced him immediately. Turning back to RJ, Ronnie crossed the extra foot separating them. This time RJ didn't move, but said in a flat tone of annoyance: "What do you want, Ronnie? I really don't have time for you right now."

If Ronnie noticed the subtle change in RJ's voice, he didn't let on.

"What do I want? I want you to follow me over to that driveway so I can welcome you back personally," he said while smiling malevolently.

RJ looked to where he was pointing. The house had a for sale sign on its lawn, abandoned at the moment. If Ronnie couldn't get him in an alleyway then the bully would have to adapt.

RJ shook his head. "Not gonna happen. Look, I'm leaving now and I don't want to see you again. You're dead to me, Ronnie. Don't talk to me and I'll return the favor." Then RJ turned away from the bully, giving the older boy his back.

Ronnie's face turned beet red with anger. Before RJ could climb onto his bike, Ronnie reached out to grab his jacket.

"Why you little shit, I guess I'll just beat you down right here in the street."

RJ spun around to face him, his clenched hand already coming up with the full force of his body behind it. RJ's right fist connected with Ronnie's cheek, breaking skin and knocking one of his molars out of his mouth.

Ronnie's head rocked away from the blow, but in less than a handful of seconds was charging at RJ, rage flooding his eyes.

RJ picked up his bicycle and jammed it into the older boy's stomach, the kickstand piercing the soft skin beneath his shirt, his light jacket unzipped. Ronnie cried out in pain and fell to the street in shock, curling up in the fetal position as tears rolled down his cheeks. By this time a few pedestrians had stopped to watch. Most of them knew both RJ and Ronnie. They had seen Ronnie picking on RJ countless times and were surprised to see the strange turn of events.

No one helped Ronnie. All just stood silent and watched.

RJ set his bike down, his face set in stone, his eyes cold.

Ronnie sat up, his hand going to his stomach as he regained his composure, shrugging off the blow. He had a minor flesh wound from the kickstand, a small amount of blood staining his shirt, but otherwise was fine.

He stood up, wiping the tears from his cheeks. "Why, you little shit, I'm gonna kill you for that," he growled.

RJ stood perfectly still, his fists raised in front of him while he waited for Ronnie's next move. If Ronnie had been smart, he would have ended the fight then, but he wasn't smart. He was a bully, and had been one for far too long to be anything but. He couldn't conceive of a time when RJ wouldn't be afraid of him anymore.

But what he didn't know, and never could know, was that after what RJ had experienced in the time he'd been captured by the Snatcher was far more terrifying than anything Ronnie could ever do to him on his best day.

No, RJ wasn't afraid of Ronnie anymore, and in fact, now he kind of pitied the older boy.

With an angry howl, Ronnie came charging at RJ, hoping to knock him to the asphalt and use his superior weight to hold RJ down, but as soon as Ronnie was close enough, RJ dropped to the ground, using his legs like a scythe and knocking Ronnie's legs out from under him. The bully fell to the street hard, his jaw clacking shut from the impact. His eyes closed for a moment, and when he opened them, he saw RJ's right fist rocketing toward his face.

Knuckles met cartilage and Ronnie's nose flattened against his face. Blood spurted from the wound and Ronnie held his hands to his battered visage.

RJ was preparing to hit him again and then stopped, regaining control of his temper. After what he'd been through on the Snatcher's home world, where life was cheap, he knew he could easily kill the older boy without batting an eye. But he knew that would be wrong. He was home now and the laws said he couldn't give Ronnie what he deserved.

So instead, RJ kicked the boy in the side of his torso, pushing Ronnie over. Ronnie's head whacked the pavement and he saw stars for a moment.

RJ stepped away from his former bully. He caught movement in the corner of his eye and turned to see Chris standing there, mouth open in surprise. RJ brought up his arms in a defensive posture, but Chris backed away.

"Whoa, dude, I don't want none of this, it was all Ronnie's idea," Chris stammered.

"Fine then. Get the hell out of here and don't bother me again," RJ told him.

Chris nodded, got on his bike and pedaled away as fast as he could, leaving Ronnie alone in the street.

RJ walked over to Ronnie and knelt down next to him; the older boy was trying to staunch the flow of blood seeping through his fingers, but was having little luck. Years later, Ronnie would need plastic surgery to fix the damage done this day.

RJ leaned down close so only Ronnie could hear him. RJ's eyes were cold as ice, his voice level as he whispered into Ronnie's ear.

"Next time will be worse. So just leave me alone and I'll leave you alone." Without waiting for a reply, RJ stood up walked to his bike, climbed on it, and began to ride away.

"You better get home and have your father look at your nose before you bleed to death, Ronnie," RJ said over his shoulder so the surrounding people could hear. Then he pedaled away from his defeated foe.

From that day on, every time Ronnie saw RJ coming down the street, he would make sure to be on the opposite side.

Ronnie never bothered him again, which was just fine with RJ.

# DEAD RECKONING: DAWNING OF THE DEAD
By Anthony Giangregorio

## THE DEAD HAVE RISEN!

In the dead city of Pittsburgh, two small enclaves struggle to survive, eking out an existence of hand to mouth.

But instead of working together, both groups battle for the last remaining fuel and supplies of a city filled with the living dead.

Six months after the initial outbreak, a lone helicopter arrives bearing two more survivors and a newborn baby. One enclave welcomes them, while the other schemes to steal their helicopter and escape the decaying city.

With no police, fire, or social services existing, the two will battle for dominance in the steel city of the walking dead.

But when the dust settles, the question is: will the remaining humans be the winners, or the losers?

When the dead walk, the line between Heaven and Hell is so twisted and bent there is no line at all.

# RISE OF THE DEAD
By Anthony Giangregorio

## DEATH IS ONLY THE BEGINNING!

In less than forty-eight hours, more than half the globe was infected.

In another forty-eight, the rest would be enveloped.

The reason?

A science experiment gone horribly wrong which enabled the dead to walk, their flesh rotting on their bones even as they seek human prey.


Jeremy was an ordinary nineteen year old slacker. He partied too much and had done poorly in high school. After a night of drinking and drugs, he awoke to find the world a very different place from the one he'd left the night before.

The dead were walking and feeding on the living, and as Jeremy stepped out into a world gone mad, the dead spotting him alone and unarmed in the middle of the street, he had to wonder if he would live long enough to see his twentieth birthday.

BOOK 6

# DEAD UNION

By Anthony Giangregorio

## BRAVE NEW WORLD

More than a year has passed since the world died not with a bang, but with a moan.

Where sprawling cities once stood, now only the dead inhabit the hollow walls of a shattered civilization; a mockery of lives once led.

But there are still survivors in this barren world, all slowly struggling to take back what was stripped from their birthright; the promise of a world free of the undead.

Fortified towns have shunned the outside world, becoming massive fortresses in their own right. These refugees of a world torn asunder are once again trying to carve out a new piece of the earth, or hold onto what little they already possess.

## HOSTAGES

Henry Watson and his warrior survivalists are conscripted by a mad colonel, one of the last military leaders still functioning in the decimated United States. The colonel has settled in Fort Knox, and from there plans to rule the world with his slave army of lost souls and the last remaining soldiers of a defunct army.

But first he must take back America and mold it in his own image; and he will crush all who oppose him, including the new recruits of Henry and crew.

The battle lines are drawn with the fate of America at stake, and this time, the outcome may be unsure.

In a world where the dead walk, even the grave isn't safe.

# THE DARK
By Anthony Giangregorio

## DARKNESS FALLS

The darkness came without warning.

First New York, then the rest of United States, and then the world became enveloped in a perpetual night without end.

With no sunlight, eventually the planet will wither and die, bringing on a new Ice Age. But that isn't problem for the human race, for humanity will be dead long before that happens.

There is something in the dark, creatures only seen in nightmares, and they are on the prowl.

Evolution has changed and man is no longer the dominant species.

When we are children, we are told not to fear the dark, that what we believe to exist in the shadows is false.

Unfortunately, that is no longer true.


ANOTHER EXCITING CHAPTER IN THE DEADWATER SERIES!

# DEADRAIN
By Anthony Giangregorio

Welcome to the New America, population: 0

When a bacterial outbreak contaminates America's lower atmosphere, the resulting rain mutates into a deadly conduit for death.

Human's all over America are exposed and within a matter of days society has crumbled and the walking dead rule the land.

The America we know is gone, replaced by a new order; where the dead walk and humans are the prey.

Henry Watson and his small group of companions travel the country, searching for someplace better, someplace where the rain is safe.

In the New America the rules have changed; survive or perish.

# DARK PLACES
By Anthony Giangregorio

A cave-in inside the Boston subway unleashes something that should have stayed buried forever.

Three boys sneak out to a haunted junkyard after dark and find more than they gambled on.

In a world where everyone over twelve has died from a mysterious illness, one young boy tries to carry on.

A mysterious man in black tries his hand at a game of chance at a local carnival, to interesting results.

God, Allah, and Buddha play a friendly game of poker with the fate of the Earth resting in the balance.

Ever have one of those days where everything that can go wrong, does? Well, so did Byron, and no one should have a day like this!

Thad had an imaginary friend named Charlie when he was a child. Charlie would make him do bad things. Now Thad is all grown up and guess who's coming for a visit?

These and other short stories, all filled with frozen moments of dread and wonder, will keep you captivated long into the night.

Just be sure to watch out when you turn off the light!


# DEAD TALES: SHORT STORIES TO DIE FOR
By Anthony Giangregorio

In a world much like our own, terrorists unleash a deadly dis-ease that turns people into flesh-eating ghouls.

A camping trip goes horribly wrong when forces of evil seek to dominate mankind.

After losing his life, a man returns reincarnated again and again; his soul inhabiting the bodies of animals.

In the Colorado Mountains, a woman runs for her life, stalked by a sadistic killer.

In a world where the Patriot Act has come to fruition, a man struggles to survive, despite eroding liberties.

Not able to accept his wife's death, a widower will cross into the dream realm to find her again, despite the dark forces that hold her in thrall.

These and other short stories will captivate and thrill you.

These are short stories to die for.

# DEADFREEZE
By Anthony Giangregorio

THIS IS WHAT HELL WOULD BE LIKE IF IT FROZE OVER.

When an experimental serum for hypothermia goes horribly wrong, a small research station in the middle of Antarctica becomes overrun with an army of the frozen dead.

Now a small group of survivors must battle the arctic weather and a horde of frozen zombies as they make their way across the frozen plains of Antarctica to a neighboring research station.

What they don't realize is that they are being hunted by an entity whose sole reason for existing is vengeance; and it will find them wherever they run.

# DEADFALL
By Anthony Giangregorio

It's Halloween in the small suburban town of Wakefield, Mass.

While parents take their children trick or treating and others throw costume parties, a swarm of meteorites enter the earth's atmosphere and crash to earth.

Inside are small parasitic worms, no larger than maggots.

The worms quickly infect the corpses at a local cemetery and so begins the rise of the undead.

The walking dead soon get the upper hand, with no one believing the truth.

That the dead now walk.

Will a small group of survivors live through the zombie apocalypse?

Or will they, too, succumb to the Deadfall.

# THE MONSTER UNDER THE BED
By Anthony Giangregorio

Rupert was just one of many monsters that inhabit the human world, scaring children before bed. Only Rupert wanted to play with the children he was forced to scare.

When Rupert meets Timmy, an instant friendship is born. Running away from his abusive step-father, Timmy leaves home, embarking on a journey that leads him to New York City.

On his way, Timmy will realize that the true monsters are other adults who are just waiting to take advantage of a small boy, all alone in the big city.

Can Rupert save him?

Or will Timmy just become another statistic.

# DEAD RAGE
### By Anthony Giangregorio

An unknown virus spreads across the globe, turning ordinary people into bloodthirsty, ravenous killers.

Only a small percentage of the population is immune and soon become prey to the infected.

Amongst the infected comes a man, stricken by the virus, yet still retaining his grasp on reality. His need to destroy the *normals* becomes an obsession and he raises an army of killers to seek out and kill all who aren't *changed* like himself.

A few survivors gather together on the outskirts of Chicago and find themselves running for their lives as the specter of death looms over all.

The Dead Rage virus will find you, no matter where you hide.

Also available as The Rage Plague by Permuted Press.


**THE NEXT EXCITING CHAPTER IN THE DEADWATER SERIES!**
**BOOK 7**
# DEAD VALLEY
### by Anthony Giangregorio

## Untouched Majesty

After nearly drowning in the icy waters of the Colorado River, the six weary companions come upon a beautiful valley nestled in the mountains of Colorado, where the undead plague appears to have never happened.

With the mountains protecting the valley, the deadly rain never fell, and the valley is as untouched as the day it was created.

But the group is soon captured by a secret, military research base now run by a few remaining scientists and soldiers.

On this base, unholy experiments are being carried out, and the group soon finds themselves caught in the middle of it.

Mary, Sue, Raven and Cindy are taken away to be used as breeders, the scientists wanting to create a new utopia, which the living dead can't reach, but the side effect of this is the women will lose their lives.

Henry and Jimmy, now separated and captured themselves, must find a way to save them before it's too late; the scientists unleashing every conceivable mutation at their disposal to stop them.

In the world of the living dead, the past is gone and the future is non-existent.

# LIVING DEAD PRESS

Where the Dead Walk

www.livingdeadpress.com